JOHN PRINE

American Music Series

Peter Blackstock and David Menconi, Editors

JOHN PRINE

In Spite of Himself

EDDIE HUFFMAN

University of Texas Press
AUSTIN

Requests for permission to reproduce material
from this work should be sent to:
Permissions
University of Texas Press
P.O. Box 7819
Austin, TX 78713-7819
utpress.utexas.edu/rp-form

The paper used in this book meets the minimum requirements of
ANSI/NISO Z39.48-1992 (R1997) (Permanence of Paper). ∞

Design by Lindsay Starr

Library of Congress Cataloging-in-Publication Data

Huffman, Eddie, author.
John Prine : in spite of himself / Eddie Huffman. — First edition.
pages   cm — (American music series)
Includes bibliographical references and discography.
ISBN 978-1-4773-1399-2 (pbk. : alk. paper) —
1. Prine, John. 2. Composers—United States—Biography.
3. Folk musicians—United States—Biography. I. Title.
II. Series: American music series (Austin, Tex.)
ML410.P846H84 2015
782.42164092—dc23 2014031677
[B]

Frontispiece: Photograph of John Prine by Michael Wilson.

doi:10.7560/748224

Contents

▼

JOHN PRINE

Introduction

▼

Stephen Colbert wasn't a pompous, reactionary moron, but he played one on TV. On this episode of the long-running Comedy Central show *The Colbert Report*, he struggled to maintain his trademark insincerity. The star, trim and youthful as he pushed fifty, was still months away from being tapped to replace David Letterman as host of *The Late Show*. He had just made his nightly glory-hog jog across *The Colbert Report* set and taken a seat next to his guest. He couldn't contain his enthusiasm. "I'm an enormous fan, an enormous fan," the host said. Colbert was born in 1964, the last year of the Baby Boom. His guest was born at the front end, in 1946.

Now it was 2013, and John Prine had grown corpulent in his golden years, his once-luxuriant mane of black hair a distant memory, its remnants gray and receding. His head tilted at an odd angle, as if its weight were a bit much for his neck. With his round face and gray mustache, Prine had started to resemble Wilford Brimley, the veteran character actor best known in recent years as the TV pitchman who talks about his "diabeetus." Colbert's guest had had dramatic health problems of his own, but lived to tell the tale. The host introduced him as "a Grammy Award–winning singer-songwriter," "a folksinger's folksinger," and a "songwriter's songwriter." He also noted that Prine started his professional career delivering mail. "Were you a mailman's mailman?" Colbert asked. "Were you the kind of mailman that other mailmen wanted to get their mail from?"

Prine grinned and looked at Colbert the way he looks at the world in his songs: from a cockeyed angle. "I was the kind of mailman that dogs couldn't wait to see coming down the street," he replied. Prine is modest to a fault, perpetually countering the vicissitudes of life with a funny story.

His appearance on *The Colbert Report* happened a couple of weeks after an infamous appearance on the MTV Video Music Awards by Miley Cyrus. The twenty-year-old singer, a former teenage star of the Disney Channel TV show *Hannah Montana*, shed her good-girl image by taking the stage in rubber underwear, dangling her tongue out of her mouth, and grinding around singer Robin Thicke in a jiggling dance called twerking, popularized by hip-hop artists.

"I've got a beef with you, John Prine," Colbert told the singer. "I'm an enormous fan of yours, but you like to keep it simple. It's mostly just vocals and guitar. Why not flashpots? Why not face paint? Why not someone twerking against you while you're doing your songs?"

Prine paused for a moment before responding: "That would put me in a different tax bracket."

The singers who made it had one thing in common, Barry Poss once told me: They were obsessed with making it. They bet everything on a shot at stardom—often to the exclusion of friends, family, and all the other trappings of a normal life. Poss founded Sugar Hill Records in 1978 and helped launch the careers of Ricky Skaggs, Robert Earl Keen, and Nickel Creek. "Even artists who appear to be calm on the outside, who are in the big leagues, they are driven," Poss said. "They are really driven. They want it badly." For a brief time in the early eighties, it looked as if Sugar Hill was going to sign John Prine, too.

But Prine, in a rare show of ambition, decided to start his own record label instead. Prine seldom displayed a drive for stardom. If he ever wanted it badly, he kept it to himself. For years he didn't even consider himself a songwriter, just a Midwestern kid who liked to "make up songs." When he realized he could earn more money playing those songs than delivering mail, he quit his job at the Post Office—and slept a lot. Where other singers went to extraordinary lengths to get their music heard—moving to New York or Los Angeles, pestering song publishers and club owners—Prine was happy just to have a place to play. He got his first gig on a dare: Somebody challenged him to show what he could do after he grumbled about the talent at an open-mike night. Opportunities seemed to fall into his lap. A few nights a week he would drive his Chevy to Old Town, Chicago's answer to Greenwich Village or the French Quarter, play a few sets, hang out with his friends, then head back home to the apartment out in the suburbs he shared with his wife. One night in the spring of 1971, a friend called him at an Old Town hole-in-the-wall to say that Kris Kristofferson and Paul Anka were on the way there to hear him sing. Somebody at the club had to wake Prine up to come to the phone.

That friend, Steve Goodman, had enough ambition for the both of them. Diagnosed with leukemia a couple of years earlier, Goodman knew he was living on borrowed time and hustled constantly to get his songs heard. He did the same thing for his friend Johnny, who might still be just another local hero playing for tips in Chicago bars if Goodman hadn't dragged Kristofferson and Anka over to the Earl of Old Town that night. A few weeks later Prine and Goodman flew to New York on Anka's dime, and they each landed record deals immediately. Just like that, the singing mailman from Maywood, Illinois, had become a labelmate to Led Zeppelin, Aretha Franklin, and Crosby, Stills and Nash.

That's one way to look at it. Another way to look at it is that Prine worked hard for years on one of the few things he had ever really been good at, honing his craft to the point where people would compare him to one of the greatest songwriters who ever lived. He watched his father bust his ass for decades at a factory job, making just enough to keep the family in a nondescript rental house on the Midwestern plains, four hundred miles away from his beloved Kentucky hills. Bill Prine would have headed back south in a heartbeat if there had been any other job prospects down there besides mining coal. He died prematurely up north, but his son would eventually find a way to live down south on his own terms. He got there in part by spending countless hours alone in his room learning guitar licks, listening to records, making up songs. He worked for hours with his fiddle-playing brother, took lessons year after year at a folk music school in Chicago, went to see legends play live. He made up in woodshedding, raw talent, and songcraft what he lacked in ambition.

Goodman may have gotten him the audition, but Prine landed the gig all by himself.

"Prine's stuff is pure Proustian existentialism," Bob Dylan told veteran music critic and MTV producer Bill Flanagan in 2009 during a *Huffington Post* interview. "Midwestern mind trips to the nth degree. And he writes beautiful songs." Dylan was one of Prine's formative influences, and for much of the seventies Prine and the best of his singer-songwriter peers got labeled, one after the other, "the new Dylan." Unlike other new Dylans such as Bruce Springsteen and Loudon Wainwright III, Prine never had even a fluke hit—though others would top the country charts with his tunes, and Bonnie Raitt would make his "Angel from Montgomery" one of her signature songs.

Born in a working-class suburb of Chicago, he was the son of a beer-drinking union man, a father who loved country music and never got over having to abandon the rolling hills of rural Kentucky for work in a flatland can factory. Prine got drafted as the Vietnam War ramped up, ran an army motor pool, and returned home to his old job as a mailman before another singer-songwriter helped him land a deal with Atlantic Records. "I remember when Kris Kristofferson first brought him on the scene," Dylan told Flanagan. "All that stuff about 'Sam Stone' the soldier junky daddy and 'Donald and Lydia,' where people make love from ten miles away. Nobody but Prine could write like that."

When he was a kid Prine would stand in front of a mirror strumming a broom, pretending to be Elvis Presley. On his very first album he recorded with the same Memphis musicians who played on Elvis's "Suspicious Minds" and "In the Ghetto"—not to mention Aretha Franklin's "Do Right Woman, Do Right Man" and Dusty Springfield's "Son of a Preacher Man." The producer of Prine's first three albums, Arif Mardin, had helped create some of the Rascals' biggest hits in the sixties and would go on to do the same for the Bee Gees in the mid-seventies. Over the years Prine would record or write with such luminaries as Steve Cropper, Sam Phillips, John Mellencamp, and Trisha Yearwood. But their hit-making magic never rubbed off on him. He even tried a couple of brief forays into Hollywood.

Prine's triumphs have been deceptively modest, though; he has created a rich and varied career for himself flying under the radar. Film critic Roger Ebert was the first person to champion Prine's music in the media. ABC Television used a Prine song as the theme for a short-lived sitcom. He was an early musical guest on *Saturday Night Live* and appeared on *Austin City Limits* almost as many times as Willie Nelson himself. Scores of artists have covered Prine's songs, from Johnny Cash and Bette Midler to George Strait and Miranda Lambert. He showed a DIY spirit by walking away from the major-label machine in the early 1980s and pioneering his own record company, which is still in business long after many other labels have bitten the dust or gotten swallowed by corporate conglomerates. Prine has earned many honors, including two Grammy Awards, induction into the Nashville Songwriters Hall of Fame, and an exhibit at the Country Music Hall of Fame. Over the years he crossed paths with John Belushi, Phil Ochs, Raitt, Springsteen, Dustin Hoffman, David Geffen, Phil Spector, Tom Petty, Billy Bob Thornton, and Andy Griffith. He sobered up after years of serious partying, made the third time the charm when it came to marriages, and survived a bout with neck cancer. (Almost halfway through the second decade of the twenty-first century, Prine would face a new health challenge: lung cancer.) He surrounded himself with a family late in life, and now divides his time between Nashville and Ireland when he's not on the road, still playing dozens of dates every year in theaters across America and Europe. He has been able to count some of the greatest music legends of the twentieth century among his biggest fans, including Cash and Dylan, and his songwriting is cited as an influence by virtually every young songwriter with a twang in his or her voice.

Prine's songs will be his most lasting legacy. A big chunk of his legend rests on the tunes from his self-titled 1971 debut album: "Angel from Montgomery," a remarkably sensitive portrait of a middle-aged Southern housewife written by a Midwestern kid in his early twenties, and the two songs cited by Dylan. "Donald and Lydia," inspired by Prine's days in basic training, may be the sweetest song ever written about masturbation, while "Sam Stone" was years ahead of its time as the story of a Vietnam veteran turned dying addict. The album also included the antiwar "Your Flag Decal Won't Get You into Heaven Anymore," the hippie anthems "Illegal Smile" and "Spanish Pipedream," and "Paradise," a song about the destruction of his family's little Kentucky hometown that would become a bluegrass standard. Bill Monroe, the man who invented bluegrass and gave the genre its name, grew up in the same little corner of Kentucky as Prine's parents, a music-rich region that also spawned early country music star and fingerpicking legend Merle Travis, along with fifties teen heartthrobs and harmony singers the Everly Brothers.

The first time Prine ever met Monroe, somebody told him Prine was the guy who "wrote that song about Muhlenberg County," Prine told writer David Fricke, who penned the liner notes for *Great Days: The John Prine Anthology*, a definitive two-CD collection of the singer's work released in 1993. (And sadly out of print two decades later.) Monroe replied, "Oh yeah, I thought that was a song I overlooked from the '20s." Prine and his old buddy Steve Goodman cowrote the classic country parody "You Never Even Called Me by My Name" (aka "the perfect country and Western song," a hit in the seventies for David Allan Coe), though Prine let Goodman take all the credit for it. Over the years Prine wrote and recorded memorable comic songs ("Dear Abby," "The Bottomless Lake"), tragic songs about divorce and death ("Bruised Orange [Chain of Sorrow]," "Lake Marie"), and surreal story songs that defy easy categorization ("Sabu Visits the Twin Cities Alone," "Jesus the Missing Years"). He did take credit for the No. 1 country hits he cowrote for Don Williams and George Strait. The way he spins tall tales and evokes American folklore has earned him repeated comparisons to Mark Twain. Elvis once asked one of his band members to play a Prine song for him over and over, late into the night.

Two Prine concerts bookended my work on this biography. Toward the early phase of my research on the book, in October 2012, I left my home in the rolling hills of the North Carolina Piedmont and drove up to the mountains to see Prine perform in the Thomas Wolfe Auditorium at the venue formerly known as the Asheville Civic Center. (Insert generic corporate sponsor name here.) It was the fifth or sixth time I had seen Prine play live, and not one of his better shows. His voice was rough but serviceable, and he seemed disengaged from the audience, talking little between songs, telling remarkably few stories compared to previous concerts I had seen. It was a solid performance, but not a particularly memorable one. Longtime Prine sideman Jason Wilber made the biggest impression on me that night, playing like ten guitarists rolled into one.

Fourteen months later, toward the end of both the writing process and 2013, I had tickets to see Prine again, this time much closer to home, at War Memorial Auditorium in Greensboro, North Carolina. Three weeks before the show, I got a Google News alert that Prine had been diagnosed with cancer—again—and was postponing some shows in December as a result. Fortunately, the Greensboro show was still on, along with a concert the following night in Charlotte—the last one before he would go under the knife. During a fine opening set, Justin Townes Earle paused between songs to praise Prine, with whom he had toured periodically over the course of several years: "He's one of the sweetest people I've ever met, and he's one of the most consistent performers I've ever seen." That consistency seemed questionable during Prine's first two or three songs—he could barely croak out his lyrics. "I've got a little frog in my throat tonight," he said after "Picture Show." That was an understatement. "I hope it's just a little one," he continued. "I'm trying to get rid of it by singing." While I felt bad for Prine because of his health problems and struggles to perform, I was disappointed at the prospects of a mediocre concert. "I'm starting to sound like Louis Armstrong," Prine cracked after his third song, "Speed of the Sound of Loneliness."

Then something remarkable happened: Prine *did* get rid of it by singing—and, perhaps, by taking a few swigs from what looked like a bottle of cough syrup. By the time he sang "Six O'Clock News," four songs into the show, he was starting to sound like his old self again (well, at least his post-neck-cancer, post-chain-smoking self). It was all uphill from there: Prine chatted amiably after almost every song, reminiscing about Goodman and a festival they played nearly forty years earlier in nearby Galax, Virginia, called Stompin 76, a kind of bluegrass Woodstock. It brought more than 100,000 people to a farm outside a tiny mountain town ill-prepared to host such a horde. Prine and his band played a full half hour longer than the ninety-minute show I had seen the year before, delivering songs recorded throughout his career, from old favorites such as "Grandpa Was a Carpenter" to obscure numbers such as "Iron Ore Betty." He was the second performer I had seen in that same venue sing "Angel from Montgomery" in the span of a week—Bonnie Raitt had given a gorgeous rendition with an extended introduction just a few days before. Prine delivered an early Christmas present, "I Saw Mommy Kissing Santa Claus," and introduced "Hello in There" with his customary self-deprecating humor. "I kinda grew up thinking I wanted to be an old person," Prine told the Greensboro crowd. Then he spread his arms wide.

"Voilà!"

I heard a John Prine song at the first concert I ever attended. It was a hot Saturday in April 1980, Spring Fest on campus at the University of North Carolina at Chapel Hill. Bonnie Raitt shared the bill that day with the Atlanta Rhythm Section and the band I had been obsessed with since sixth grade, the Beach Boys. The stage was out on the football field facing the visitors' side of Kenan Stadium, and Raitt played "Angel from Montgomery." I managed to get my adolescent mind off of her tight striped T-shirt long enough to appreciate hearing this gorgeous, heartfelt ballad. I had already gotten to know the song via Raitt's live version on the soundtrack to the documentary *No Nukes*.

Like Colbert, I was born at the end of the Baby Boom. I was a month shy of my sixteenth birthday that day I saw Raitt in Chapel Hill, winding down my sophomore year of high school in a mill town twenty-five miles up Highway 54. I would eventually catch up to classic rock, soul, funk, hip-hop, country, jazz, and world music, but in 1980 my sights were set mostly on singer-songwriters. Jackson Browne had been my favorite, with his old buddy Warren Zevon about to overtake him. (Zevon also had an indirect Muhlenberg County connection: He had served as the Everly Brothers' pianist and band leader, was onstage with them when they fell apart in 1973, and wrote "Frank and Jesse James" in tribute to them.) I liked well-crafted, emotionally honest songs, as well as funny songs that showed a twisted sense of humor.

The big FM rock station out of Raleigh, WQDR, played the hell out of Jimmy Buffett, Don McLean, James Taylor, Dan Fogelberg, Harry Chapin, Gordon Lightfoot, Arlo Guthrie, and a bunch of other singer-songwriters, but it rarely, if ever, played Prine. In those pre-Internet days, the word on artists spread primarily via word of mouth, radio play, and magazine reviews and features. I eventually picked up on Prine the same way I picked up on a lot of other music, via the recommendations of rock critics—particularly Dave Marsh. His newsletter, then called *Rock & Roll Confidential*, convinced me to take a chance on Prine's *Aimless Love*, in 1984, the first album on his new record label, Oh Boy. It was a lot more country than most of the music I listened to in those days, but it still resonated with me.

Prine immediately felt like a kindred spirit, a funny, irreverent guy with a serious side. Anybody who had the audacity to sing the pickup line "I won't do nothin' wrong / Till you say it's right" was OK by me, and "The Bottomless Lake" was a hilarious tall tale that was way up my alley. The most undeniable track on the record was "Unwed Fathers." In the era of *Thriller* and *Born in the USA*, Prine stood out from the multiplatinum, stadium-filling rockers via understatement. He offered up a raw emotional tale of a scared teenager facing motherhood alone, singing in a neutral drawl that let the emotions Prine poured into his lyrics speak for themselves. A 1988 live album caught me up on a lot of classic Prine songs that I had missed as a kid in the seventies. That year I did a phone interview with him for a North Carolina newspaper and saw him in concert for the first time.

"When the presidents of CBS or Warner Brothers call to tell me about their problems I can understand, because I'm a mogul, too," Prine cracked. He was chatty and funny, easy to talk to. He talked with me about playing music at home as a child, writing "Sam Stone" a decade before the plight of Vietnam veterans became a common theme for songwriters, and appreciating the latest resurgence of acoustic-based popular music, led at the time by Suzanne Vega and Tracy Chapman. That short phoner merely whetted my appetite. The more I learned about him over the years, the more I wanted to know. Prine held steady as countless genres came and (sometimes) went, from Southern rock and jazz fusion through disco, funk, punk, hip-hop, indie rock, cowpunk, electronica, house, new jack swing, grunge, pop punk, complaint rock, alt-country, crunk, neo-soul, emo, and many others.

In recent years Prine's style of music has fallen under an umbrella term, Americana, that embraces everyone from the Byrds and Emmylou Harris through Steve Earle and Wilco to the Avett Brothers and Mumford and Sons. (Americana from England!) Despite my ongoing love for artists across many genres, Americana is the genre that—in one form or another—has called me back over and over again, year in and year out. I like the earthiness and emotional honesty, the fiddles and mandolins, the roots in the cultural traditions of a region my ancestors first settled three centuries ago. Those Jackson Browne records I loved as a kid—which showcased the brilliant slide guitar and fiddle work of David Lindley—had been, in retrospect, Americana when Americana wasn't even a thing yet. Some of my favorite latter-day country/Americana artists (Elizabeth Cook, Drive-By Truckers, Those Darlins, Josh Ritter, Brandi Carlile, Miranda Lambert) duet with Prine or cover his songs.

Another favorite, Todd Snider, recorded for Prine's label. When I find a new Americana artist I like, a Prine connection often surfaces. In June 2012, shortly after I started working on this book, I stumbled into a show by a fine young Americana band called Wayne Graham from a tiny town in eastern Kentucky, on the opposite end of the state from Muhlenberg County. They quickly earned my respect with their inventive, passionate country rock and their cover of one of my favorite Prine songs, "Fish and Whistle."

When the opportunity came along to make Prine the subject of my first book, I didn't hesitate. Nor did I let it slow me down when I learned that the singer and his manager through most of his adult life, Al Bunetta, would not cooperate with me. (The official reason from Oh Boy headquarters in Music City was that Prine Inc. was working on a documentary and a songbook and considered my book to be "competition." My arguments that my book would complement rather than detract from their projects fell on deaf ears.) Fortunately, Prine has left an exhaustive paper and audio trail over the years—first and foremost being his twenty-two albums (if you count best-of collections and live recordings), but also radio interviews, TV appearances, and a wealth of other sources. During a year of extensive research I happened across dozens of great Prine anecdotes, about topics ranging from brief encounters with Dustin Hoffman and Phil Spector to the incidents that inspired some of his greatest songs. I traveled to Prine's hometown, wandering through the halls of his old high school and the yard of his modest boyhood home. I had lunch at one of Prine's favorite greasy diners in Nashville, hung out with thumbpickers in Muhlenberg County, and wandered the banks of the Green River in the shadow of the giant cooling towers that rose into the skies of rural western Kentucky more than four decades ago as Paradise evaporated. The more I learned about Prine, the stronger a sense of kinship I felt with him. We each grew up in blue-collar families eating our mother's fried chicken, obsessively listening to records for clues about life beyond our hometowns. We spent our summers playing in the woods and exploring a river. He was the third of four boys; I was the fourth of four. We share a love of language, humor, classic movies, and good stories, and in adulthood we have each dealt with divorce, grave health threats, and the challenges of raising sons of our own.

Like the other books in this series, this one focuses on the artist's recorded output, his place in the world, and the mark he has left on it. Writing it has given me a chance to fill in the blanks of Prine's long career, catch up on any music I had missed along the way, and explore the threads that run from song to song, album to album, decade to decade. Some of his albums are better than others, of course, and I offer my perspective on all of them as I explore the brilliant records and the ill-advised side trips, the underappreciated gems and the hard-earned comebacks. I have lived and breathed John Prine's life and music and emerged with a renewed appreciation for his songwriting skills and his ability to make vital records for much of his forty-plus years in the music business. While I note some of his personal ups and downs along the way, I keep the focus primarily where it belongs: on his music. "It's a big old goofy world," Prine reminds us, and his life and work bear that out.

CHAPTER 1

Special Delivery

▼

The Earl of Old Town had closed for the night, and John Prine was snoozing in a booth after his performance, waiting to get paid. He woke up to a call from his friend Steve Goodman, another Chicago singer-songwriter. Goodman was on his way across town with Kris Kristofferson and Paul Anka, and he had convinced them to give Prine a listen.

The chairs were already up on the tables so the floors could be cleaned, but a few were pulled down for Prine's command performance. "I had this moment of compassion for him, thinkin' what this kid must be thinkin' gettin' up in front of a couple of strangers, showin' your stuff," Kristofferson said in a video interview for a 2003 DVD of Goodman performances. "He proceeded to sing 'Sam Stone,' 'Paradise,' 'Donald and Lydia,' 'Hello in There.' Absolutely destroyed it. One after the other. 'Spanish Pipedream.' It was the most incredible thing." (As the guy who wrote "Me and Bobby McGee" and "Sunday Morning Coming Down," Kristofferson knew a thing or two about songwriting himself.) Anka was also impressed. "John Prine was something else," he told *Zoo World* magazine in 1973. "This guy, a mailman, singing those songs, with those lyrics!" After Prine finished, Kristofferson requested an encore. "I got up and sang about maybe seven songs or so, because I wasn't sure how long they wanted to be held up for," Prine said on the Goodman DVD. "And I got off the stage, and Kris asked me to go back and sing the same songs, and sing anything else I got."

Anka, an old-school crooner who had recently added a Kristofferson song to his repertoire, was looking to branch out into management. It wasn't long before he followed up with Goodman, suggesting he and Prine go to New York to cut demos and try to get a record deal. For Goodman it was a no-brainer, but Prine took some convincing. "Anka came to town and met with Stevie and me, and I was still basically undecided because I was kind of bewildered by the whole thing," he told William Ruhlmann in an interview for a 1992 *Goldmine* magazine article. "I mean, once I got a job in a club, I'd sing three nights a week and sleep all week. To me, it was the perfect job." Prine figured he would get around to making a recording sooner or later, but he wasn't in any particular hurry. True to form, his friend refused to take no for an answer.

Goodman already knew his way around the city from a stint four years earlier at the Cafe Wha? They flew into LaGuardia and headed to Greenwich Village. Kristofferson happened to be playing at the Bitter End. Alabama native Donnie Fritts had worked with Kristofferson in Nashville and now played keyboards in his band, which would prove fortuitous for Prine. Fritts had written "Rainbow Road" for Arthur Alexander with another Alabama songwriter, Dan Penn, and collaborated with others to write songs recorded by the Box Tops and Dusty Springfield. Penn and another keyboard player, Spooner Oldham, had cowritten several rock and soul classics, such as "I'm Your Puppet" for James and Bobby Purify and "Cry Like a Baby" for the Box Tops. Fritts, Penn, and Oldham had all emerged from the scene that coalesced into FAME Studios in Muscle Shoals, Alabama, which for the previous few years had competed with Stax in Memphis as the capital of funky Southern soul. FAME was the studio where Percy Sledge recorded "When a Man Loves a Woman," Wilson Pickett cut "Mustang Sally," and Aretha Franklin unleashed "I Never Loved a Man." Atlantic Records vice president Jerry Wexler, a former music journalist who produced Ray Charles's breakthrough hits in the mid-1950s, had gotten to know the Muscle Shoals boys through his work producing records for Pickett and Franklin.

"We were there playing the Bitter End and it just so happened, I kept begging Jerry to come meet Kris and he wanted to meet Kris, so he comes to the show," Fritts told Eric Gebhardt in a 2009 interview for the website Blues in London. "John and Stevie come in to the second show and Kris gets John up to do a couple songs and I go out to sit with Jerry." Like

Kristofferson and Anka before him, Wexler was blown away by Prine. "He said, 'Who the hell is this kid?'" Fritts said. "'Cause he did 'Sam Stone' and 'Hello in There' and everybody just went crazy. So I said, 'I'll introduce you to him when the show's over.'" Some musicians spend a lifetime angling for a break; for Prine, the breaks just kept jumping right in the boat.

Through the late sixties Atlantic had been best known as the home of hard soul music, from the classic records made in New York by Charles and Franklin to the partnership with Stax/Volt in Memphis that produced records by Otis Redding, Sam and Dave, and Booker T. & the M.G.'s. The soul music out of Chicago, Philadelphia, and Detroit's Motown label leaned toward the melodic, radio-friendly end of the spectrum, while Southern soul had more grit and funk, with deeper roots in gospel. (There were plenty of exceptions in both directions, of course.) By the beginning of the seventies, Atlantic had fully embraced rock 'n' roll. The label had directly signed Led Zeppelin, Crosby, Stills and Nash (and sometimes Young), Boz Scaggs, Mott the Hoople, and Yes, and worked out a distribution deal with the Rolling Stones.

Its roster was short on singer-songwriters, however. Loudon Wainwright III had released critically acclaimed albums on Atlantic in 1970 and '71, but neither album had sold much and he would soon jump ship to Columbia. For other labels the genre was hitting its commercial peak in 1971. Bob Dylan and Paul Simon recorded for Columbia; James Taylor and Arlo Guthrie for Warner Brothers; Carole King for Ode; and Cat Stevens for A&M. Reprise had cornered the market on the Canadian contingent: Neil Young, Joni Mitchell, and Gordon Lightfoot all recorded for the label Sinatra founded in 1960. Atlantic did have a distribution deal with a brand-new singer-songwriter-oriented label, Asylum Records, founded by a couple of former agents with the William Morris Agency, David Geffen and Elliot Roberts, but it was still in its formative stages. King and Taylor both had No. 1 hits in the summer of '71: A two-sided single for King, "It's Too Late" backed with "I Feel the Earth Move," and, for Taylor, the King-penned "You've Got a Friend." Wexler may have seen Prine as an artist who could help Atlantic make up lost ground.

Prine sang three songs at the Bitter End. "Wexler talked to me in the dressing room and asked me to come see him in the morning," Prine told

Ruhlmann. "I came over, and he offered me a $25,000 recording contract. I hadn't been to New York 24 hours." The average annual salary in the United States in 1971 was about $10,000. That night Anka gave the guys from Chicago a taste of life at the top of the music-biz food chain. "Me and John, Billy Swan and Kris went to Paul's penthouse," Fritts told Gebhardt. "He said 'Y'all like movies?' I said 'Shit, I love them!' He said 'Do you want to see any that's out now?' I said 'John Wayne's new movie.' He had all the brand new movies at his house"—and a 35mm projector. Later that night, the Welsh Elvis joined the party. "It was like four in the morning and somebody knocks on the door so me and Billy go to the door and Tom Jones is there with a couple of his bodyguards and some gorgeous gal," Fritts said. "It was just one of those weird damn nights, you know?"

Goodman, meanwhile, landed a deal with the label Anka had recently signed with, Buddah Records. "We were there about a week, and we both got contracts together," Prine told John Platt. "It was like about ten years passing in front of us. It was a very strange week in New York." On a subsequent trip to New York, he and Goodman were sharing a room at the Hotel Roosevelt. When Prine came back from hearing some music in the Village, he found Goodman hard at work. "He's sittin' there writing," Prine said on the Goodman DVD. "And I look over his shoulder, and it says, 'It was all that I could do to keep from crying / Sometimes it seems so useless to remain.' And I jumped up on the bed and I started playin' an imaginary fiddle, and I went, 'You don't have to call me darlin', darlin', but you never even call me by my name.' And we started laughing." Pretty soon they had a complete song, but Prine refused to take credit for it. "I was young and sensitive, and I said, 'It makes fun of country music!'"

The offer from Atlantic called for Prine to record ten albums over the next five years, a common pace in the sixties, when artists routinely released multiple records in a single year. ("Such requirements were a polite fiction by the '70s," Ruhlmann wrote.) Wexler didn't land his catch right away. "I told him I needed a little time," Prine told Ruhlmann. "I wanted to go home and talk to my father about it. I wanted somebody to look at the contract. I went over and I saw Anka before I went back home, to see what his involvement in this was, because he bought me the plane ticket." He admitted he and Goodman were pretty naïve at this point. Since Anka had paid for their plane tickets to New York, Prine said, they made him their manager.

The return to Chicago was triumphant. "We were like conquering heroes," Prine told Lydia Hutchinson in an interview for a 1995 article in *Performing Songwriter* magazine. "If they could've given us a ticker-tape parade, they would have." Prine accepted Wexler's offer and began making plans to record his debut album, which he discussed on *The Studs Terkel Program* on 98.7 FM, WFMT, the home of the folk radio show *The Midnight Special*. Terkel, born in New York in 1912, had lived in Chicago since he was eight years old. A regular at the Chicago Folk Festival, he served as master of ceremonies for local folksinger Bonnie Koloc at the record-signing party for her debut album. He was a long-time radio personality who had broadcast on WFMT since 1952, as well as an oral historian who had published three books by 1971: *Giants of Jazz*, *Division Street: America*, and *Hard Times: An Oral History of the Great Depression*.

Terkel didn't so much interview Prine as offer effusive words of praise and then wait while Prine awkwardly fumbled around for a response. Prine opened the show by singing "Hello in There." He had made a studio recording at the station the previous year, but he sounded considerably more relaxed this time around. "I don't know what to say," Terkel said. "I think that's gonna be a classic. You have everything in it, don't you? The complete shutting out of old people, and the feelings they undoubtedly have that you're able to evoke an experience. Quite remarkable." Prine went on to sing "The Frying Pan," "Sam Stone," "Donald and Lydia," and "Spanish Pipedream." They talked about Prine's Kentucky roots, as well as his military service and writing "Sam Stone." The singer discussed his upcoming recording session for Atlantic, with Muscle Shoals on the short list as its location. "It's kind of a toss-up between there and New York, and I hope we end up down in Muscle Shoals," Prine said. Before Prine closed with "Flashback Blues," Terkel called him "the most powerful and important songwriter in America today." Heady words for a twenty-four-year-old kid from Maywood who had only quit his Post Office job a few months before.

CHAPTER 2

Thursday's Child

▼

John Edward Prine, conceived in the depths of a Midwestern winter, was born 10 October 1946 at Westlake Hospital in Maywood, ten miles west of downtown Chicago. He was the family's third son, a Thursday's child who had far to go.

Bill, thirty-one, and Verna, twenty-six, brought Dave and Doug's baby brother home to the unassuming two-story worker's cottage they rented on First Avenue, which they shared with Bill's parents. Prine may have been born up north, but the family had deep roots in Kentucky. They took him on a prenatal tour of his ancestral home in the family's 1939 DeSoto. "It's like I'm from there, but just wasn't actually born there," he told Ronni Lundy in an interview for the 1991 book *Shuck Beans, Stack Cakes, and Honest Fried Chicken: The Heart and Soul of Southern Country Kitchens.* "When my mother was carrying me—about eight months along—they came down to Kentucky and the Smokies and the Grand Ole Opry, so I was nearly born down south. Hell, I'd already been to the Opry in 1946, before I was even born."

A black-and-white family photo from the late forties shows an instantly recognizable, toddler-sized John standing between his brothers in a sun-dappled clearing at the edge of a patch of woods. Doug, a goofy grin on his face and a shock of dark hair cascading over his forehead, clutches John's left arm. Doug wears suspenders over a University of Illinois T-shirt with a profile portrait of the school's mascot in those days, Chief Illiniwek, in full feathered headdress. Bespectacled Dave, on John's right with his left hand draped over his baby brother's shoulder, sticks his tongue out at the camera. John has an unfamiliar crop of fine blond hair on his head but he looks off into the middle distance with a familiar expression: thoughtful, preoccupied, a little sad.

Dave had come along first, in November 1937, less than a year after sixteen-year-old Verna married Bill in Muhlenberg County, Kentucky, and returned with him to Maywood. The village, founded in 1869 on three square miles of prairie along the western banks of the Des Plaines River, had 25,829 people in the 1930 census. An academic paper describes the village during the Depression, when the Prines arrived: "Maywood may not have had the reputation of being wealthy as did nearby Oak Park or Elmhurst, but it was a comfortable suburb. Indeed, the planning done by Colonel Nichols in the 1870s still gave the town something of an 'elite' reputation fifty years later."

Oak Park, just east of Maywood toward downtown Chicago and Lake Michigan, was the hometown of literary titan Ernest Hemingway and the home base and proving ground for pioneering architect Frank Lloyd Wright. Maywood had its own celebrity claims to fame: Charles Lindbergh flew a mail route out of the village a year before he flew the *Spirit of St. Louis* across the Atlantic Ocean in 1927, and, a decade before that, poet Carl Sandburg sired two of his three daughters and one of his most famous poems, "Chicago," while living in Maywood.

> HOG Butcher for the World
> Tool Maker, Stacker of Wheat,
> Player with Railroads and the Nation's Freight Handler;
> Stormy, husky, brawling,
> City of the Big Shoulders

Blue-collar Maywood was considerably huskier and more brawling than tony, leafy Oak Park, if no less flat. Bill, son of a carpenter, had moved up from the Kentucky coalfields to the plains of Illinois to become a toolmaker. He worked at the American Can Company, where the beer can was born in 1935. He served as president or vice president of the union for about thirty years.

Music also meant a lot to Bill—even if he lacked the gift himself. The family owned records by artists from across the musical spectrum: Duke

Ellington, Spike Jones, and Roy Acuff. They went to a lot of concerts at the Oriental and Chicago Theatres, including shows by Count Basie, Louis Armstrong, and Johnny Cash. One of Prine's first concerts was a performance by Spike Jones and His City Slickers. Jones was like a Tex Avery cartoon character made flesh. "I think the whole time I was waitin' for Johnny Puleo, the [dwarf] harmonica player, to run out and bite Spike Jones on the leg," Prine told his longtime guitarist, Jason Wilber, in a 2011 radio interview.

A bouncy song by a Kentucky homeboy, Muhlenberg County native Merle Travis, began a fourteen-week run at the top of the country charts the week after Prine was born. "If you want your freedom PDQ, divorce me C.O.D.," Travis sang in "Divorce Me C.O.D." The Windy City's big country radio station, WJJD, delivered the accents and stories of home to the Prines and families like them who followed the hillbilly highway north in pursuit of jobs and opportunity. Most evenings Bill would sit in the kitchen, put the radio in the window to improve the reception, and drink beer while listening to songs by Roy Acuff, Lefty Frizzell, Hank Williams, and Webb Pierce. John's mother had a good sense of humor. "My mom was pretty dry, but she was a real funny person," Prine told Nick Spitzer in a 2008 interview for *American Routes Radio*, broadcast on WWNO in New Orleans. He felt loved and cared for growing up. "Everybody picked me up when they came in the door and swang me around," Prine told writer Lloyd Sachs in a 2005 interview for *No Depression* magazine. "It was a really great childhood."

His grandmother, Idell, taught her daughter-in-law a lot about cooking, such as how to whip up a plate of hash. Other Verna specialties included chili, fried potatoes, pot roast, steak and gravy, biscuits and gravy, roast turkey and mashed potatoes, and fried chicken. The family traveled down to Muhlenberg County every summer. Prine recalled fishing trips far and near, to the White River hundreds of miles south in the Ozark Mountains of rural Arkansas, or to a lake just outside Maywood. The Prines were mainstream Protestants in a sea of Cook County Catholics, Methodists from way back. Bill's grandfather listed his occupation on census forms as Methodist minister (as well as mechanic). Bill's father, Empson Scobie Prine, served as a steward at First Methodist Church in Maywood. He died at home at age sixty-four on 18 July 1953, and the family took him home to Muhlenberg County to bury him in Central City.

That same year the fourth Prine boy, Billy, was born. Billy came along three weeks before John's seventh birthday. "I was supposed to have been the baby," Prine told Meg Griffin in a 2005 interview on Sirius satellite radio. Dave graduated from high school and headed downstate to attend the University of Illinois at Champaign. He got married not long afterward. A photo from the wedding shows Bill, forty-one, staring confidently into the camera, his meaty toolmaker's hand resting on his left knee, the proud patriarch surrounded by his family. On workdays, after his shift had ended at American Can, Bill would come home and drink a quart of Old Style on the front porch, stashing an extra on reserve in the freezer. Sometimes he would take his sons to bars with him. Bill would "take us with him to hillbilly bars, set me up, order an orange pop for me, go play the jukebox, and give me money for the pinball machine," Prine told Sachs. Bill made the best of his blue-collar existence, but it wasn't the life he dreamed about. Prine's parents had "an unqualified love of the land and an elemental pride in a job well done; a painful awareness of the toll hard work and shoestring budgets can take on love and family; [and they appreciated] the simple pleasures that make the big hurts a little more bearable," writer David Fricke wrote in 1993 for the liner notes to Prine's *Great Days* collection.

One year Prine got a guitar for Christmas, an aqua blue department store Silvertone, he said in a 1993 spoken-word recording, "A John Prine Christmas." "The model was called Kentucky Blue. And man, I saw that sittin' under the tree—I just couldn't wait. First year or so I didn't know how to play it. I'd just stand in front of the mirror with a string around my neck with that guitar and I'd try and look like Elvis." Rock 'n' roll cast a shadow as long as the tailfins on a Cadillac, and Prine got caught up in the excitement like millions of other kids. He bought 45s at the local hardware store and appliance fix-it shop. "I'd go in and buy a record and I'd take it home and I'd play it twenty times, and if by the twentieth time I wasn't as passionate about it as the first time I heard it, I would take it back and tell 'em there was a flaw or defect," Prine told Wilber. Artists who generally made the cut: Johnny Cash, Johnny Horton, Little Richard, and Buddy Holly.

Prine wasn't much of a student, but he gradually evolved into an accomplished storyteller. "In school, the only thing I used to be able to do at all was when they gave me a free hand at writing dialogue," he told

Bruce Pollock for a collection of songwriter interviews, the 1975 book *In Their Own Words*. "Writing nothing but dialogue. Everybody else, all these kids who were straight-A students, would just bang their heads against the wall, and I'd just go, 'Whoosh!' and hand it in. The teacher would say, 'Who'd you buy this from?' Because I was a horrible student otherwise." Prine was a thinker, a daydreamer. "I get very far away," he told Ted Kooser, the U.S. poet laureate, during a 2005 appearance at the Library of Congress. "I tried to explain it to some friends. Once I had one of these spells when I was about 13. I told my parents and they sent me to an eye doctor. I just told them sometimes I felt very far away, yet I felt like I could see things as if I was looking down into the room. This went on for a good long while."

As a teenager Prine started dabbling in juvenile delinquency, like a stereotype from a fifties educational film. Chicago mob boss Al Capone had died three months after Prine was born and was buried in neighboring Hillside, but his legacy lived on in Maywood's young thugs. "Maywood was a mixture of everything," Prine told a hometown audience during a 2000 concert at his old high school, Proviso East. "Melrose Park was on one side and that was Italian American. Forest Park . . . leaned toward German Americans and Polish Americans. You can tell by the restaurants. Oak Park? To Maywood it was where the rich people lived. In River Forest everybody would point out [mobster] Tony Accardo's house. We'd ride by it on our bicycles." Capone had given Accardo the nickname "Joe Batters" because of the skill he showed bashing two Chicago Outfit turncoats with a baseball bat. He was the son of Sicilian immigrants who eventually succeeded Capone. That Italian mob heritage filtered down to Prine's little gang, the Parts Brothers. "If somebody was talking about robbing something or there was going to be a big fight, somehow I would manage to not be there," Prine told the *Chicago Sun-Times* in 2010.

Clearly Prine needed a hobby, something to keep him off the streets besides avoiding rumbles between the Jets and the Sharks. One night in 1960 or '61 his big brother gave him one. He was shocked to learn his oldest brother could play. "I walked in the kitchen one night and he was playin' a song for our dad on the guitar, and I didn't know any of my brothers could play music," Prine told Griffin. "And I was just stunned.

He saw my face—I was definitely headed to be Juvenile Delinquent 101 right then. He knew I didn't pay attention much, and he said, 'If you'll listen, I'll teach you three chords. But you gotta pay attention.' And so I did, and it totally caught my attention. It probably saved me from a lot of bad stuff I was headed for."

Thus began years of Prine sitting in his room, playing guitar. "The first time I held down a chord and I didn't muffle it, well, I just sat there with my ear on the wood, even after the sound died, feeling the vibrations," he said, according to a 1995 promotional interview released by Prine's own Oh Boy Records. "From there, it was me sitting there alone in a room singing to a wall."

Camelot-era kids were feeling the vibrations from the redwood forest to the Gulf Stream waters. The Kingston Trio had topped the charts in 1958 with "Tom Dooley," a slick update of an old ballad about a nineteenth-century murder in the North Carolina mountains. The Great Folk Scare was tuning up across the country, from Dinkytown in Minneapolis to Old Town in Chicago to Greenwich Village in New York City. Minnesota-born folksinger Bob Dylan, a complete unknown, had just rolled into Manhattan.

Dave passed along records for his brother to learn that expanded Prine's musical horizons and gave him a firm foundation in country, folk, and blues: one by the first family of country music, Virginia's Carter Family; one by self-taught North Carolina guitarist Elizabeth "Libba" Cotten, best known for the buoyant Piedmont blues song "Freight Train"; and one by the most playful, lighthearted bluesman around, Mississippi John Hurt. The fingerpicking especially caught Prine's ears—"Freight Train" was one of the first songs he learned. To please his father he learned a repertoire of country classics by Hank Williams, Roy Acuff, Jimmie Rodgers, and Webb Pierce. Once he learned an entire album. "I think it was an old radio show that they'd released as a live Hank Williams thing, with the Drifting Cowboys and Miss Audrey," Prine told Meg Griffin in 2005. "I had memorized all the in-between patter, and I would sit and do the whole Hank Williams record in my bedroom—I'd introduce Miss Audrey and everything."

Eventually he decided it would be more fun to write his own songs. "After I learned my first couple of songs, I found it easier to make up songs than to try to learn my favorite ones," he told Kooser in 2005.

"They never sounded anywhere near as good as the records sounded, so I would just make something up and I would sing it till I got tired of it. Then I discovered girls, and I would make up songs to try and impress 'em—which didn't always work. I did that for awhile. It was more or less a hobby I kept to myself."

Big changes came to his family as the sixties revved up. Doug, who got the nickname "Tippy Toes" from his time on the high school gymnastics team, followed Dave out the door, joining the U.S. Air Force in 1961. Dave would become a father in April, when Pat gave birth to Verna and Bill's first grandchild, Anne, making Prine an uncle at age fourteen. With all the changes came reassuring glimpses of home: A new TV series, *The Andy Griffith Show*, offered a weekly visit to the small-town South and comic explorations of rural mountain culture.

Prine gradually got more serious about playing. He had his eye on a Gibson Hummingbird at a local music store, so he found another job in order to save up and buy it. "They took money off of it because it was sittin' in the window of the store and the sun had kinda ruined the finish on it," Prine said during an interview segment for a 1980 appearance on the TV show *Soundstage*. Prine set to work shoveling snow and doing other odd jobs at the Episcopal Church of the Holy Communion to save $250 for the guitar. "I was a pew dustin', cross polishin', lawn mowin', snow shovelin' son of a gun," he told David Fricke in an interview for the *Great Days* collection. A photo from 1962 shows a rail-thin Prine standing and strumming, the sleeves on his white T-shirt rolled up. He wears a slouch hat and blows a kazoo. A coltish Billy sits on the sofa across the room from him in his stocking feet, blowing into a tuba.

Despite Dave's new parental responsibilities, he still made time for plenty of woodshedding with his little brother, Dave learning fiddle as John learned rhythm guitar. The brothers would head into the city for inspiration from veteran musicians, catching artists such as Doc Watson and the Stanley Brothers at the annual University of Chicago Folk Festival. Dave's attention was an act of love that would permanently alter the direction of Prine's life. "I couldn't concentrate on anything besides daydreaming," Prine told writer Greg Kot of the *Chicago Tribune*. "My brother saw this in me, and he saw music as a way of getting through to me." Once they taught themselves the basics, Dave started taking classes at the Old Town School of Folk Music in downtown Chicago.

Chicago's first folk club, the Gate of Horn, had opened in 1956 in the basement of the Rice Hotel on North Dearborn Street. Owner Albert Grossman hired Frank Hamilton, a guitarist and banjo picker from California who had played with Woody Guthrie, as one of the club's house musicians. Hamilton cofounded the Old Town School a year later. One of its first students was a Chicago teenager named Jim McGuinn, who learned about the school when another Gate of Horn house musician did a show at his high school.

Out in the suburbs, Prine eventually followed his older brothers to Proviso East High School. He showed athletic prowess, following Doug's footsteps on the gymnastics team—and forcing the family to adjust their nicknames. Doug became Tippy Toes One, while John was dubbed Tippy Toes Two. A picture in the 1963 *Provi*, Proviso's yearbook, shows a thin, muscular Prine wearing tights and a Proviso East tank top, sitting cross-legged with his fellow Pirates from the varsity gymnastics squad. Another photo shows Prine looking ripped as he goes through a pommel horse exercise, body extended, biceps bulging. "Concentrating on his position, John Prine combines strength, form, and timing on side-horse," the caption read. "Prine, probably the most improved player on the squad, demonstrates his skill in the 'loop off.'"

Even though he still wasn't much for academics, Prine had become an avid reader, taking a shine to the novels of John Steinbeck. Music began to play a larger role in his life. The Old Town style of group lessons suited Prine, because students didn't have to read music and could learn in the anonymity of a cacophonous crowd of strummers. The stamped dates on his Old Town School registration card show that he attended classes there steadily about once a week beginning in September 1963. Like his brother, Prine took lessons with Ray Tate, learning licks by the likes of Doc Watson.

Frank Hamilton had left the school in 1962 to replace Erik Darling in the Weavers, the pioneering folk group. Hamilton's old boss at the Gate of Horn, Albert Grossman, had also moved on. Grossman, a first-generation Chicagoan born to Russian Jewish immigrants in 1926, helped start up the Newport Folk Festival in Rhode Island in 1959. Then he assembled the folk group Peter, Paul and Mary before becoming Bob Dylan's manager. In the summer of 1963 Peter, Paul and Mary's cover of "Blowin' in the Wind" reached No. 2 on the charts and introduced America to Dylan.

Dave made sure his brother knew "Blowin' in the Wind" did not originate with Peter, Paul and Mary. "He had given me a coupla Ramblin' Jack [Elliott] records, and I just really dug the way he sang and everything," Prine told country singer Bobby Bare during a 1985 appearance on The Nashville Network. ". . . my brother said, 'You know that song "Blowin' in the Wind"?' And I said, 'Yeah,' and he said, 'The guy that wrote that sounds a lot like Ramblin' Jack. You oughtta go pick up his album.' So that's how I got my first Bob Dylan album." Elliott performed at the Chicago Folk Festival in 1962. Dylan himself was popular enough by December 1963 to play at the city's 2,500-seat Orchestra Hall.

A mid-sixties Prine family photo shows a mature Dave, now in his late twenties, sporting a mustache and a dark long-sleeved dress shirt, sawing away on his fiddle. Billy, now approaching adolescence, sits in the background. He wears a striped sweater and plucks on a strawberry blond spruce-top Hofner bass with a sunburst finish, the same kind Paul McCartney plays. Bill and Verna smile in the background. In the left foreground stands a hawk-faced Prine, wearing a dark vest and tie, his hair styled in a neat pompadour. He gazes intently at Dave's fingering, strumming a guitar. But it's not the Hummingbird acoustic: Now he plays an electric Fender Jaguar.

Bill's mother, Idell, died on 23 June 1964. She was eighty-five. As with Empson the previous decade, the family took her home to Muhlenberg County for burial.

Prine continued to make up songs. He had girls to impress. "I remember this gorgeous girl," he told Dave Hoekstra of the *Chicago Sun-Times* in 2010. "She was so pretty the word was that she only went out with college guys. My senior year I'm sitting behind her in art class. She had a voice like Marilyn Monroe, real soft. She turned around and said, 'Hi Jimmy.' I went out with her for four months and never corrected her." She told Prine he reminded her of Roger Miller. Texas-born Miller, a country songwriter and singer, was taking America by storm during Prine's last year of high school. He had found his niche writing high-energy country songs with a twisted comic bent. In 1964 "Dang Me" and "Chug-a-Lug" made the Top 10 on both the country and pop charts. "I loved the way he put words together, the sounds of the words, whether they made sense or not, whether it sounded like nonsense, it'd just really get to me," Prine told Bill Flanagan in an interview for the 1986 book

Written in My Soul: Rock's Great Songwriters Talk about Creating Their Music. Because of the Marilyn-soundalike girlfriend, Prine said, "I became a huge Roger Miller fan."

Another girlfriend, Ann Carole, came from Italian stock. She was the daughter of a Proviso East janitor. He had access to one of the school's tape recorders, and recorded Prine singing "The Frying Pan," "Sour Grapes," and "Twist & Shout." "The Frying Pan," the stronger of the two originals, is a rollicking comic tale of domestic disharmony, showing a definite Roger Miller influence: "I miss the way she used to yell at me / The way she used to cuss and moan / And if I ever go out and get married again / I'll never leave my wife at home." "Sour Grapes" is a darker, moodier (and slightly clunky) tale of lost love: "I couldn't care less if she never come back / I was gonna leave her anyway / And all the good times that we shared / Don't mean a thing today." Both songs demonstrate a solid grasp of song form and lyrical economy, creating vivid images with few words that conjure real emotions.

Eventually his songwriting fell by the wayside. Prine muddled through the rest of high school, and had to go an extra semester. He finally finished half a year late, at the beginning of 1965. "I graduated in January, and went to the office to pick up my diploma," Prine told the crowd at his 2000 homecoming concert. "The custodian was there and he said, 'Hey, you got your diploma?' And that was my ceremony."

CHAPTER 3

Call of Duty

▼

The same month Prine graduated from high school in Maywood, Old Town School veteran Jim McGuinn went to Columbia Studios in Hollywood to record a Dylan tune, "Mister Tambourine Man." The ringing tone of McGuinn's twelve-string electric Rickenbacker quickly became the signature sound of folk rock. "Thanks to the Old Town School of Folk Music, I had a solid foundation to work from," McGuinn said years later in an interview for a history of the school. "The sound of the Byrds was a direct result of the fingerpicking techniques that I'd learned."

Though Prine continued attending classes at Old Town on a regular basis, it never occurred to him to follow McGuinn's lead. "It was always a hobby to me," he told William Ruhlmann. "I only wrote songs to amuse myself or to get some girl's attention." But high school was over and he needed to earn his keep, so he got a job delivering mail for the U.S. Post Office. The job required no training, offered good benefits, and gave Prine a way to make money while he figured out what he wanted to be when he grew up. "I read everything," he told Ted Kooser in 2005. "If there was ketchup on page 57 of *Time* magazine, it was me, you know? I read it at lunch."

A year after he got his high school diploma, his own mailman delivered a surprise from the U.S. Selective Service System: An Order to Report for Induction. Like Elvis before him, Prine had been drafted into the U.S. Army.

Prine said his carpenter grandpa, Empson, "voted for Eisenhower, 'cause Lincoln won the war." Empson's father, William Walker Prine, fought for the Union with the Thirtieth Illinois Volunteer Infantry Regiment, which helped starve out the Confederates in the siege of Vicksburg and marched to the sea with Sherman. Empson's father-in-law, William Henderson "Billy" Smith, also wore Union blue, fighting with the Eleventh Kentucky Volunteer Infantry Regiment and sustaining a minor wound at Shiloh in the spring of 1862. Eventually the U.S. Army sent Smith to a recruiting station in Paradise—just across the Green River from his native Ohio County, Kentucky.

World War II hit Maywood harder than most American towns: Company B of the 192nd Tank Battalion, aka the Maywood Tank Company, served under Generals Douglas MacArthur and Jonathan Wainwright IV in the Philippines. The company provided cover as U.S. troops withdrew in the face of a Japanese invasion and were among the seventy thousand hungry, poorly equipped American and Filipino soldiers captured when Bataan surrendered on 9 April 1942. Maywood has honored their sacrifice annually ever since.

The Prine family did what they could on the home front. Empson and Bill both gave blood, and Empson served as an air-raid warden. Plenty of the town's families experienced the horrors of war in a devastatingly personal way. But a movie-mad guy like Prine—born thirteen months after Japan's surrender ended World War II—was just as susceptible as the next kid to violent fantasies inspired by the glamorous, relatively bloodless way Hollywood depicted combat. "All of us kinda grew up with Audie Murphy movies and stuff like that," Prine told Bobby Bare. "After I saw *To Hell and Back*, I passed an Oldsmobile car lot on the way home. I jumped up on the hood and I shot everybody on the street."

Murphy, who earned more medals than any other American soldier in World War II, played himself fighting across Europe in *To Hell and Back*, released in 1955. A decade later, the Vietnam War gave another generation of Americans a chance to experience the difference between play-acting in their hometowns and slogging through the jungles of Southeast Asia with an M16 rifle. President Lyndon Johnson doubled the number of troops drafted each month beginning in the summer of 1965. A new batch of Maywood boys got swept up in the rising tide of the latest war. A handwritten note on Prine's Old Town School registration card reads "drafted 1/31/66."

He went through basic training at Fort Polk outside Leesville, Louisiana, where the Maywood Tank Company had trained a quarter century before. Prine and his friends called it "Disease-ville." Treating a military aptitude test as a joke, he selected answers at random on a multiple-choice form, only to qualify as a "mechanical genius." By the luck of the draw, he avoided the hot war in Southeast Asia and followed Elvis's footsteps to a Cold War base in West Germany. There he headed up a motor pool working on construction equipment. "I remember one morning we had an inspection and we had one too many bulldozers," he told an Alaska audience in 2002, according to a review in the *Fairbanks Daily News–Miner*. "That's just as bad as being one short, so we buried it." He eventually earned a second stripe as a corporal, his highest rank in the army.

Doug, meanwhile, wrapped up his service in the air force and returned home. He went to Chicago's City Hall one day to apply for a job doing maintenance work, but wound up taking a test to become a police officer instead. Chicago's police detectives had a grisly case to investigate that summer, when Richard Speck systematically raped, tortured, and murdered eight student nurses. On the other side of the Atlantic, Prine found that he couldn't entirely elude the horrors of Vietnam even in West Germany. "It was something that disturbed me on a personal level," he told Ruhlmann. "I had friends over there. I spent my time in Germany, but some of the guys that were over in Germany with me had volunteered to go over there to get some time cut off their tour of duty. You only had to pull thirteen months over in Vietnam, and some of those guys didn't come back, either."

Home on leave in late 1966, Prine married his high school sweetheart, Ann Carole, the day after Christmas. A wedding photo shows the happy couple beneath a "Merry Christmas" banner, the bride's mane of a veil dwarfing her head. Soon enough it was back to West Germany. Life in his hometown had prepared Prine well for the random mix of strangers he would bunk with in the service. "Maywood stuck out because it was integrated," he told Dave Hoekstra in 2010. "Later on, especially when I got in the Army, I was glad I grew up in that situation. I was with kids from Mexico, black kids." It had been years since Prine had written a song, but the boredom of army life eventually brought him back to it. "I'd taken quite a long break before the Army, and to kinda entertain myself, one of the guys in the barracks had a [German-made] guitar, an old Framus, and he was singing Lefty Frizzell songs," Prine told Jason Wilber. "He'd lend me his guitar and I'd sing him some of the folk songs I knew and some of the country stuff. We got along pretty good, and the guys all started coming and listening to us play."

The one song he definitely recalls writing in the army, "Aw Heck," owes a debt to Roger Miller, like "The Frying Pan" before it: "The cannibals can catch me and fry me in a pan / Long as I got my woman," he sang, forcing a comic rhyme by saying "woo-man." "I was sittin' on my bunk makin' up the words to this one night and this buddy of mine from Louisiana walked in and sat on the bunk across from me and started listening to the words I was writing," Prine told an audience in a story heard on his 1988 album *John Prine Live*. "I guess he thought they struck him kinda funny, so he slapped his leg and said, 'Aw, heck!' So I put that in the song and I made him a songwriter, too." Even this goofy song dipped into darkness, making reference to an assertion by fifties mass murderer Charlie Starkweather that if he were to be executed, his girlfriend and coconspirator, Caril Fugate, ought to go out with him: "I could get the electric chair for a phony rap / Long as she's sittin' in my lap."

Prine's few songs up to this point had focused on domestic concerns and affairs of the heart, but as the world changed around him, his focus expanded. When he returned home in 1968, he couldn't help but notice the impact of military service on his friends. "I had a buddy come home from Germany, and a month after he got out I called his house and he was in a veterans hospital havin' shock treatments," Prine told Bare. "He just went bananas. I knew it when I seen that all of his shoes was pointed the same way under his bed, that he wasn't really out of the army. He had those hangers the right way—I said, 'Oh, he's in trouble. If somebody blew "Reveille" right now, he'd run out the window.'" Maywood had remembered veterans of the Bataan Death March with a parade every September since 1942, but for Vietnam veterans, "They weren't no parades or nothin'," he said.

Marriage and two years running an army motor pool overseas had done nothing to change Prine's career path. He liked the freedom he found walking his mail routes in Maywood, Broadview, and Westchester. The job gave him plenty of time to think—when he wasn't dodging stray dogs. It was an era when unfenced, unchained, and fertile dogs commonly roamed the streets, and the notion of hounds ambushing mailmen was more than a comic-strip cliché. "There was a couple of dogs on the route that had actual vendettas against me," Prine told Meg Griffin.

The trouble his friends were having adjusting to civilian life gave him plenty to think about. He started putting together a song he would call "The Great Society Conflict Veteran's Blues." President Johnson's Great Society program was an ambitious attempt to create a sixties version of FDR's New Deal with programs such as Head Start and Medicare, but Vietnam would overshadow Johnson's domestic accomplishments. As the sixties waned, the war escalated abroad, American cities erupted in flames during race riots at home, and illegal drugs replaced alcohol as the mind-altering substance of choice for many young people. Pop music, meanwhile, got louder, weirder, and psychedelicized, the Bobby Fuller Four and the Dave Clark Five giving way to the Chocolate Watchband and the 13th Floor Elevators. Jim McGuinn now had a long string of hit singles under his belt with the Byrds, from a rocking cover of Pete Seeger's "Turn! Turn! Turn! (To Everything There Is a Season)" to a band original, "Eight Miles High." In 1967 McGuinn changed his first name to Roger because the leader of an Indonesian spiritual movement told him the new name would better "vibrate with the universe."

Prine reacted to all the heaviosity by going in the opposite direction, keeping his lyrics plainspoken and rooted in everyday life. The writing process for "Sam Stone," he said, started with two lines: "Sweet songs never last too long on broken radios" and "There's a hole in Daddy's arm where all the money goes." The part about broken radios originated in his workplace. The carrier who sorted mail next to him at the Post Office had a radio that "had fell so many times, 'cause people tripped over the cord, that [he] had it wrapped up in electrician's tape," Prine told Ruhlmann. "I liked the idea of a broken radio, and I started thinking about that on the mail route, and it developed into the story about a soldier." The hole in Daddy's arm was an image inspired by political cartoons, Prine told Studs Terkel: "I had just kind of a picture of a fella shooting money into his arm, you know, like a rainbow of money just falling down into his arm."

He based the story in part on a 1957 movie, *A Hatful of Rain*, a melodrama with a film noir feel directed by Fred Zinneman on the heels of *From Here to Eternity* and *High Noon*. Don Murray, previously known for his comic roles, played a Korean War vet turned addict named Johnny Pope. "They had him on morphine for a wound, and when he came home he couldn't kick it," Prine told John Platt in a 1971 interview on WGLD in Oak Park. He brought the story from the film into his own era: "All my friends I knew, they just felt so empty when they got out— they felt like it was a complete waste, no matter where they were, whether they were in 'Nam or they stayed in the States, they felt like it was completely wasted, that they had just taken a couple of years of their life and done nothing, not gone backwards, forwards, sideways, or anything." He called the Vietnam veteran Sam Stone.

The song was quiet, deeply personal, zooming in to examine the smallest details of a broken man's life, the vacant stare on a dying man's face:

> And the gold rolled through his veins
> Like a thousand railroad trains
> And eased his mind in the hours that he chose
> While the kids ran around wearin' other people's clothes

But Prine was still writing for the walls, singing behind closed doors. Soon enough it was back to delivering bills and catalogs.

After Grossman opened the Gate of Horn, a series of folk clubs followed, concentrated in the Old Town neighborhood adjacent to Lincoln Park on Chicago's Near North Side. Arlo Guthrie, the folksinging son of the legendary Woody Guthrie, quickly became a regular. In 1969 the Quiet Knight opened on North Wells Street, later moving to the second floor of an old brick building on West Belmont. Other folk clubs of the era included the Earl of Old Town, the Old Town Pub, and Scot's Cellar.

The city had been a hotbed for music and culture since the Jazz Age, when King Oliver, Jelly Roll Morton, and Louis Armstrong rolled in from New Orleans to play steady gigs for gangsters and society swells. Bluegrass founder Bill Monroe first left Kentucky at eighteen to work at an oil refinery in Whiting, a Chicago suburb just over the Indiana state line. Bill and his brother Charlie began their career as the Monroe Brothers on WJKS, a radio station a few miles away in Gary, Indiana. Chicago's clear-channel WLS set the stage for the Grand Ole Opry with the *National Barn Dance*, a country show broadcast every Saturday night from 1924 to 1952. Bill Prine's beloved *Suppertime Frolic* aired on WJJD during the same era and beyond. When it came to black music, Chicago had it all, from down-home blues to soaring gospel to the sweetest soul music this side of Smokey Robinson courtesy of Sam Cooke, Jerry Butler, and Curtis Mayfield. As the sixties progressed, Chicago produced some of the heaviest rock bands on this side of the pond, including the Paul Butterfield Blues Band and the Electric Flag.

It was also the era when Oak Park's Ray Kroc introduced the world to McDonald's hamburgers, Hugh Hefner made smut semirespectable when he founded *Playboy* magazine in his hometown of Chicago, and a long line of performers emerged from the city to transform the face of modern comedy: Elaine May, Mike Nichols (who also hosted *The Midnight Special* radio show), Joan Rivers, and Bob Newhart, many of them associated with the Second City improv theater established in Old Town in 1959.

Dave formed a band with other guys from the Old Town School. They played old-timey music, with a name, National Recovery Act, that harked back to the thirties and FDR's New Deal programs. Dave played fiddle and Tyler Wilson played guitar, with Fleming Brown sometimes joining them on banjo. Doug got married in early 1968. It would prove to be an eventful year for the Chicago Police Department—and other government institutions around the world. Nineteen sixty-eight quickly became a year of bloodshed, riots, and chaos. The Chicago ghetto went up in flames after Martin Luther King was assassinated, with Mayor Richard J. Daley authorizing the police to kill suspected arsonists on sight.

Chicago played host to a national cataclysm during the final week of August, when the Democratic National Convention returned to the city, twelve years after the peaceful 1956 convention. Hundreds of antiwar protesters showed up, as well. A clash between police and protesters—later dubbed a "police riot"—resulted in widespread use of tear gas and mace, and in violence that spread out of Grant Park and into the streets of the city. Several prominent organizers were later charged with conspiracy and incitement to riot, including Abbie Hoffman, Jerry Rubin, Tom Hayden, and Bobby Seale—part of a group that would come to be called the Chicago Eight. (Later Chicago Seven, after Seale was given a separate trial.) As the trial progressed in 1969, daily demonstrations took place outside the courthouse, led by the chairman of the local Black Panther Party, Fred Hampton, a 1966 honors graduate of Proviso East High School in Maywood. A sleeping Hampton died in a hail of gunfire on 4 December 1969 when local and federal officers raided his apartment.

Eventually five members of the Chicago Seven were convicted on charges of intent to incite a riot while crossing state lines, and sentenced to stiff prison terms by Judge Julius Hoffman. Their convictions were later reversed on appeal.

Inspiration comes from unpredictable sources. John Lennon in a hollow log inspired Prine to write an homage to the elderly while sitting in a mailbox. "I'd heard John Lennon sing the [Beatles] song 'Across the Universe,' and there was a bit of echo on his voice and the guitar," Prine told Paul Zollo in an undated interview for *Bluerailroad: A Magazine of the Arts.* ". . . And I was thinking about what you would say if you stuck your head in a hollow log: 'Hello! Hello in there!' And that developed into a song about old people."

Living with one set of grandparents and frequently visiting another in Kentucky had fueled his affection for senior citizens. Delivering mail carried him back to his time a decade earlier helping his friend Mike deliver newspapers to the Baptist Retirement Home in Maywood. "They were all glad to see us, but some of the women would talk to other women as if we were grandchildren of theirs," Prine told the *Soundstage* camera. "Don't trust anyone over thirty" was the watchword of the era. But Prine's song was radically traditional—despite an offhand aspersion on the previous decade's military adventure in East Asia, a sentiment far more resigned than defiant: "We lost Davy in the Korean War / And I still don't know what for / Don't matter anymore," the song's protagonist sings.

> You know that old trees just grow stronger
> And old rivers grow wilder every day
> Old people just grow lonesome
> Waiting for someone to say, "Hello in there, hello"

The old man also mentions Rudy, a former coworker "at the factory." The inspiration for the name walked on four legs—Prine heard his neighbors calling their dog while he was writing the song. Prine wrote part of the song in a USPO relay box—an unmarked drop box without a slot used to transfer mail between carriers. "I hopped in there to eat my ham sandwich for lunch and to hide from the Chicago wind," he wrote in the liner notes for a 2011 collection of vintage songs called *The Singing*

Mailman Delivers. He played the song in a G form transposed to C by putting a capo on the fifth fret of his guitar. ("It's a good thing for the little guitar capos," Prine told a North Carolina audience in 2013. "Otherwise, everything I played would be in G.") He called the song "Old Folks."

All that remained now was for Prine to find a stage to sing his songs on—and a push to get him up on it in the first place. In the meantime, he was starting to treat his songs less like time-killing distractions and more like artistic creations with potential financial value. He was writing them down, finally, and thinking about intellectual-property issues. He copyrighted his first batch of songs under the name "Bruised Orange," an impromptu name for an imaginary musical. (Someone told him it was cheaper to copyright a batch of songs as a musical rather than copyrighting each song individually.) Another Chicago folksinger, Fred Holstein, captured Prine's songs on tape during informal recording sessions at his apartment.

Fred's brother, Ed Holstein, approached Prine about cowriting early on. "Let's write a song about old people," Holstein told him, Prine said in his interview with Nick Spitzer. "I said, 'I can't do that, because I put everything I felt about old people into that one song. How about a woman who's middle-aged but feels older than she is?' And he says, 'Nah.' So I went home and wrote 'Angel from Montgomery' by myself."

Prine was starting to populate his songs with a rich ensemble cast, and his capacity for empathy looked boundless. "I am an old woman, named after my mother," he sang. "My old man is another child that's grown old." (Prine's handwritten lyrics showed that "child" replaced his original "kid.") "Angel from Montgomery" shared with the Vietnam veteran song a series of well-chosen details that made vivid a sense of dreams gone sour. But this wasn't the tragedy of war's aftermath and physical death; this was a Henry David Thoreau observation ("The mass of men lead lives of quiet desperation") crossed with Glen Campbell's "Dreams of the Everyday Housewife." It was thunderous desire and dreams written with lightning reduced to the buzzing of flies in the kitchen: "How the hell can a person go to work in the morning / And come home in the evening and have nothing to say?" Prine thought he chose Montgomery, Alabama, as the setting because it was Hank Williams's hometown.

CHAPTER 4

Open-Mike Night

▼

After a guitar lesson at the Old Town School, Prine would check out the talent playing the weekly open-mike night at a neighborhood bar. For a while the Old Town crowd would hit the Saddle Club, near the Earl of Old Town. When the school moved to new digs, they would gather across the street at the Fifth Peg, a two-hundred-seat club on Armitage Avenue. Prine's guitar teacher, Ray Tate, would be there, along with other teachers and students. (The club's name referenced the separate peg on the neck of a banjo for tuning the drone string. Folk clubs in Toronto and Greenwich Village also used the name, though years before a dispute between co-owners had transformed New York's Fifth Peg into Gerde's Folk City.) "What happened there after school was as important as what happened in the school," Prine told Greg Kot of the *Chicago Tribune* in 2010.

But he lacked the gumption to test his own songs before a real live audience. "I was very nervous about singing the songs in public for the first time," he told Paul Zollo. "Because I thought that they would come across as too detailed, too amateurish. Because I hadn't heard anybody being that detailed. And I thought there must be a reason for that. I must not be doing it the right way, whatever the right way is. But I knew the songs were very effective to me. And they reached me. And I was very satisfied with the songs. But I didn't know how they would relate to other people because I didn't consider myself a normal person." He loved to sing, however, even if he wasn't crazy about the sound of his own voice.

One Sunday night in 1970, after a couple of beers at the Fifth Peg, Prine started talking shit under his breath about the open-mike talent. The people sitting with him challenged him to put his money where his mouth was. He struggled through "Old Folks," "Paradise," and "Sam Stone." "I was writing these songs totally for myself, not thinking that anybody was going to hear them," Prine told Zollo. "And I went from that to being a very nervous public performer. Who had no voice whatsoever. I would kind of speak the words. Very fast or very slow, depending on how the melody went. And I'd hold certain notes to let people know I was going to the next idea. And that's about how limited it was."

He got the songs out, only to be greeted by silent stares. If it had been a Bugs Bunny cartoon, there would have been crickets chirping. "I started shuffling my feet and looking around," he told Ken Paulson during a 2004 appearance at Nashville's First Amendment Center. "And then they started applauding, and it was a really great feeling. It was like I found out all of a sudden that I could communicate. That I could communicate really deep feelings and emotions. And to find that out all at once was amazing." The owner of the Fifth Peg came over and asked him if he wanted a job. "Doing what?" Prine responded. "I wasn't tryin' for a gig," he told Meg Griffin. "I didn't know what a gig was." The owner offered to pay Prine to sing. "And I said, 'Man, I can't sing,'" Prine said. "And he said, 'Just come in here and sing three forty-minute sets on a Thursday night.' And he says, 'And you can keep half of the door.' So, I did. And I started doing that, and I was delivering mail during the day." He was twenty-three years old.

Holding the stage for that long would require Prine to flesh out his sets with a few covers by Dylan, Tom Paxton, John Denver ("Leaving on a Jet Plane"), and James Taylor ("Sweet Baby James"). Even so, he scrambled to write a whole new batch of tunes before his first paying gig. He quickly padded his portfolio with a couple of songs about the pains of leaving childhood behind, à la Joni Mitchell's "The Circle Game" and Neil Young's "Sugar Mountain" ("Souvenirs" and "Flashback Blues"); a wistful breakup song ("Blue Umbrella"); an extended metaphor about America betraying its citizens via overseas military misadventures in the guise of a romantic melodrama ("The Great Compromise"); and a song that was either about Prine's fertile imagination or about smoking pot, depending on how plausible you find Prine's denials ("Illegal Smile," the chorus of which began "fortunately I have the key to escape reality"). Prine wrote the song at home in Melrose Park, "in the kitchen of our three-room flat while my wife Ann Carole was sleeping in the next room," he told a crowd years later, as documented on *John Prine Live*. "I was a mailman. It was 1969, and nothing seemed to make much sense to me. I liked to laugh and when I can't laugh I like to smile. Some people think you should have a reason to smile or they think you're up to something, so it must be an illegal smile."

His day job inspired another political song, but a funny, satirical one this go-round. It all started with *Reader's Digest*, a homespun, broadly popular magazine founded in 1922 that served up extremely conservative ideas about politics ("Let's Set Black History Straight") and culture ("Must Smut Smother the Stage?") among such recurring features as "Humor in Uniform," "It Pays to Increase Your Word Power," and "Laughter, the Best Medicine." The magazine's back covers were like Norman Rockwell paintings stripped of their humor and spark. They showcased old-fashioned images of flowers, birds, kittens, and well-scrubbed white people engaging in such wholesome activities as fishing, watching a Fourth of July fireworks display, and buying vegetables at a roadside stand next to a country church. *Reader's Digest* offered a comforting vision of a pre-sixties—almost nineteenth-century—WASP America, a world where Black Panthers, acidheads, and Yippies existed (if at all) only as incomprehensible juvenile aberrations, the remote objects of paternalistic lectures delivered by responsible grown-ups. In 1970 its cover boasted that readers bought more than twenty-nine million copies of *Reader's Digest* in thirteen languages. The magazine was ubiquitous in Middle America, and a perfect reflection of how Middle America saw itself.

The magazine's editors and Prine might have found some common ground on the subjects of senior citizens and picturesque Southern hamlets, but they parted company when it came to war. It wasn't just the magazine's politics that Prine took issue with—delivering it on his mail route in Westchester was no picnic, either: It was small and bulky, requiring dozens of separate bundles of mail. One issue featured a free flag decal, suitable for sticking on car windows, storm doors, or anywhere else Middle America felt inspired to show its fealty to the U.S. government.

"The next day, I came out, and people had them stuck everywhere," Prine told Ted Kooser. ". . . And I thought, 'Wow, you know? Shoot, things are even worse than I thought they were.'"

In the opening lines of the song, singing over simplified Carter picking, Prine gleefully lobbed an issue of *Reader's Digest* into a smut shop: "While digesting *Reader's Digest* / In the back of a dirty-book store / A plastic flag with gum on the back / Fell out on the floor." Prine proceeded to turn heartland hawks into cartoon characters: "I stuck them stickers all over my car / And one on my wife's forehead." Shifting perspective, the singer critiqued his protagonist's jingoistic zeal: "Now Jesus don't like killin' / No matter what the reason's for." "Your Flag Decal Won't Get You into Heaven Anymore" was no grim portrait of death and decay like Prine's Vietnam veteran song, no moody portrait of betrayal like "The Great Compromise."

In 1970, Edwin Starr's "War (What Is It Good For?)" competed for the hearts and minds of America with Merle Haggard's "The Fightin' Side of Me." During the late summer Prine settled into his weekly gig at the Fifth Peg. He earned fifty cents for each paying customer; twelve people showed up for his first gig. He wasn't ready to quit his day job just yet. But the next appearance drew a bigger crowd. He would come up with songs while driving his '65 Chevy Malibu downtown for a Thursday night gig. "About the fifth time I was driving down there I thought, 'God, the same people are gonna be sitting there. I better have a new song,'" Prine told Zollo. "So I wrote 'Souvenirs' in the car on the way down."

It would prove to be one of his mother's favorite songs, a sweet song of loss. "I hate graveyards and old pawn shops / For they always bring me tears," Prine sang. He would have to wait to see how it worked on guitar. "I came up with the melody in my head, and I thought that the melody must surely have six or seven chords to it, it was so complex," he told Kooser. He was afraid it might even require some jazz chords: "Jazz chords to me are anything that takes more than three fingers to hold. I got down to the club and couldn't wait to take my guitar out to see if I could even get close to it." The result surprised him. "I went to the men's room with my Martin guitar around my neck in these cramped quarters and played the song, and I thought, 'Hell, it's only three chords!'" Prine told Jason Wilber. "I went onstage and sang it and everybody loved it. 'Here's what I just wrote.'"

Word began to spread around the Chicago club scene. Bonnie Koloc, born a few months before Prine in 1946, had left her hometown of Waterloo, Iowa, in 1968 to try her hand at folksinging in the Windy City. She quickly became a fixture on the Earl of Old Town stage. Koloc dropped by the Fifth Peg one night and heard Prine sing the Vietnam veteran song and "Old Folks"—sometimes called "Hello in There." "Afterwards I walked up to him and said, 'John, you don't have to worry about a thing,'" Koloc told the *Chicago Tribune* in 1990. On Saturday, 1 August 1970, Prine did an interview on 98.7 FM, WFMT, the home of folk radio show *The Midnight Special*. After the interview, he got permission to document his songs with a professional recording at the radio station. He wanted a copy to send to the Library of Congress for copyright purposes. *The Midnight Special* host Ray Nordstrand served as recording engineer. Prine recorded eleven songs: "Hello in There," "Souvenirs," "Great Society Conflict Veteran's Blues," "Paradise," "Blue Umbrella," "Aw Heck," "Illegal Smile," "Flashback Blues," "The Frying Pan," "Sour Grapes," and "A Star, a Jewel, and a Hoax."

He sang alone, accompanying himself on acoustic guitar, just as he would at the Fifth Peg. Prine made the most of his limited guitar chops, giving the songs an energetic bounce and shimmering emotional resonance that his voice failed to convey. The songs were stunning; his delivery had yet to catch up to them. Making his first real recording, singing in a sterile environment with no audience to egg him on, Prine sounded uptight. His vocal phrasing was stiff and regimented, his tone emphatic and largely humorless, his range limited. His accent was an odd mix of city and family, Chicago burr meets Muhlenberg twang. "Illegal Smile" kicked off with some nice Merle Travis–style guitar picking, but Prine rushed the song, undermining the humor of the lyrics and making its tempo changes sound forced. (The song transitioned from straight 4/4 time in the verses to waltz time, 3/4, on the choruses.) Not surprisingly, he sounded most relaxed and comfortable on the oldest, most familiar songs, "Sour Grapes" and "Frying Pan."

The last track was a cryptic little eighty-two-second throwaway Prine dared the listener to decipher (a dig at the Dylan fans Prine would criticize for "picking the vowels apart"?) while he coined a new word: "Great thoughts don't come / To those who try too hard / To interpretate what's going on / In the mind's backyard." The longest song, "Hello in There," clocked in at 4:05, while a couple of others raced to a finish before they'd hardly gotten started good. "Aw Heck" was over after 1:38, while "Frying Pan" wrapped up in a record seventy-nine seconds.

On stage, by contrast, he talked for long stretches, his introductions frequently overshadowing the songs themselves. "I talked a whole lot when I first started singing, because I was really nervous," Prine told Paulson. "I couldn't wait to get the singing part over so I could start talking again." The contrast between lighthearted spoken introductions and dark lyrics sometimes confused audiences. For example, Prine would tell funny stories about his army service as a lead-in to the song about Sam Stone, the Vietnam veteran. "When people would hear 'There's a hole in Daddy's arm where all the money goes' for the very first time, a lot of times there would be kind of nervous laughter," he told Paulson. "And then the second time it would come around, they would talk about the song right then and there. They would start talking—sometimes to me. And by the time it'd come around the third time, it was absolute silence."

A couple of months after the WFMT recording session, the film critic for the *Chicago Sun-Times* dropped by the Fifth Peg for a Prine show. Roger Ebert was four years older than Prine, growing up downstate in a college town, Urbana. He had been at the paper since 1967, and moonlighted as a screenwriter, cowriting the latest Russ Meyer breastacular, *Beyond the Valley of the Dolls*, released in the summer of '70. Ebert also liked music, and he knew how to have a good time. Old Town was his stomping grounds. "We were a shifting population of people who knew one another, sometimes well, sometimes barely, and saw one another night after night in the same places," Ebert wrote in 2004. "For me the anchor was O'Rourke's Pub at 319 W. North, and no night was complete without touching base there. But many nights a crowd would gather and move down the street, maybe to the Old Town Ale House, maybe to the Quiet Knight, very often to the Earl of Old Town. Even later we might work our way up Lincoln to Sterch's or Orphan's or Oxford's."

Ebert didn't customarily write about music, but when he heard Prine sing, he made an exception. "I knew from the moment I heard him how good he was," Ebert wrote in his blog decades later. "I wasn't a music critic, but I wrote about him in the *Sun-Times* because after hearing him sing 'Old Folks' and 'Sam Stone,' how could I not?" The article appeared in the *Sun-Times* on Friday, 9 October 1970—which happened to be John Lennon's thirtieth birthday. The accompanying photo is a tight shot of

Prine strumming and singing, a rug hanging on the wall behind him. He wears a jean jacket and his hair is still short enough to pass USPO muster. The headline: "Singing mailman who delivers a powerful message in a few words." It opened with a description of "Your Flag Decal Won't Get You into Heaven Anymore" and quoted the chorus. "Lyrics like this are earning John Prine one of the hottest underground reputations in Chicago these days," Ebert wrote. He described Prine's performing style: "He appears on stage with such modesty he almost seems to be backing into the spotlight. He sings rather quietly, and his guitar work is good, but he doesn't show off. He starts slow. But after a song or two, even the drunks in the room begin to listen to his lyrics. And then he has you." Ebert also talked about "Sam Stone," which "says more about the last 20 years in America than any dozen adolescent acid-rock peace dirges." He praised the "hole in Daddy's arm" line for its "stunning power." "You hear lyrics like these, perfectly fitted to Prine's quietly confident style and his ghost of a Kentucky accent, and you wonder how anyone could have so much empathy and still be looking forward to his twenty-fourth birthday on Saturday."

Ebert's work as a critic showed that he valued honesty, emotional openness, and plain language, and he seemed to view Prine as a kindred spirit. After hearing the Vietnam veteran song, Ebert wrote later, "I said to my pals at my table, 'He is the best singer-songwriter in America. That song is a great short story.' He *is*, not *will be*, because that first night I also heard his 'Old Folks.'" The singer's efforts to keep his set fresh with new material paid off in Ebert's *Sun-Times* critique: "Prine's songs are all original, and he only sings his own. They're nothing like the work of most young composers these days, who seem to specialize in narcissistic tributes to themselves. He's closer to Hank Williams than to Roger Williams, closer to Dylan than to Ochs." When Ebert got around to quoting Prine speaking rather than singing, it was a comment about songwriting: "In my songs, I try to look through someone else's eyes, and I want to give the audience a feeling more than a message."

Prine's wife also got a mention in the article. Ann Carole, Ebert wrote, "says she finds scraps of paper around the house with maybe a word or a sentence on them and a month later the phrase will turn up in a new song." The article contained a minor error, implying that Prine only began taking lessons at the Old Town School that same year. Ebert praised Prine's sense of humor and quoted from "Hello in There," "Illegal Smile," "Angel from Montgomery," and "The Great Compromise." Toward the end of the article he noted Prine's growing popularity: "His crowds grew so large that the Fifth Peg is now presenting him on Friday and Saturday nights; his opening last weekend was a full house by word-of-mouth."

Prine hadn't seen anything yet. The Ebert profile "busted things wide open," he told Kot. "I had people waiting outside in line on Armitage, and I'd do two or three shows a night." Prine started getting offers to perform in other clubs, including the Earl of Old Town on Wells Street, which drew a diverse clientele. "The audiences were so varied," Ed Holstein told the *Tribune* in 1999. "You had people from the neighborhood, conventioneers, doctors and lawyers, all kinds of crowds."

Steve Goodman had been playing the Old Town clubs for about a year before Prine got started. Prine had been impressed with an original train song, "The City of New Orleans," that Goodman sang on *The Midnight Special* radio show. "I just got this vision that the guy singin' that song wore turtleneck sweaters and had kind of a crew cut and maybe a little beard," Prine said in a video interview for a 2003 Goodman DVD. "And a really tall guy." The Holstein brothers had brought Goodman to hear Prine play at the Fifth Peg, but they didn't meet that night. Prine was backstage at the Earl of Old Town on another night when Goodman walked in—all five feet, two inches of him. "Here comes this guy stormin' through the door, looks like Edward G. Robinson," Prine said in the DVD interview. "And walks up to me and says, 'Hi, I'm Steve Goodman! You're all right!' Like previous to that I wasn't. He, just like, solidified it, you know? And we became kinda instant friends."

The Earl of Old Town was also a favorite haunt for Ebert: "The Earl, across the street from Second City, was the holy ground of the Chicago folk music renaissance, and there I heard for the first time Steve Goodman and Fred Holstein—and Bonnie Koloc, Michael Smith, Jim Post, Bob Gibson, Ginny Clemons, and the remarkable string band Martin, Bogan and the Armstrongs. I was there after hours one night when Goodman sang a song he said he had just composed called 'City of New Orleans.'" Goodman was born on Chicago's North Side in 1948. Before establishing himself in the Old Town scene he attended the University of Illinois for a year, playing covers in a rock band called the Juicy Fruits.

He also spent some time in Greenwich Village in 1967, performing regularly at the Cafe Wha? before returning to his hometown. He was diagnosed with leukemia back in Chicago. "He was nineteen when I met him, and that's when he got sick and almost died," Koloc said. But Goodman responded well to treatment, continuing to perform while resuming his studies at Lake Forest College. "He was a real fireball," Prine told Nick Spitzer. "I've never met anybody like him."

For a while Prine kept his day job, delivering mail in the suburbs when the sun was up, singing downtown after dark. But the balance quickly shifted. After six years delivering mail, he told the postmaster he was quitting. The postmaster advised him not to withdraw his retirement funds in case he decided to return. "I said, 'Oh, no—you don't understand. No matter what happens, I ain't comin' back here,'" Prine told William Ruhlmann. Performing paid better and kept him out of the elements; he would write no more songs while hiding from the wind in relay boxes. "I was making so much singing on three nights a week, I was making more than I was walking in the snow," he said. "Most people would have kept both jobs, I guess, and doubled their money, and I just quit and slept all week."

Leukemia gave Goodman a sense of urgency that Prine lacked, and he quickly became Prine's unofficial promo man. "Steve Goodman was the most supportive friend-slash-fan I could've had," Prine told *American Songwriter* magazine in 2005. "He used to corner people and sing two of my songs and one of his." "Illegal Smile" earned Prine an invitation to appear on a local public-access TV show—and helped to cement the song's status as a weed-smokers' anthem. "I went on this underground TV program, and the only stage set they had was two chairs and this fake marijuana plant," he told Lydia Hutchinson. "I came on and sang 'Illegal Smile,' and they kept having the camera pan in, real psychedelic-like, on the plant. On top of that, I got fined by the musicians' union for not taking any money to do the show."

One November night in 1970 someone recorded a Fifth Peg performance for posterity. A bass player accompanied Prine. The singer "needs no introduction," but got one anyway. While he hadn't magically turned into Frank Sinatra since August, his singing for a live audience sounded markedly better than his singing on the WFMT studio recording. He was much looser and more relaxed, and his phrasing had improved dramatically. He still had trouble holding notes—he positively yowled as he stretched out "hello in tharrrrrrrr." His voice cracked near the beginning of the second verse of "Flag Decal," but that was part of the charm of a live recording. Prine sang about half of the originals he recorded during the WFMT session, with "Souvenirs," "Aw Heck," "The Frying Pan," "Sour Grapes," and "A Star, a Jewel, and a Hoax" omitted—or missing from the surviving tapes, at least. Several new songs made an appearance: "Flag Decal," "The Great Compromise," "Angel from Montgomery," "A Good Time," "Quiet Man," and "Spanish Pipedream." And, for good measure, he threw in a two-song Hank Williams medley ("Hey, Good Lookin'" and "Jambalaya [On the Bayou]").

"A Good Time" was the weakest of the new originals, a sophomoric, moody, self-consciously poetic ballad in the vein of early Simon and Garfunkel: "And you know that I'd survive if I never spoke again / And all I'd have to lose is my vanity." "Quiet Man" was its opposite number, a much more plainspoken and naturally clever song, reveling in Dylanesque wordplay: "Hocus-pocus, maladjusted / Don't you think my tears get rusted?" Prine revealed the emotional cost of his natural empathy in his spoken introduction to "Quiet Man": "This is about people's problems. Sometimes it's nice—somebody comes up to me and they got a problem and I help them with it, or they'll help me with my problems. But some people come up and they've got all these problems, and they tell 'em to ya for about an hour, and then they walk away laughin'. And you're stuck with their problems for the rest of the day." (His speaking voice was all Chicago—Prine's accent must have stuck out like a sore thumb among the mushy vowels of Muhlenberg County with that hard "I" sound and the way he pronounced "O" like "ahh," turning "problem" into "prahhblem.") In the chorus he transformed emotional pain into gorgeous imagery. "Oodles of light what a beautiful sight," he repeated as the song wound down. "Both of God's eyes are shinin' tonight / Raisin' beams of incredible dreams / And I am the quiet man." The audience erupted into some of the most raucous cheers of the night when he finished.

They already knew Prine's material well, even if they didn't know the song titles yet. They shouted requests for "Muhlenberg County" and "Hole in Daddy's Arm." He claimed to have cowritten "The Great

Compromise" with "Star-Spangled Banner" author Francis Scott Key. "It's a hate song to a woman I love," Prine said. "It's about a kid that went out lookin' for America, and he found her in a barroom, drinkin'. She was feelin' bad, so he felt sorry for her and asked her out to the drive-in. She was only an Okie from Muskogee, and I was a Battle Creek freak." Just in case anyone missed the Vietnam War metaphor, after he sang the part about America hopping into "a foreign sports car," he interjected, "a Hanoi Hudson!"

Prine closed the show with a song every bit as rousing as "Flag Decal," "Spanish Pipedream." It was a hilarious Age of Aquarius anthem, the hippie commune ideal summed up in less than four minutes. He sang in the voice of a draft dodger—"a soldier on my way to Montreal." The soldier met a stripper "on the road to alcohol." ("I figure if I can't get a song out of that, then I couldn't write anymore," Prine told Studs Terkel.) The stripper offered the soldier words of Woodstock Nation wisdom: "Blow up your TV / Throw away your papers / Go to the country / Build you a home." He feigned naïveté, "For I knew that topless lady had something up her sleeve." They ended up leaving the bar together, moving to the country, and raising a litter of children who "all found Jesus on their own." (Not unlike Dylan and his ex–Playboy Bunny wife Sara raising their family in the actual village of Woodstock.) The crowd erupted once again. In response to a woman shouting "More! More!" the emcee announced, "If you wanna hear more of John, remember: He's gonna be here three nights, each week, indefinitely—Friday, Saturday, and Sundays."

Prine's reputation continued to grow. A Chicago-based record label specializing in blues and jazz, Delmark, started sniffing around. Owner and founder Bob Koester took Prine out to lunch one day—"my first show-biz lunch," he told Kot. "We went for a burger somewhere, around the corner from the Jazz Record Mart on Grand. He offered me a one-album deal, said I could sing Hank Williams and Jimmie Rodgers covers, 'Sam Stone' and 'Hello in There' and three or four of mine. I wouldn't have to tie up all my own stuff." Prine declined: "I knew Delmark was a great label that had great people on it, and here I had a chance to be on that roster. So by me saying no, that's when it clicked: I must have something in mind that I'm not telling myself."

Prine had created a catalog of great songs, a well-polished stage show complete with between-song patter, and a strong reputation on the Chicago club scene. All he needed now was a break, and Goodman made it his mission to get him one. Fortunately for both singers, Kris Kristofferson was coming to town.

By 1971, after stints sweeping floors at Columbia Records' Nashville studio and piloting choppers for an oil company in south Louisiana, Kristofferson had established himself in the upper echelon of Music City songwriters. The ex–army captain had progressed far beyond his right-wing anthem "Viet Nam Blues," a mid-sixties hit for Dave Dudley. Roger Miller recorded Kristofferson's "Me and Bobby McGee" in 1969, taking it to No. 12 on the country charts. Ray Stevens's recording of "Sunday Mornin' Comin' Down" stalled at No. 55 on the country charts in 1969, but Johnny Cash's version made it all the way to No. 1 the following year. Prine was a fan. "What we were tryin' to do, Kris was doin' already," Prine told the cameras for the Goodman DVD. "He was writin' these songs that just kinda brought everything together, like country music and folk music and all this stuff." By the time Kristofferson rolled into Chicago in the late spring of 1971 for a series of shows at the Quiet Knight, Janis Joplin's version of "Me and Bobby McGee" had become a massive hit, reaching No. 1 on the pop charts a few weeks before. Joplin had recorded the song shortly before her death on 4 October 1970, making it the biggest posthumous single since Otis Redding's "(Sittin' on) The Dock of the Bay" in 1968. Goodman got the nod as Kristofferson's opening act.

Prine, meanwhile, was playing at the Earl of Old Town and continuing to write. His time in basic training at Fort Polk inspired a song called "Natural" about two young lovers failing to connect with anybody but themselves. Prine described the army barracks as "a warehouse of strangers with sixty-watt lights." While fat townie Lydia pleasured herself at home on a Saturday night, the young PFC Donald took carnal matters into his own hand "after midnight in the stillness of the barracks latrine." He got the characters' names from a book to help expectant parents name their baby.

Masturbation was America's dirty little secret. Everybody did it (made abundantly clear by the popularity of *Playboy* magazine, which brought photos of naked female bodies out of smut shops and into the mainstream), but nobody admitted it—except when talking to clinical researchers. The nation was still reeling from—or doing its best to ignore—two reports from William Masters and Virginia Johnson: *Human Sexual Response* in 1966 and *Human Sexual Inadequacy* in 1970, which scandalously asserted that masturbation was common practice. The number of porn theaters in the United States had swelled from about 20 in 1960 to 750 in 1970. Philip Roth had become a national figure on the strength of his 1969 novel *Portnoy's Complaint*, which describes its protagonist's masturbatory habits in lurid detail. Despite its undeniable popularity, religious leaders still characterized masturbation as a grave sin. For decades puritanical adults had tried to steer teens away from the practice with spurious scare tactics—warnings that it would lead to physical maladies ranging from shameful (hair growing on the palms of one's hands) to crippling (blindness).

Prine didn't let any of that slow him down. The first lines of the song played like a scene behind the opening credits of a movie: "Small town, bright lights, Saturday night / Pinballs and pool halls flashing their lights." His ability to flesh out a character with a few choice words reached new heights: "Lydia hid her thoughts like a cat / Behind her small eyes sunk deep in her fat." Young PFC Donald, meanwhile, was an anonymous grunt in a room full of "bunk beds, shaved heads."

> They made love in the mountains, they made love in the streams
> They made love in the valleys, they made love in their dreams
> But when they were finished there was nothing to say
> 'Cause mostly they made love from ten miles away

On the surface the song may have been about masturbation, but on another level Prine aimed at a deeper truth about loneliness and isolation. He eventually renamed the song "Donald and Lydia," modeling it after Dylan's "The Lonesome Death of Hattie Carroll" "as far as telling a story and having the chorus be the moral to the story," he told Paul Zollo. "A wider moral than what the story's saying. Like where the chorus is all-consuming, and a much bigger subject than what you're detailing. Yeah, that was much in the same way that any upbeat song I modeled after Chuck Berry, I modeled a ballad after specific songs, and that song of Bob Dylan's, 'The Lonesome Death of Hattie Carroll,' to me was to be held up as a real model for songs, as was a lot of Hank Williams Sr. songs."

The same week Goodman was opening for Kristofferson, Paul Anka was singing for an exclusive crowd in the 250-seat Empire Room at the upscale Palmer House hotel. Though he was the same age as Dylan and the Beatles—and five years younger than Kristofferson—the Canadian-born Anka had more in common with the smooth-voiced, orchestrated crooners of the prerock generation. He had gained fame as a teen idol in the late fifties and early sixties with such romantic hits as "Diana" and "Put Your Head on My Shoulder." He also wrote English lyrics for the French pop song "Comme d'habitude" ("As Usual"), which had recently been a hit for Frank Sinatra under its new title: "My Way." Yet Anka didn't just peddle nostalgia: By 1971 he had freshened up his set list with a Kristofferson song, "Help Me Make It through the Night."

When they weren't performing, Kristofferson and Anka painted Old Town red, along with Kristofferson's girlfriend. At the time he was dating Samantha Eggar, an English actress who had starred in *Walk Don't Run* with Cary Grant and *Doctor Dolittle* with Rex Harrison. "There we were gettin' juiced and fallin' in around the clubs, and Kris told me he had this fantastic guy he wanted me to hear," Anka told *Zoo World*. But Goodman wasn't content merely to bask in the glow of celebrity adoration, Prine said.

In fact, Goodman pestered Kristofferson to check out Prine throughout their Quiet Knight stand. Kristofferson liked a Prine song he had heard Goodman sing, but he just couldn't be bothered to go hear him play. "He kept sayin', 'You gotta see this guy!'" Kristofferson told Bill Flanagan in an interview for *Written in My Soul*. "Well, everybody always tells me that. I didn't want to go." Goodman's persistence finally overcame Kristofferson's resistance on Sunday night. Kristofferson, Eggar, Goodman, and Anka crowded into a cab and headed across town to Wells Street.

CHAPTER 5

In the King's Footsteps

▼

Though the publicity photos of the time show the crew dressed in stylized "hillbilly"
costumes and sitting on bales of straw, the members were not
exactly fresh from the mountains.

CHARLES K. WOLFE,
writing about the Cumberland Ridge Runners, a Depression-era band,
in *Kentucky Country: Folk and Country Music of Kentucky*

After getting discovered by Kristofferson and Anka and signing with
Atlantic, Prine thought he would make his first record in Muscle Shoals
or New York. Instead, Atlantic sent him down to Memphis, home of
W. C. Handy and B. B. King, Elvis Presley and Al Green. His producer
would be one of the label's veterans, Arif Mardin, born in Istanbul in
1932. Mardin met Dizzy Gillespie and Quincy Jones there in 1956, and
moved to Boston two years later to attend the Berklee College of Music
as the school's first recipient of the Quincy Jones Scholarship. In 1963 he
went to work with fellow Turks Ahmet and Nesuhi Ertegun at Atlantic.

Over the next eight years Mardin mostly worked with soul artists, such
as King Curtis, Donny Hathaway, and Brook Benton. Mardin landed his
biggest hits when he coproduced sessions for the Rascals that resulted in
"Good Lovin'," "Groovin'," "How Can I Be Sure," and "People Got
to Be Free." Jerry Wexler called him the Pasha (the Ottoman Empire's

equivalent to the British "lord"), "his soulful Turkish eminence." Mardin branched out into singer-songwriter territory in 1970 when he coproduced *Christmas and the Beads of Sweat* for Laura Nyro with Felix Cavaliere of the Rascals. That album was recorded in New York, but featured several musicians associated with Muscle Shoals, including Duane Allman.

The Prine sessions would take place at American Sound Studio, which opened in a nondescript north Memphis storefront in 1967. Mardin and Wexler had coproduced *Dusty in Memphis* for Dusty Springfield, a 1969 masterpiece that featured the hit single "Son of a Preacher Man." Though Springfield ended up tracking most of her vocals in New York, the music was played by the house band at American. The studio had become a red-hot hit factory by 1971, with a warm, distinctive, full-bodied sound. (Any album recorded at American in the late sixties and early seventies seemed to end up with Reggie Young's electric sitar on at least one track.) Other hits recorded at American were "The Letter" and "Cry Like a Baby" by the Box Tops, Aretha Franklin's "Do Right Woman, Do Right Man," Bobby Womack's "What Is This," B. J. Thomas's "Hooked on a Feeling," and Neil Diamond's "Sweet Caroline." Not to mention the singles that cemented Elvis Presley's comeback in 1969 after years of mediocre movie soundtracks: "In the Ghetto," "Kentucky Rain," and "Suspicious Minds."

A little more than a decade earlier Prine had been a kid standing before his mirror in the Chicago suburbs strumming a broom, trying to look like Elvis. Now he was literally walking in the King's footsteps and feeling out of place. Mardin, by contrast, felt right at home in the small studio. "I did many, many recordings there," he told Tom Doyle in a 2004 interview for the website Sound on Sound.

Memphis had been a mecca for recording artists since the early fifties. Sam Phillips opened his Memphis Recording Service in 1950, producing the song some consider the first rock 'n' roll record ever made, "Rocket 88," in 1951. (The song was attributed to Jackie Brenston and His Delta Cats, but Ike Turner wrote it and led the band.) Phillips and his label, Sun Records, would go on to change the course of American music history with recordings by everyone from B. B. King and Howlin' Wolf to Presley, Jerry Lee Lewis, Carl Perkins, Johnny Cash, and Roy Orbison. Stax came to the fore in the sixties, introducing the world to Otis Redding, Booker T. and the M.G.'s, Sam and Dave, and Isaac Hayes. Royal Studios, established in 1956, was just coming to prominence as the home studio for Al Green, who hit with "Tired of Being Alone" in '71. Ardent Studios opened in 1966, handling some work for Stax and gradually becoming known for rock 'n' roll when Led Zeppelin, Leon Russell, and ZZ Top came to work there at the beginning of the seventies. James Taylor went to Ardent in early '71 to record *Mud Slide Slim and the Blue Horizon*, the follow-up to his smash *Sweet Baby James* album. Those sessions produced one of that year's biggest hits, "You've Got a Friend." Memphis was hot.

But funky grooves made Memphis hot, not folk stylings—despite the anomalous success of Taylor's album. The guys at American, accustomed to playing heavily rhythmic material, weren't sure what to make of the acoustic guitar-strumming storyteller Mardin had thrust upon them. "I didn't know where to put him," said Bobby Wood, piano player at American, in an interview with Roben Jones for the book *Memphis Boys: The Story of American Studios*. "Folk and piano never worked for some reason." Prine introduced his songs to the band as he always had, accompanying himself as he sang. "I remember thinking, 'How are we gonna get anything musical out of *that*?'" percussionist Hayward Bishop told Jones. "There was no evidence of groove whatever, and I was hungry for groove. Prine came off like a folk poet. This guy was nasally, he didn't have any tone to his voice, and all his songs are in the same key! I thought, 'This is gonna be like milking a dag-blasted *dog*!'"

They had a record to make, so they soldiered on. The American rhythm section cut most of the songs that had put Prine on the map: "Illegal Smile," "Spanish Pipedream," "Hello in There," "Sam Stone," "Your Flag Decal Won't Get You into Heaven Anymore," "Angel from Montgomery," "Quiet Man," "Donald and Lydia," and "Flashback Blues." Despite not knowing where to put Prine, Wood added great warmth to "Illegal Smile" and "Hello in There" with his electric piano, even managing to drop some funk into "Pretty Good," a new song. Bobby Emmons opened "Sam Stone" with a suitably funereal organ, while Young broke out his sitar for the first and only time, adding a creepy, otherworldly feel to the song that amplified the lyrics' message of disconnection and death. The musicians thought Mardin was more reserved than usual during the Prine sessions. At one point the producer squelched Bishop's attempt to liven up his drum part on a song. "He looked me right in the eye and said, 'No experimenting, please,'" Bishop told Jones. The recordings were unfailingly professional, though they lacked the spark and personality of the best material the American musicians had recorded with other artists.

In addition to "Pretty Good," newer songs recorded at American included "Far from Me" and "Six O'Clock News." "Pretty Good" was the weakest of the three, a Dylan-style abstraction with bad-dream lyrics ("I met a girl from Venus, and her insides were lined in gold"), punctuated by Young's slashing, distorted lead guitar, and an ecumenical dismissal of organized religion:

> I heard Allah and Buddha were singing at the savior's feast
> And up in the sky an Arabian rabbi
> Fed Quaker Oats to a priest
> Pretty good, not bad, they can't complain
> 'Cause actually all them gods is just about the same

The other two songs were much stronger. "Six O'Clock News" was a haunting tale of suicide based on a troubled childhood friend who got some devastating news during one of his trips to juvenile court. "The prosecutor decided to tell the court and my friend that his father was his father, but his mother was his oldest sister," Prine said. "No wonder he was always in trouble." "Far from Me" beautifully set the scene for a disintegrating romance:

> As the cafe was closing
> On a warm summer night
> And Cathy was cleaning the spoons
> The radio played the Hit Parade
> And I hummed along with the tune

Prine wrote the song "about the first girl that ever broke my heart," he told John Hiatt. "That'll make a songwriter of you right away." He picked and strummed Maybelle Carter–style on the song, and he amplified the sense of loss and displacement in the lyrics by mixing up the song structure. Sometimes he sneaked in bars with a different time signature, a technique old-time musicians call "crooked." (There's a song that dates back to the minstrel-show era that goes, "The world is round, but it's crooked just the same.") It's a technique that shows up often in mountain music and country blues played by self-taught musicians less bound to conventional song structures than their classically trained counterparts.

The real star of the American recording sessions was pedal steel player Leo LeBlanc, who anchored "Far from Me." The Massachusetts native had recently moved to Memphis after a stint in Bakersfield, California, the town where country stars Buck Owens and Merle Haggard launched their careers. He had already established himself during sessions at Muscle Shoals, but he was an interloper at American in 1971. His guitar work added an authentic country feel to "Donald and Lydia" and "Spanish Pipedream." It got buried in the mix on "Angel from Montgomery," however. One of Prine's finest songs fell victim to a plodding tempo and overkill from Emmons's organ—an admirable but ultimately unsuccessful attempt to take the song to church. The song had legs, though, and it would improve in subsequent versions. It's dense with tricky little time shifts and derives part of its drama from Prine's use of a flat seventh chord. (The Beatles had employed the flat seventh to similar effect three years earlier in "Hey Jude.")

Prine's simple, delicate acoustic guitar intros served the songs well, on the whole. Throughout the session, his voice sounded more relaxed than on the WFMT recording, though his phrasing remained stiff and unimaginative, his discomfort with studio work still audible. The songs would stand largely on the strength of his remarkable ability to tell stories, create characters, and turn memorable phrases. "He was deep into his music," Emmons told Jones. ". . . I liked it that he had the ability to look at all these subjects that other writers wouldn't touch."

Steve Goodman made a guest appearance at the Memphis sessions, adding acoustic guitar to "Flashback Blues." He and Prine's brother Dave traveled to A&R Studios in New York to record the one song cut outside American. For "Paradise," which sounded as if it could have been recorded decades earlier than the other tracks, Goodman added acoustic guitar and subtle harmony vocals, while Dave played fiddle. Playing bass on the track was Neil Rosengarden, a multi-instrumentalist whose father led the orchestra on *The Dick Cavett Show*. As in "Far from Me" and "Angel from Montgomery," Prine threw in extra (or "crooked") bars that gave the song an unconventional feel. Played straight, it would have sounded like a more predictable, formulaic Nashville tune.

John Prine introduced its namesake to the world like few debut albums before or since. Everything his fans would come to love about him—drama, humor, memorable characters, great stories, a badass outsider stance offset by a reverence for tradition—could be found, fully developed, in its forty-four minutes and seven seconds. The recordings showed ample room for Prine to grow as a musician, recording artist, and vocalist, but the songs were built to last.

The album was a perfect time capsule, capturing the era when Depression babies embraced the law-and-order conservatism of Richard Nixon while their children were dying in the jungles of Vietnam or going wild in the streets back home. (The social changes of the sixties didn't really trickle out to small-town America until the early seventies.) All the contradictions of Prine's life up to that point came through—impulses in conflict between his conventional life as a married suburban mailman/army veteran and his clear preference for laid-back hippie hedonism. In "Spanish Pipedream," he playfully advocated a wholesale rejection of Middle American values at a time when communes were a widespread social experiment. On the very next song, "Hello in There," he promoted dialogue with senior citizens in a song that could have worked (and probably has worked) as a Sunday school lesson or sermon.

In an era where countless artists and their fans were cutting virtually all ties to conventional society and sailing off into the uncharted waters of sonic experimentation, free love, rejection of religious and political traditions, and unbridled drug use, Prine kept one foot planted firmly in the world of his parents and grandparents ("Paradise," "Angel from Montgomery," "Hello in There," and his music's foundation in traditional music) while taking tentative steps forward into a new way of life ("Spanish Pipedream," "Illegal Smile," "Your Flag Decal Won't Get You into Heaven Anymore"). If the songs weren't strictly autobiographical—as many of the songs by Prine's singer-songwriter peers were purported or presumed to be—it's safe to say they reflected the ideas banging around in the head of a bright, complex, unassuming young man who had songwriting talent to burn.

With thirteen songs in the can, it was up to Atlantic to package the record and convince the American public that Prine was worth a listen. For the album cover photo, the label sent him to the San Francisco studio of photographer Jim Marshall, who had shot the Beatles' final U.S. concert in 1966, the Monterey Pop Festival in 1967, Woodstock in 1969, Johnny Cash flipping the bird at San Quentin State Prison, and the cover photo for the Allman Brothers' *At Fillmore East* album. "We were making small talk when a pickup truck arrives with three bales of hay," Prine told Lloyd Sachs. "He said, 'I'm gonna do a head shot of you and the straw will make an interesting background.'" Prine balked: "I thought they coulda had me on a bus or something. I had never sat on a bale of hay in my life." Despite the photographer's reassurances, he took more than just a head shot. Marshall captured a full-body shot of a denim-clad Prine sitting on a hay bale, one hand resting on another, his cowboy boots crossed, his head slightly tilted, his expression neutral. His hair has started to grow out in the back, but it remains short compared to many of his music contemporaries. An acoustic guitar leans against two other bales stacked up behind him. "Next thing I know it's about five days before the album comes out and I'm at the record company in New York and I saw the cover photo, and there I am sitting on a bale of hay," Prine told Greg Kot. "And I pipe up that while I like country music, this looks like 'Hee-Haw.' But it was too late to change it."

Prine took the "Paradise" recording to his parents' house before the album showed up in stores. He wanted his father to hear it. "I had to borrow a reel-to-reel machine to play it for him," Prine told Lydia Hutchinson. "When the song came on, he went into the next room and sat in the dark while it was on. I asked him why, and he said he wanted to pretend it was on the jukebox." Bill Prine died on 16 August 1971, a couple months before *John Prine* was released. He had a heart attack shortly after losing a union election at American Can. He was just fifty-six years old. "Last time I saw my dad he was sitting on the front porch drinking a beer, and looking at the traffic go by," Prine wrote in the liner notes for *John Prine Live.* "That's the way I like to remember him." As with his parents, the family took Bill home to Muhlenberg County, burying his body at a family cemetery near the former site of Paradise. The next day, Prine was back in Chicago talking to a reporter for *Rolling Stone.* "Prine kicked at the floor as if trying to scrape cowshit from his boots," Les Bridges wrote. "The eyes, tucked deep into his high-cheekboned, vaguely Indian-looking face, were red and exhausted. He wore a stubble of beard. On this particular morning Prine had reason to look tired. The day before he had buried his father, who had died suddenly of a heart attack."

The article also described Prine joining Kristofferson on stage at the Quiet Knight to sing "Sam Stone" and adding backing harmonies to "Me and Bobby McGee." "No way somebody this young can be writing so heavy," Kristofferson told Bridges. "John Prine is so good, we just may have to break his thumbs." Kristofferson wrote liner notes for the back cover of *John Prine*, telling how Goodman railroaded him into checking out Prine at the Earl: "It was too damned late, and we had an early wake-up ahead of us, and by the time we got there Old Town was nothing but empty streets and dark windows. And the club was closing. But the owner let us come in, pulled some chairs off a couple of tables, and John unpacked his guitar and got back up to sing." He compared Prine to the era's premier singer-songwriter. "It must've been like stumbling onto Dylan when he first busted onto the Village scene, . . ." Kristofferson wrote. "One of those rare, great times when it all seems worth it, like when the Vision would rise upon Blake's 'weary eyes, Even in this Dungeon, & this Iron Mill.'" Songs that stood out for him were "Sam Stone," "Donald and Lydia," and "the one about the Old Folks." "Twenty-four years old and writes like he's about two-hundred and twenty," Kristofferson wrote. "I don't know where he comes from, but I've got a good idea where he's going." In a postscript, he thanked "the people at Atlantic for making good things happen fast to someone who deserves it." The back cover also credited the musicians who played on the album—though it got a couple of their names wrong. Hayward Bishop was credited as "Bishop Heywood," while Neil Rosengarden's first name was misspelled.

Wexler gave Prine a book of short stories by Ring Lardner, a Chicago sportswriter and fiction author who had influenced Ernest Hemingway, because he thought their writing seemed similar. The Atlantic executive also sent an advance copy of Prine's record to Dylan. A week before its release, Prine and Goodman were back in New York hanging out in the Village with Kristofferson and another of his lovers, Carly Simon, before a show at the Bitter End. Simon's own debut album had appeared earlier that year, producing the Top 10 hit "That's the Way I've Always

Heard It Should Be." "Kristofferson said, 'Come on over,' and gave us Carly's address," Prine told Paul Zollo. "Carly was opening for Kristofferson at the Bitter End. He said, 'I got a surprise for you guys.' So we come over and we're sitting in Carly's place, and there's a knock on the door and in walks Bob Dylan." Somebody broke out a guitar and they started trading songs. Dylan already knew "Far from Me" and "Donald and Lydia," and sang along with Prine. Then Dylan sang a new song, "George Jackson," a tribute to a Black Panther leader shot and killed a few weeks earlier during a riot at San Quentin: "Sometimes I think this whole world / Is one big prison yard / Some of us are prisoners / The rest of us are guards." It was the first overt protest song Dylan had written in years. "Goodman looks at him and says, 'That's great, Bob,'" Prine told Zollo. "'It's no "Masters of War," though.'"

The songs were still coming fast and furious for Prine. He performed several new songs in New York. "Everybody" was a rollicking number about the need for human connection that opened with the narrator bumping into Jesus—who happened to be taking a stroll on the ocean. "I said, 'Jesus, you look tired,'" Prine sang. "He said, 'Jesus, so do you.'" "The Torch Singer" was a bluesy waltz sung from the point of view of a man left "both naked and bare" by an emotional performance. "Rocky Mountain Time," another waltz (with a couple of dramatic tempo changes), was a Dylanesque tale of dislocation, which may have reflected the whirlwind changes in Prine's life that year: "I'm too young to be where I'm going / But I'm too old to go back again." The Vietnam War reared its ugly head once more in "Take the Star out of the Window." The title referenced the service flag—a popular home decoration in the World War II era that largely fell out of favor by Vietnam. It was a small banner that displayed a blue star for each family member in the service and a gold star for any family member who died while serving. In contrast to "Sam Stone," "Take the Star out of the Window" is an up-tempo tune. The veteran in this song didn't want to talk about the war ("Don't you ask me any questions / 'bout the medals on my chest / Take the star out of the window / And let my conscience take a rest"), but for the moment, at least, he seemed to have returned with a more optimistic outlook than Stone, making "an Oriental waitress his own homecomin' queen."

The New York Times reviewed Prine at the Bitter End, calling him "a cut above the new generation of folksingers." Billboard also weighed in:

"Prine is an essentially functional singer who throws away his songs in a deceptively offhand, head-scratching manner. His songs though are exceptional, enabling him to put across some strong ideas in a simple format usually taking refuge in humor ('Illegal Smile' and 'Your Flag Decal Won't Get You into Heaven Anymore'). It is obvious that Prine is a writer to watch—he could also develop into a performer of merit if he can keep the innocence intact." (Goodman, the review says, "is more outgoing than his partner and talks a lot more between songs.") The *Billboard* review did little for Prine's name recognition—it gave his first name as Tom. Atlantic SD 8296 was just showing up in record stores. The *Rolling Stone* story came out in early December. The article mentioned a cover of "Sam Stone" ("the story of a skag-shooting ex-GI and his inevitable OD") by Gate of Horn mainstay Bob Gibson, as well as a forthcoming cover of "Hello in There" (misnamed "Old People") by folk queen Joan Baez. Prine talked about recording in Memphis, where Reggie Young told him, "Your songs are either the best I ever heard or the worst. I kind of think they might be the best; I can't tell yet. They sure are different."

Two weeks later, *Rolling Stone* ran a review of *John Prine*. "This is a very good first album by a very good songwriter," Karin Berg wrote. She went on to praise the complex ideas in his songs, his "excellent" melodies, and his compassion. But Berg found "Sam Stone" "too heavily contrived," and she thought Prine erred too often on the side of bitterness: "The stories he tells have a negative kinkiness; if pain isn't apparent, it's just below the surface." The *Los Angeles Free Press* reviewed *John Prine* side by side with *Steve Goodman*. "Of the two new albums, Goodman's is probably the better one," Chris Van Ness wrote. "Prine has written some fine songs, many of which are already well on their way to becoming classics, and the album is very well produced; but it remains simply a collection of fine songs."

Atlantic placed ads for the album in music magazines, the copy sounding like something out of *Sesame Street*: "He writes soft songs about his country childhood memories. And hard songs condemning the wrongs of the city." Cover versions of Prine songs started appearing, such as John Denver's version of "Spanish Pipedream" (which he renamed "Blow Up Your TV," after its chorus) on his *Aerie* album, released within weeks of Prine's debut. Atlantic sent Prine out on the road for the first time to promote the album. Reviewing a show at the

Troubadour in Los Angeles, Nat Freedland wrote that he "looks like a leftover Everly Brother, plays acoustic guitar in early folk style, and sings like protest-era Dylan." The Dylan comparisons were flying fast and furious. When Prine got back home and did a radio interview on WGLD in Oak Park on 19 December, he downplayed them. "Well, that whole Woody Guthrie, Jack Elliott, early Dylan—that's a whole style of singin' that may have influenced my singin'," he said. He listed other people besides Baez planning to cover his songs, such as Carly Simon ("Angel from Montgomery") and Dylan himself. "Dylan cut 'Donald and Lydia,'" Prine said. "I don't know if it'll make it—he's got an album comin' out in January."

CHAPTER 6

Singers and Songwriters

▼

In 1972, America's pop-radio airwaves resonated with the sound of acoustic guitars. Don McLean's cryptic epic "American Pie," the title track to an album released around the same time as Prine's debut, hit No. 1 in January. The song surveyed rock history from Buddy Holly to Bob Dylan, the Byrds, and Mick Jagger. It claimed the top spot from "Brand New Key" by Melanie, another singer-songwriter. That same month Paul Simon released *Paul Simon*, his solo debut, in the wake of Simon and Garfunkel's 1970 breakup. Songs that fell at least loosely into the singer-songwriter category ruled the roost for most of the first half of 1972, despite occasional incursions by soul artists Al Green, the Chi-Lites, and the Staple Singers. Those No. 1 singles were Nilsson's "Without You," Neil Young's "Heart of Gold," America's "A Horse with No Name," and Roberta Flack's "The First Time Ever I Saw Your Face."

The year brought good karma to Goodman after all his efforts to promote Prine. Arlo Guthrie recorded "The City of New Orleans" for his album *Hobo's Lullaby*, and the single made the Top 20 in the fall. More and more artists covered Prine's songs, as well. Fellow Chicago folkie Bonnie Koloc brought a woman's voice to "Angel from Montgomery," Bette Midler recorded "Hello in There" for her debut album, and John Denver cut "Paradise" for his *Rocky Mountain High* album. Singular soul man Swamp Dogg (born Jerry Williams Jr.) recorded a crying, gospel-soaked version of "Sam Stone" for his album *Cuffed, Collared,*

Tagged & Gassed. "He sings it like a sermon," Prine told Peter Cooper during an appearance at the Country Music Hall of Fame in 2014. "I never met him, but I'd sure love to tell him how much I appreciate him doing that song that way." Paul Anka even weighed in with a bluesy cover of "Pretty Good" on his album *Jubilation.* None of them were hits, though, and *John Prine*—despite the positive reviews—barely cracked the Top 200 in late February, peaking at No. 154 and falling back off the charts less than a month later. Prine continued to tour, honing his craft on the road.

Los Angeles Times critic Robert Hilburn, who had helped launch Elton John to stardom with an exuberant concert review in the summer of 1970, had tried to give Prine a similar send-off. He created significant buzz for Prine's first Los Angeles show with a two-thousand-word review of *John Prine.* Prine was scheduled to open for Brewer and Shipley during a six-day run. Unfortunately, he ended up in the hospital and Goodman was called in as a last-minute substitute. "I thought it was ulcers," Prine told author Clay Eals in an interview for his 2007 Steve Goodman biography. "It'd been diagnosed as several things. It was just a bad case of nerves. I don't mean stage fright. Everything had caught up with me. My stomach got tied up in a knot, and I could hardly breathe."

Prine landed another gig at the Troubadour after he had time to recover. Professional iconoclast Lester Bangs reviewed the show for *Phonograph Record,* declaring it "a bust on all counts." A lover of sixties garage rock and the Detroit hard rock of the Stooges and MC5, Bangs had little patience for anything with folk roots recorded by anyone besides Van Morrison. "Prine is a likeable guy—he kept making jokes about booze, which is a lot better than the aren't-we-cool snickers of head humor—but his guitar playing is mediocre, almost amateurish," Bangs wrote. ". . . It doesn't bother me that most of Prine's songs have a sameness of structure and sound—the effect of this sameness in performance is to make everybody in the audience dummy up and listen real intently for the words because they know anything this static has gotta have a message as the payload."

The Bangs review aside, Prine was well received at the Troubadour, like Elton before him. But a successful West Coast kickoff failed to translate into substantial radio play or record sales. "I was still such a believer that I called Asylum Records founder David Geffen and suggested he might want to manage him," Hilburn wrote in his 2009 memoir *Corn Flakes with John Lennon and Other Tales from a Rock 'n' Roll Life.* "David tried to buy John's management contract, but the manager would only sell 50 percent of it. David didn't want to pick up any new partners, so he passed."

Anka may have held the official title of manager for Prine and Goodman, but the day-to-day responsibilities of working with them fell to a young agent in New York, Al Bunetta. He had served as road manager for the Young Rascals and agent for a variety of other artists—Al Green, Bette Midler, the Manhattan Transfer, and comedian George Carlin. "One day our boss came in and told us that . . . Paul had signed these two artists from Chicago," Bunetta said in a 2006 interview with David Hooper of WRLT in Nashville for his *Music Business Radio* show. What started out as just another assignment quickly became a labor of love. "Before I met him, it was the boss asking me to do it," Bunetta said. "Because he thought I would do it better than anybody else there—they were all working with these other artists there at the time that were really, really hot. I had heard a song called 'Sam Stone,' and I couldn't believe it. I heard it at the Bitter End in Manhattan and I could not get the song out of my head." Bunetta and Prine had no trouble connecting on a personal level. "We're from basically the same kind of neighborhoods," Prine told William Ruhlmann. "He was from Jersey. The neighborhood I grew up in in Chicago was just almost exactly like his."

Prine would team up with Mardin to record a new batch of songs in '72, but they kept it simpler than on Prine's first album. "I told Arif after a year of touring by myself, I would rather go in and do this record like the songs are being played, like either do it with just my acoustic or an upright bass and Dobro and stuff like that," Prine told Ruhlmann. He didn't want to "dress 'em up like they were on the first album." They recorded *Diamonds in the Rough* at Atlantic's Manhattan studios with a small, tight group of musicians: Prine, his brother Dave, and Goodman joined by David Bromberg on guitar and Steve Burgh on bass and (on one cut) drums. There was nary a keyboard or electric sitar to be found this time around. Burgh was only twenty-one, but he was already a music-biz veteran—his band Jacob's Creek had released a trippy album on Columbia three years earlier. Burgh had also recorded with the genre-hopping Bromberg, who released both his debut album and a follow-up in '72. Bromberg, a multi-instrumentalist, had become the singer-songwriter's sideman of choice, recording with Jerry Jeff Walker, Tom Rush, Ed Sanders of the Fugs, Tom Paxton, Richie Havens, Carly Simon, Eric Andersen, and Dylan on both his notorious *Self Portrait* album and its better-received follow-up, *New Morning*.

Prine would record all of the new songs he had played at the Bitter End the year before, and reach back to the first songs he ever wrote, "Sour Grapes" and "The Frying Pan," to fill out the album. The version of "Sour Grapes" here was considerably darker than the WFMT version. Prine added drama to the song with a string-twanging hammer-on trick that would become one of his signature guitar techniques over the years. The album also contained familiar songs of more recent vintage: "Souvenirs" (boosted by Goodman's guitar work and subtle harmonies), "Take the Star out of the Window," and "The Great Compromise," which also featured the hammer-on technique. The newest songs ranged from "Billy the Bum," a character study not much more imaginative than its title, to "The Late John Garfield Blues," a doomy waltz with enough imagination for two or three songs. Prine elongated his vowels à la Dylan, stretching the song form by adding extra measures here and there—a full three additional measures as he yowled the song to a close. It was filled with cinematic images ("black faces pressed against the glass . . . wind-blown scarves in top-down cars") and multiple references to death mixed with gallows humor. "I heard a brand-new joke," Prine sang.

Two men were standing upon a bridge
One jumped and screamed, "You lose"
And just left the odd man holding
Those late John Garfield blues

John Garfield, a movie star in the forties and early fifties, was something of a proto–James Dean, playing moody characters in such films as *The Postman Always Rings Twice* and *Body and Soul* before dying prematurely of a heart attack in 1952 at age thirty-nine. But Prine said the song was less a character study than an attempt to capture a particular feeling. "It was a song about late Sunday night / early Monday morning," he told Bill Flanagan. "A weird time, I always thought. One night I was watching a John Garfield movie; it was the only thing on. I couldn't call the song 'The Late Sunday / Early Monday Blues.' John Garfield would get a certain look on his face—the way he shifted his head or something—that I felt like sometimes."

While none of the up-tempo numbers rose to the level of "Spanish Pipedream," several came close via sheer enthusiasm, especially "Everybody," "The Frying Pan," and "Yes I Guess They Oughta Name a Drink after You," a rousing number enlivened by Dave's fiddle and Dobro. It's about a lovelorn man trying to drown his sorrows—complete with shouted suggestions for those drink names: "Bloody Mary!" "Near beer!" Prine's instincts for a more stripped-down record were good, and the album felt considerably more organic than its predecessor—even if only three of its songs ("Souvenirs," "The Late John Garfield Blues," "The Great Compromise") approached the best tunes on *John Prine*. It sounded as if Mardin mostly sat back and let the band play. "I'd usually go with featuring the artist, build the arrangements around the artist," Mardin said in a 2003 interview for the website Turks.US. "I didn't want to bring the artist into a preset situation. I guess that's why I was able to work with various artists of different styles."

Prine had finally overcome his stiffness in the studio, but the trade-off was vocal control: He came off like a hell-raising redneck on *Diamonds in the Rough*, frequently indifferent to pitch. His voice actually cracked here and there, but the surge in energy and good humor more than compensated for the lack of polish. The last song was the most carefully sung: A chorus of voices joined Prine for his first recorded cover, reaching back to his early days as a musician for an a cappella version of the Carter Family's "Diamonds in the Rough." "We cut the record for $6,200," Prine told Ruhlmann. "We were afforded a lot to do the record, but that's what we spent on it. That was including beer. We did it in two and a half days, mixed. So, just about everything on there was cut live in the middle of the floor. We didn't have any baffles up or anything."

Rolling Stone caught up with Prine in New York shortly before the album's release. The opening paragraph of Ed McCormack's story described Prine on stage at the Bitter End, halfway through a six-night stand, calling out for a special guest: "Whar's that harmonica player?" The "nervously nondescript figure" who joined him was none other than Bob Dylan. Prine said Dylan "was so fucking nervous, man . . . because he hasn't played in front of people for so long." Dylan had surfaced a year earlier for short sets at the benefit Concert for Bangladesh, staged by former Beatle George Harrison at Madison Square Garden. Otherwise his public appearances had become less frequent than NASA moonwalks. "I thought he was just a quiet, unassuming guy," Prine told an interviewer in 1981. The audience was skeptical: "I introduced Dylan and about two people were clapping. No one believed it. They thought Dylan was either dead or on Mount Fuji." Dylan wound up singing and playing on "Sam Stone," "Far from Me," and "Donald and Lydia." David Bromberg accompanied them on guitar. "I was knocked out at simply being in New York, so to have Dylan play with me seemed surreal," Prine said.

The *Rolling Stone* article addressed Prine's alcohol consumption: "He chugalugged a mouthful of beer, replaced the mug on the stool he eschews—preferring to stand while he plays—and balanced his cigarette precariously on its edge." (After pulling "a crumpled pack of Salems out of the pocket of his shapeless suede jacket.") As with his father before him, drinking was starting to become one of Prine's defining characteristics. "Everybody's been gettin' on me about my drinkin'," he told the writer. "My wife, my manager, the guy who owns the Bitter End. Hell, man, how else'm I s'pose to face all them people every night?" Ann Carole accompanied Prine on this trip, and was rewarded with a condescending characterization in the nation's leading music magazine, which described her as "a pleasant-looking girl with small-town housewife written all over her." She talked about Prine's excitement the night he first sang in public at the Fifth Peg: "That night after he came home he just kept tossing and turning and saying over and over, 'They liked me, they liked me!' I said, 'I know they did, John, and that's wonderful—but now go to sleep!'" She worried out loud about how the upheavals in his life were affecting him. "Sometimes I have to keep looking to make sure he's still there, and that he hasn't been changed by all of it," she said.

Opening the Bitter End show were a couple of fellow folkies and Dylan fanatics: Keith Sykes and Loudon Wainwright III. Goodman joined Prine for "Paradise." Prine, McCormack said, writes "songs that are wholly and unmistakably in the American grain, jukebox songs, barroom songs, blue neon light songs, liquor store songs, hobo songs, back porch songs, whorehouse songs, barnyard and graveyard songs, sad-funny songs with steel pedal guitars weeping like heartbroken la-dies—songs like early American primitive paintings, bittersweet and filled with humor and Gothic irony."

Other writers had qualified praise for *Diamonds in the Rough* after its release later in October, just before President Richard Nixon's land-slide reelection victory over George McGovern. Veteran New York critic Robert Christgau declared the album "not as rich as the debut, but more artlessly and confidently sung." Critic Stephen Holden, writing in *Saturday Review*, deemed the album "a disappointment." "Prine's songs are inevitably suffused with pessimism and bitterness," he wrote. "Since the gloom they evoke is nearly absolute, there appears to be a kind of conde-scending oversimplification underlying Prine's work that makes it more attractive to the urban sophisticates he is *not* writing about than to the victimized Middle Americans that he *is*." The record fared little better than its predecessor in terms of airplay and sales, peaking at No. 148 during a ten-week run on the charts.

The album did help Prine land a nomination for a Grammy Award as Best New Artist of 1972, along with the Eagles, Loggins and Messina, America, and Harry Chapin. (Both of Prine's first two albums were re-leased during the award's eligibility period.) Prine was the only artist in the group without a hit single. Chapin's story song, "Taxi," had climbed to No. 24 on the charts. Loggins and Messina had made the Top 10 with "Your Mama Don't Dance," a feat matched by the Eagles with "Witchy Woman." America's "A Horse with No Name" spent three weeks at No. 1 in late March and early April. The fifteenth annual Grammy Awards ceremony took place on 3 March 1973 at the Tennessee Theater in Nashville. The middle-of-the-road soul group the Fifth Dimension an-nounced the Best New Artist winner after singing snippets of songs by each of the award's previous winners. The telecast showed Chapin and Loggins and Messina in the audience, but the other nominees appeared to be no-shows. Illustrations of their faces appeared on a screen at the back of the stage—with a big purple picture of Prine materializing when Florence LaRue said his name. In typical Grammy fashion, the award went to the biggest-selling artist: "America," the members of the Fifth Dimension announced in unison. "Accepting the award for America is Dusty Springfield," the show's announcer said as the house orchestra played an arrangement of "A Horse with No Name."

The folks back home in Chicago continued to be Prine's most reliable audience. Some of the city's young improv comics were big fans. "A lot of 'em hung out at the Earl of Old Town," Prine told Bobby Bare. "Goodman liked to play over there all the time. Right across the street was Second City, and John Belushi was over there at the time. He used to come around over to the Earl of Old Town when they had breaks at Second City—Belushi'd come across the street. And when we had breaks, we'd go watch Second City." Belushi, the son of an Albanian immigrant, was born fifteen miles west of Maywood, in Wheaton, in 1949. His Canadian comic partner, Dan Aykroyd, was also a fan of Prine and Goodman. "Belushi used to do Marlon Brando singin' my songs"—including "Angel from Montgomery," Prine said.

"Paradise" helped get Prine's name out to the American public, one cover at a time, starting around 1972. Besides John Denver, artists recording the song were pop singer Jackie DeShannon, a native of Hazel, Kentucky; the Muhlenberg-rooted Everly Brothers; the Country Gentlemen, a veteran bluegrass band with a constantly evolving lineup that featured a young Kentucky native, Ricky Skaggs, on fiddle at the time the group recorded "Paradise" in 1973; and West Virginia bluegrass duo Jim and Jesse (who added an interesting key change to the final verse). Jim and Jesse "kinda introduced it to the bluegrass world for me," Prine told Jeremy Tepper in a 2005 interview that aired on the Sirius satellite radio channel Outlaw Country. He also appreciated the Everlys' version, which appeared on their 1972 album *Pass the Chicken and Listen*, produced by Merle Travis protégé Chet Atkins. "Don and Phil did it, and they're from there, so that made it kinda double trouble," Prine told Tepper. "It was just really good, them singin' about 'Daddy, won't you take me back to Muhlenberg County?'" In the spring of 1973 Prine traveled to the capital of West Virginia to headline a benefit concert for a reform faction of the United Mine Workers. When Prine sang "Paradise" for the miners, *Rolling Stone* reported, "before he is finished every gravel-throated coal miner and southern West Virginia factory worker in the hall is singing along."

Prine never lived in Kentucky, but his father made sure the Bluegrass State lived in him. "Our dad raised us kinda like anytime we were going back to Kentucky," he told John Hiatt in an interview for a 2001 appearance on *Sessions at West 54th*. "So we spent some of our summers there on vacations." Bill always told his sons they were "pure Kentuckians." Prine related to the colorful stories in traditional music because of his family's roots in the rural South. "I remember in third grade they asked us to go home and find out where our heritage was, and I didn't know what they meant," Prine told Jason Wilber. "I asked my dad where our heritage was, and the next day in school, the little girl behind me said, 'Swedish and English, British.' The next person said, 'German and Italian.' And I stood up and said, 'Pure Kentuckian, last of a dyin' breed!'"

Muhlenberg County, pop. 31,499, lies along the west bank of the Green River in western Kentucky, part of the Ohio River Valley. The county was named after Peter Muhlenberg of Pennsylvania (1746–1807), a Lutheran minister, brigadier general during the American Revolution, and a U.S. congressman and senator. Founded in 1798, roughly equidistant from Tennessee, Illinois, and Indiana, it has dirt farms on the surface and coal mines underneath. Speculators started breaking ground to unearth the county's rich mineral deposits as early as 1820. Prine's ancestors made their way there from North Carolina, Virginia, and Indiana. Spelling variations on the family name included Prin, Prinn, Perrin, Pryn, Prynn, and Prynne—as in Hester Prynne, shunned protagonist of Nathaniel Hawthorne's classic 1850 novel of Puritan New England, *The Scarlet Letter*. The family originated in old England, where an earlier incarnation of John Prine did time as a prisoner in the Tower of London. He carved Latin graffiti in 1568 that read "VERBUM DOMINI MANET"—"The word of the Lord remains."

All four of Prine's grandparents were born in Kentucky. Bill's mother, Laura, was born in Paradise on 29 December 1878. Her husband, Empson, was born 15 February 1889 in Buffalo, about one hundred miles east of Muhlenberg County. Verna's father, John Luther Hamm, was born in 1884 and Verna's stepmother, Rhoda Hamm, in 1887. (Her mother, Agnes Leona Yonts Hamm, died when Verna was five.) By 1930 Luther was running a grocery store in Central City, about ten miles west of Paradise. He was an occasional Methodist minister who also played the guitar and fiddle, picking with Ike Everly (father to the Everly Brothers) occasionally in Drakesboro. But coal mining was a much more reliable source of income than music. Prine got a glimpse of his grandfather in action when he was about five and Luther pulled his guitar out from under his bed to play a couple of songs.

Across the Green River, Bill Monroe was born in 1911 in the Ohio County town of Rosine, about ten miles northeast of Paradise. In a region where great pickers are outnumbered only by Baptist churches, Muhlenberg and Ohio Counties hit a rich seam. At its heart was another Ohio County native, an African American guitarist named Arnold Shultz, born in 1886 to a father who had been enslaved. Monroe first saw him play at a square dance in his hometown. Toward the end of his life he was playing with banjo player Clarence Wilson and fiddler Pendleton Vandiver, the relative Monroe memorialized in the song "Uncle Pen."

Another guitarist, Kennedy Jones, learned Shultz's style and passed it on to Mose Rager, an Ohio County native who never managed to see Shultz play firsthand. The lively fingerpicking style Prine gleaned from his brother Dave, Old Town School instructors, and records by the Carter Family, Libba Cotten, and Mississippi John Hurt bore a close resemblance to Muhlenberg County thumbpicking. A guitar thumbpicker, wearing a banjo pick only on his thumb, plucks a steady rhythm of bass notes with his thumb while picking out the melody and fill notes on the high strings using his index and middle fingers—effectively playing lead and rhythm simultaneously.

Rager was born in 1911 and lived most of his life in the Muhlenberg town of Drakesboro, a crossroads about halfway between Greenville and Paradise. Just as Rager had been in awe of Jones, Merle Travis—born in 1917 a few miles south of Drakesboro in Rosewood—was in awe of Rager. Travis thought Rager could have been a star. "If Mose had decided to go into show business, he could have run us all out," Travis said, according to a 1977 article in the *Louisville Courier-Journal*.

Travis never worked in a coal mine, despite writing such classic miners' laments as "Sixteen Tons" and "Dark as a Dungeon" (the latter inspired by a motorcycle ride on a pitch-black night). His father was a miner, but Travis managed to find steady work as a musician apart from a brief stint in the U.S. Marine Corps toward the end of World War II. After the war, Travis moved to the West Coast, where his friend Gene Autry helped land him a series of minor roles in Western movies. Travis signed with Capitol Records in 1946, already a major label a mere four years after its founding, and quickly wrote and recorded a series of clever, high-energy hits: "Divorce Me C.O.D.," the song that hit No. 1 on the country charts the week after Prine was born; "Smoke, Smoke, Smoke (That Cigarette)," a big hit for Tex Williams; and "So Round, So Firm, So Fully Packed," in which Travis revisited the cigarette theme to turn a double entendre Lucky Strikes slogan into a single entendre.

Twenty years before music critics lauded the Beatles for creating the first concept album in Sgt. *Pepper's Lonely Hearts Club Band*, Travis released an album of four 78 RPM records, *Folk Songs of the Hills*, that featured a number of songs about coal mining: "Nine Pound Hammer," "Dark as a Dungeon," "Sixteen Tons," "The Powder Explosion," and "The Miner's Wife." A 1955 recording by Tennessee Ernie Ford would turn "Sixteen Tons" into one of the biggest hits of the fifties and make it his signature song. A decade later, in 1968, Johnny Cash recorded "Dark as a Dungeon" on his historic live album *At Folsom Prison*. That same year, Roger McGuinn and the Byrds recorded their take on another cut from *Folk Songs of the Hills*, the gospel standard "I Am a Pilgrim," modeled after the Travis version. It showed up on *Sweetheart of the Rodeo*, on which the Byrds teamed up with country-rock pioneer Gram Parsons to veer away from folk rock and create a traditional country album. With the Muhlenberg County thumbpicking tradition as his foundation, Travis had become a country music institution. He acknowledged Shultz by making the fretboard-frying "Cannonball Rag" a regular part of his repertoire, and he never failed to credit Rager for his success.

While Travis was starting his path to Hollywood and country music stardom, the other man he credited as one of his "tutors," Ike Everly, was trying his luck with relatives in the Chicago area, much like the Prine family. Two decades before his sons made the Everly Brothers a household name, Ike and two of his brothers, Charlie and Leonard, headed north to look for work above ground and play music. In 1935 Ike married a Central City girl, Margaret Embry. Their first son, Don, was born two years later in Brownie, a coal-mining camp outside Central City. Phil was born in 1939 after the family moved to Chicago.

The boys joined their parents on the air by the time Phil was six, and in 1950 *The Everly Family Show* was born. By the mid-fifties, with musical tastes changing and steady gigs drying up, Ike and Margaret quit the music business and moved back to Illinois after years spent in Iowa and Tennessee. Don and Phil, meanwhile, settled in Nashville and eventually signed with a small New York label, Cadence. Their first single in the spring of 1957, "Bye Bye Love," soared to No. 2 on the pop charts, kept from the top slot by Elvis Presley's "Teddy Bear" and Pat Boone's "Love Letters in the Sand." The song, propelled by the Everly Brothers' tight harmonies and driving acoustic guitars, peaked at No. 5 R&B and No. 1 country, eventually selling more than a million copies. Their next single, "Wake Up Little Susie," would not be denied the top spot, perching at No. 1 for four weeks that fall.

Prine's Kentucky kin had more modest musical ambitions. Verna Valentine Hamm (nicknamed "Cotton" for the white-blonde hair she had as a child), Luther and Agnes's eighth child, was born in Muhlenberg County on Valentine's Day in 1920. Verna completed eighth grade at a one-room schoolhouse, but family duties kept her from attending high school. She learned to play guitar and mandolin, and enjoyed going to neighborhood dances. William Mason Prine was born 24 August 1915. Bill may have clung to his Kentucky roots in part because his father's carpentry work frequently displaced the family.

The family finally put down new roots in the flat grid of Maywood, even if Bill's heart never left the rolling hills of Kentucky. He graduated from Proviso High School (later renamed Proviso East) in 1932, during the depths of the Depression. He found work through the Civilian Conservation Corps, signing on at a camp in northern Wisconsin. He later worked in Chicago with his father, Empson, doing carpentry work for A Century of Progress International Exposition—aka the 1933 World's Fair. Bill drove his Dodge back to Kentucky regularly to court Verna, helping fund the trips by selling whiskey purchased in Illinois to people in Muhlenberg, a dry county. Eventually he had to pony up one hundred dollars for a marriage bond: Judge Peck O'Neill married Bill and Verna at the courthouse in Greenville, the county seat, the day after Christmas, 1936. They would become parents less than a year later.

The next family trip to Paradise was never far off. Summer vacations in Muhlenberg County gave the young Prine and his brothers a window into another world. Driving out of the industrial bustle and traffic of mid-century Chicago, the family would head south to rural isolation, far from factories and freeways, racial and religious divides. Muhlenberg County was sparsely populated, mostly white, and Protestant, and moved at a much slower pace. Paradise felt like Mark Twain's Hannibal, Missouri, or a movie set. "It was a real Walt Disney kind of town," Prine told Ted Kooser. "It had two general stores. It had this one old fella, Bubby Short, and he would sit around and tell us ghost stories all the time. All there was to do was go fishing for catfish."

The Prine boys would explore the surrounding countryside, making their way downriver to the Airdrie furnace, a century-old iron-smelting facility about a mile away that had been abandoned shortly after it was built—Muhlenberg County's coal may have been worth a fortune, but its iron ore proved worthless. Airdrie had once boasted a hotel, more than a dozen houses, and an assemblage of Scotsmen imported to ply their trade, but all that remained by the 1950s was the overgrown ironworks. Paradise was on a similar trajectory. Originally called Stom's Landing, the settlement on the Green River was renamed Monterrey for a brief period after the Mexican-American War, but locals eventually settled on Paradise. (Competing theories for the name's origin abound.) The population would grow to about eight hundred at the town's twentieth-century peak.

Heavy surface-mining operations in the area had already taken their toll by the early 1950s. Rather than send miners down shafts to dig out coal in underground tunnels, mining companies began to access deposits closer to the surface by stripping away the rock and soil above them, profoundly altering the landscape and ecosystem. P&M Coal Company started buying up farms in eastern Muhlenberg County for strip mining, and about fifty families had left Paradise by 1952. Chicago-based Peabody Coal Company also got in on the action, eventually buying up tens of thousands of acres of land and mineral rights in Muhlenberg and Ohio Counties. In 1959 the Tennessee Valley Authority (TVA), a corporation established by the federal government during the New Deal to bring electricity and development to the rural South, announced plans to build a massive coal-burning power plant less than a mile from Paradise. Work began on two 650,000-kilowatt-capacity steam generators, the likes of which the world had never seen. There were still thirty-five families left in Paradise, but they wouldn't stick around much longer.

The beginning of the end came in 1965, when TVA announced that it would add a third generating unit to the Paradise Steam Plant. As smokestacks and eighty-story cooling towers climbed into the Kentucky sky, ash and coal dust occasionally rained down on the town's few remaining residents. "Giant shadows fall across the countryside, created by the huge chimneys at the nearby TVA plant, and the earth trembles underfoot when the world's largest strip-mining shovel takes a mammoth bite out of the soil," the Owensboro paper reported in 1967. ". . . The ground and everything above it [are] darkened with coal dust and the earth, a victim of its own riches, is scarred by deep pits. And as the last remaining residents leave this sleeping little town they glance back over their shoulders and wonder how there can be hell on earth but no place for Paradise."

Prine received word of the town's demise across the Atlantic in West Germany. A newspaper clipping was enclosed in a letter from home. When he got back to Illinois, he decided to write a song commemorating Paradise, a song his beloved dad could appreciate: "When I was a child my family would travel / Down to western Kentucky where my parents were born." Prine wrote of a "backwards old town," recalling trips out to the Airdrie ironworks, which he mistook for an abandoned prison. (It was a common misconception around Paradise, perhaps related to a period in the 1880s when prisoners from the state pen in Eddyville were brought to Airdrie to quarry stone.) The overgrown area "smelled like snakes and we'd shoot with our pistols / But empty pop bottles was all we would kill." The third verse described the fall of Paradise, when "the world's largest shovel . . . tortured the timber and stripped all the land." In the final verse, Prine soars above the devastation, asking for his ashes to be scattered on the Green River as he seeks solace on a higher plane: "I'll be halfway to Heaven with Paradise waitin' / Just five miles away from wherever I am." He had written a song that was country enough for Bill, with the chorus a direct shout out:

> And Daddy won't you take me back to Muhlenberg County
> Down by the Green River where Paradise lay
> Well I'm sorry, my son, but you're too late in asking
> Mister Peabody's coal train has hauled it away

"I thought if I wrote him a song—a true song about something that he'd lived through—he would at least listen to it," Prine told Nick Spitzer. "Because he would always ask me to sing Roy Acuff and Hank Williams, which I loved doing, but I wanted him to know. So I sang this song for him in the middle of a bunch of Hank Williams songs one day. He couldn't believe it, because he knew every word of the song was true."

Down in Muhlenberg County, reactions to "Paradise" were mixed. Though Prine was about to cross the Atlantic for his first shows in England and France in the spring of '73, he told the *Louisville Courier-Journal* he had yet to play a paying gig in Kentucky. "I've just played down there for the family reunions," he said. A store manager in Muhlenberg County reported brisk sales of DeShannon's "Paradise" single—six hundred to eight hundred copies in less than a month. Radio stations reported steady requests for the song. WTTL in Madisonville, in adjacent Hopkins County, "played it very heavy" despite "a few accusations thrown at us, about biting the hand that feeds us." Another Madisonville station, WFMW, said "people really ate it up here. We had a lot of coal miners call up early in the morning, before they go on shift, and request it." But the program director at WNES in Central City acknowledged that "some of the miners said it was degrading to them," though most of the feedback the station received had been positive. Prine said he meant the song more as "a lament for the town" than an anti-strip-mining anthem. "I liked the town a lot," he said. "If it had been a tornado that knocked the town down, I would still have written the song."

Peabody Coal tried to put a positive spin on the "Paradise" phenomenon. A cover story in the August 1973 issue of the company magazine, *Power for Progress*, celebrated "the progress the coal industry has brought to Muhlenberg County." An editor's note at the beginning of the magazine quoted the song's lyrics before mounting a defense: "Of course, our train did not 'haul it away' and the whole incident merely highlights the constant battle of emotions we are faced with each day. Peabody and its customers can be justly proud of the fact that our product—coal—helps supply the energy that gives so many people the conveniences of electricity and helps in the manufacture of many consumer products. Indirectly, we probably helped supply the energy to make the recording that falsely names us as 'hauling away' Paradise, Kentucky." *Penthouse* published an article about Paradise in December 1973 called "American Moonscape: The Peabody Strip-Off," which printed the chorus of Prine's song on its title page. The article quoted James Gilmour, an old man descended from one of the original Airdrie ironworkers, who describes a hundred square miles of desolate land in eastern Muhlenberg County that once held farms and forests. "Paradise?" Gilmour said. "There's just nothing there now—absolutely nothing. It makes me heartsick to go over there. A lot of people can grow older and go back home and say, 'Well, here's where I played as a boy.' I can't go back. There's not even any ground that I can walk over."

Talking New Bob Dylan

▼

By the time Prine released his debut album, American rock fans—or at least American rock critics—were hungry for a new Dylan. The old one had been around for more than a decade, practically retirement age in the career math of the time. ("The *old* Dylan was only thirty, so I don't even know why they needed a fucking *new* Dylan," Bruce Springsteen would say years later.) Pioneering rockers such as Elvis, Rick Nelson, Little Richard, and the Everly Brothers, all still in their thirties in 1971, were considered nostalgia acts, aging remnants of a previous musical generation.

Dylan himself seemed to be living in semiretirement with his wife and children in the backwoods of upstate New York. After a handful of brilliant mid-sixties rock albums, he had gone semiacoustic (*John Wesley Harding*), country (*Nashville Skyline*), and off the rails (*Self Portrait*). By the early seventies, he mostly seemed to have gone away. So when a new batch of singer-songwriters came along strumming acoustic guitars and singing wordy, unconventional songs in ragged, unconventional voices, music journalists and publicists started to stamp each one in turn the "new Dylan." There were Loudon Wainwright III, whose 1973 novelty hit "Dead Skunk" bore little resemblance to his brilliant, deeply personal songs about family relationships; Tom Waits, the jazzbo hipster and neo-beatnik pianist whose gravelly voice brought barflies and hustlers to life;

Steve Forbert, who pioneered the Americana genre and scored a 1980 hit with the sprightly "Romeo's Tune"; and Springsteen, who traded in his acoustic guitar for a Fender Telecaster, tightened up his lyrics, and became one of the biggest rock stars the world has ever known.

Also in the running for new Dylan over the years: Eric Andersen, Elliott Murphy, Patti Smith, Willie Nile, Billy Bragg, and Beck, among others. While it may have provided a shortcut to some easy publicity, it wasn't a label anyone seemed to wear with pride for very long, if ever. By 1975 Prine was already telling interviewers he was tired of being thought of as a "next Dylan." When Atlantic Records sent out a publicity sheet likening *Common Sense* to Dylan's 1965 classic *Highway 61 Revisited*, Prine hit the roof: "I said, 'What do you guys wanna send something like that along for?'" Prine told Bill Conrad.

Prine and Springsteen talked about their own new Dylan days after a Prine show in the late eighties, Prine told an interviewer in 1993: "I knew Springsteen from way back in '74—I met him when we were basically trying to do the same thing, trying to bust loose, and Bruce got *Born to Run* and all hell broke loose. I reminded him about a *New York Times* article in about '73, maybe, and it was like the new Bob Dylan contest. It was Springsteen, Loudon Wainwright, Keith Sykes, Elliott Murphy, and myself, this big article about who's gonna be the new Bob Dylan."

By the early nineties, enough time had passed that the whole phenomenon could be treated as a joke. Loudon Wainwright III looked back with sarcasm on his new Dylan days in a song on his 1992 album, *History*, name checking Prine as well. Wainwright had written "Talking New Bob Dylan" the previous year in honor of Dylan's fiftieth birthday:

Yeah, I got a deal and so did John Prine
Steve Forbert and Springsteen, all in a line
They were lookin' for you, signin' up others
We were new Bob Dylans—your dumbass kid brothers

"Well, we still get together every week at Bruce's house," Wainwright continued. "Why, he's got quite a spread, I tell ya. It's a twelve-step program."

More than forty years after the new Dylan phenomenon began, an NPR blog tried to stir it up all over again while marking the fiftieth anniversary of Dylan's debut at the Newport Folk Festival: "Question of the Week: Who's the New Bob Dylan?" "Tell us: Who's this generation's Dylan?" *All Songs Considered* producer Robin Hilton wrote. "And by 'this generation' I mean the 20-somethings. Who today has the vision, the reach, the imagination and voice to inspire or even unite the current generation of young people?" He continued, "We've tossed interesting suggestions around the NPR Music team, from Kanye [West] to Fiona Apple, Jeff Tweedy, The Tallest Man On Earth, Cat Power, Sufjan Stevens and Jay-Z. (I think Jay-Z is a pretty compelling one.)" In more than one hundred comments, fans weighed in with their own choices: Conor Oberst, Radiohead front man Thom Yorke, Josh Ritter, Jake Bugg, Lady Gaga, Justin Vernon, Macklemore, Jack White.

Of course, not everyone was on board with the concept: "Guys like Ritter, Oberst, Jim James & Ryan Adams have the fire but they are never gonna be as Iconic," wrote tyler samler, making random use of his Shift key. "There are no Beatles and no living Elvis to counterweight the need for a Dylan, and fame is so corporate now that a real genuine voice will never reach the mainstream that dylan hit." A music fan going under the name hetero habilis wrote, "There is and never was a 'new Dylan.'"

CHAPTER 7

Scattered, Smothered, and Covered

▼

Prine was settling into a regular pattern of recording and touring, slowly building his audience. In the summer of 1973 he did a summer tour of "little ski towns" in the Rockies with one of his early heroes, Ramblin' Jack Elliott. It was the off-season for tourists, so the crowds were small. "Jack showed up with this Winnebago and had a coupla interesting characters with him—and his dog, Caesar." A "black and gay" comedian named Kelly Green opened the shows. "He'd go out and sing, 'I'm an Old Cowhand (From the Rio Grande),'" Prine told Bare. "A lot of the cowboys down on the front row—I don't know if they liked that or not." Prine also appeared that summer at Willie Nelson's Fourth of July Picnic, a concert the country music veteran staged outside of Austin. The lineup mixed country and rock artists, such as Nelson, Kristofferson, Billy Joe Shaver, Doug Sahm, Tom T. Hall, and Leon Russell.

For his third album, Prine headed back to Tennessee. He and Arif Mardin met up in Nashville this time, recording at Quadrafonic Sound Studios, founded in 1970 by former Elvis sideman Norbert Putnam and Neil Young producer David Briggs. Goodman recorded his debut album there in 1971, and the studio had quickly become Music City's go-to destination for rockers and other artists who didn't fit into the country music scene, such as the James Gang, Young (who recorded his smash 1972 album *Harvest* at Quadrafonic), Dan Fogelberg, Grand Funk, and J. J. Cale. Prine's return to the Volunteer State also meant a return to the full-bodied sound of his debut album. Most of the musicians who played on *Diamonds in the Rough* (Goodman, Burgh, brother Dave) made an appearance, joined by some of the featured players on *John Prine* (Reggie Young, Mike Leach). One new face was another Elvis accompanist: singer Cissy Houston of the Sweet Inspirations.

The album's title track, "Sweet Revenge," kicked off with an electric guitar, organ, and drums, heralding a very different feel for the album than that of its rootsy predecessor. Sassy call-and-response backing vocals from Houston, Deidre Tuck, and Judy Clay answered the most confident, controlled lead singing Prine had ever captured on tape. He retained a ragged hillbilly edge, still miles away from the smooth delivery of such hit-making contemporaries as James Taylor and John Denver. But his singing on *Sweet Revenge* demonstrated a confidence and presence far beyond anything he managed on his debut album, and was a step up from the aptly titled *Diamonds in the Rough*. The large cast of musicians also worked more in tandem with Prine than on his first album, creating his first fully realized LP, one where the quality of the performances equaled that of the songs. Prine liked hanging out in Nashville, and by the time he made *Sweet Revenge* he felt "a little more comfortable with the full-band sound in the studio." The third time was the charm for Prine and Mardin. "I had a great deal of freedom," Prine told William Ruhlmann. "Arif allowed me all kinds of room, was wide open to any suggestions I had, and never tried to box me in a particular corner on anything. Certainly no pressure on song selection."

Prine cleared his closet of most of the rest of his old tunes ("Blue Umbrella" and "A Good Time," the latter featuring some nice Travis picking) and recorded a batch of new ones that numbered among his best to date. The title track was a misfit's defiant middle finger to the world, marking the second Prine album in a row to begin with a comic tune full of religious imagery: "I got kicked off of Noah's ark / I turn my cheek to unkind remarks." The defiant attitude carried over into the second song, "Please Don't Bury Me"—which also featured some uncharacteristically intricate guitar interplay: "Send my mouth way down south / And kiss my ass goodbye." Prine's irreverent sense of humor shone on several songs. In "Dear Abby," a solo number recorded in concert, the Chicago-based syndicated newspaper columnist gave the same pat answer ("You are what you are and you ain't what you ain't") to a series of increasingly more outlandish advice-seekers:

Dear Abby, Dear Abby
Well I never thought
That me and my girlfriend would ever get caught
We were sitting in the back seat
Just shooting the breeze
With her hair up in curlers
And her pants to her knees
Signed: Just Married

"The Accident (Things Could Be Worse)" carried on in a similar vein, reveling in life's smallest details. The song described an inconsequential fender bender at "the corner of Third and Green"—a couple of blocks from Prine's boyhood home in Maywood. The bumped and bruised victims "don't know how lucky they are," he sang. "They could have run into that tree / Got struck by a bolt of lightning / And raped by a minority." "Christmas in Prison" mixed humor with pathos, romantic longing with some of Prine's most cinematic imagery to date:

The searchlight in the big yard
Swings round with the gun
And spotlights the snowflakes
Like the dust in the sun

Mardin had commissioned the song, Prine told a North Carolina audience in 2013, telling him they needed one more song for the record. The singer went back to his hotel room to write it, thinking, "I'm gonna fix him—I'm gonna write the worst song he ever heard. After singing this about three hundred times, I started liking it."

The men in Prine's family had a strong presence in the lyrics to a couple of songs. "Grandpa Was a Carpenter" was a lively ode to Empson Scobie Prine, Bill's father, painting a picture through the accumulation of spare, telling details: "Brown necktie and a matching vest / And both his wingtip shoes / He built a closet on our back porch / And put a penny in a burned-out fuse." Prine had clearly done some ruminating on his father, as well, devoting a verse of the funky, Little Feat–flavored "Mexican Home" to Bill's death two years before:

My father died
On the porch outside
On an August afternoon
I sipped bourbon and cried
With a friend by the light of the moon

The churning "Often Is a Word I Seldom Use" is a major musical departure for Prine, a harbinger of the left turn he would take on his next
album. He played in G with a capo on the second fret that transposed the
key to A. (Paul Simon had used the same guitar configuration on Simon
and Garfunkel's "I Am a Rock.") The song also featured a subdued horn
section and heavy use of the high hat in a manner very close to disco, a
genre still in its infancy in 1973. Prine closed *Sweet Revenge* as he had
closed *Diamonds* the year before—with a cover that harked back to his
musical roots. This time he looked to Muhlenberg County, rolling away
with a casually rocking, acoustic-guitar-driven version of "Nine Pound
Hammer" by Merle Travis. Prine and Goodman would perform "Nine
Pound Hammer" together on the BBC music show *The Old Grey Whistle
Test*.

Sweet Revenge played like a successful do-over of Prine's debut album. It
was a full-band LP recorded in Tennessee, but the singer had grown dramatically as a vocalist and recording artist over the previous two years.
He sounded fully integrated with the backing musicians this go-round,
and once again he rose to the challenge of writing a compelling batch of
tunes in far less time than the decade he had leading up to the recording
of his first album.

Thematically, *Sweet Revenge* paralleled the debut almost song for
song. Early counterculture tall tales such as "Spanish Pipedream" were
matched this time by rejections of polite society more in a Western,
biker, or James Dean antihero mode (the title track, "Please Don't Bury
Me"). The new "Dear Abby" and "The Accident" matched the goofball
humor of "Illegal Smile" and "Flag Decal." There were no antiwar songs
on *Sweet Revenge*, but the Vietnam War was winding down by 1973, and
it was time for Prine to take a break from the theme after releasing three
war-themed tunes in two years. (Four if you count the line from "Hello
in There" about the Korean War casualty.) "Blue Umbrella" matched

the debut's "Far from Me" as a gorgeous, fully realized tale of romantic heartache. For bittersweet, "Paradise"-style paeans to home and family, *Sweet Revenge* offered "Grandpa Was a Carpenter" and "Mexican Home." *John Prine* took the prize for character studies, though: Apart from "Grandpa," nothing on *Sweet Revenge* really came close to "Angel from Montgomery," "Sam Stone," or "Donald and Lydia."

The album had plenty of compensating glories to counter that minor shortcoming. From its rock 'n' roll swagger to its "Do I look like I give a shit?" cover, *Sweet Revenge* oozed attitude and delivered the musical goods to back it up.

The cover photo of *Sweet Revenge* is a far cry from the hay bale shot on *John Prine* or the *Diamonds* cover, a nondescript concert close-up. This time a bearded, denim-clad Prine—wearing sunglasses and pointy-toed cowboy boots, a cigarette jutting from his lips—sprawls across the leather front seats of a 1959 Porsche convertible, looking like he just woke up on the side of the road after an all-night bender. "That was my first toy I bought with record-company money, that Porsche I'm sitting in," Prine told Ruhlmann. "I wanted to make sure I got a picture of me and my car on the cover." That record-company money still couldn't buy Prine a hit, though: *Sweet Revenge* made no more of a dent on the sales charts than its predecessor, peaking at No. 135 during an eleven-week run in the Top 200 at the end of 1973. Robert Christgau gave the album a rare "A" rating, praising his songs' "everyday detail" and "his elementary insight that social circumstances do actually affect individual American lives." Reviewing the album for *Rolling Stone*, Tom Nolan called *Sweet Revenge* Prine's "best record yet." "It's a more human work, more mature, and a step forward artistically and toward a wider audience," he wrote.

His label pushed for a "Dear Abby" single. Loudon Wainwright had cracked the Top 20 for the first time earlier that year with a novelty song, "Dead Skunk"—after leaving Atlantic for Columbia Records. "Atlantic wanted to put out 'Dear Abby' *bad*, but I said, 'Hell no,'" Prine told Ken Tucker in a 1977 *Rolling Stone* interview. "If it went big then people who hadn't heard me before but liked it would expect me to come out and sing a lot of funny, cute songs, to come on like Roger Miller." On one hand, Prine felt pleased with where his career had taken him so far. "A lot had happened in three years' time," he told Ruhlmann. "At that time I was rolling, and the press that those records were getting was usually so great. I was just starting to realize that not everybody is afforded that, that if nothing else I was getting great press, and I was going around playing. I was playing in large clubs, but turning people away, and small concert halls. They're the perfect-sized theaters, I think—anything from one thousand to three thousand seats. So I figured, 'What could be better than that?'" On the other hand, the low sales of yet another album discouraged him. "I thought when I put that one out that it really had a great chance of actually selling and being representative of what I do," he said.

Toward the end of 1973 Prine and Goodman filed suit to get out of their management contracts with Anka, making Al Bunetta the official manager for both artists. (The singers' timing was good, allowing them to distance themselves from Anka before his godawful "[You're] Havin' My Baby" became a No. 1 hit.) As 1974 began Prine told an interviewer he was thinking seriously about moving south to Nashville or Austin. One of his drinking buddies in Austin was a wild man who called himself Dep'ty Dawg, after an early sixties cartoon character. They spent a lot of time at Armadillo World Headquarters, aka the 'Dillo, a music club and pothead oasis that opened in 1970. Everybody who was anybody played there. "There was a party all the time in Austin," Prine told Jeremy Tepper. "The backstage area of Armadillo World Headquarters was like the backstage area at the Wizard of Oz."

Covers of his songs appeared regularly, some now coming from across the Atlantic. Manfred Mann's Earth Band, a progressive English rock band that had rocked Randy Newman's "Living without You" and various Dylan tunes, tackled Prine's "Pretty Good" on their 1973 album *Get Your Rocks Off.* (Christgau labeled their version "pretty great.") Scottish singer Maggie Bell turned "Souvenirs" into a slow, Janis Joplin–style blues on her 1974 album *Queen of the Night.* But the real coup came in September 1974, with the release of *Streetlights,* the fourth album by Bonnie Raitt. The singer and slide guitarist, daughter of Broadway star John Raitt, was born in 1949 and, like Prine, had released her self-titled debut album in 1971. The two singers had often crossed paths on the road and hung out together at folk festivals. Her passionate, beautifully sung version of "Angel from Montgomery" instantly became the definitive version of the song, Raitt giving full voice to its female protagonist. Working with veteran soul producer Jerry Ragovoy, Raitt added vocal embellishments to the song far beyond Prine's limited capabilities, sing-ing over an incremental, slow-building arrangement worthy of the Band. The song is "just such a tender way of expressing that sentiment of long-ing—like 'Hello in There'—without being maudlin or obvious," Raitt said in a story that appeared in *Acoustic Guitar* in 2006. "It has all the different shadings of love and regret and longing."

The same month Raitt released her cover, Prine's voice hit the Amer-ican television airwaves. A new ABC comedy called *The Texas Wheelers*, produced by Mary Tyler Moore's MTM Enterprises, used an abbrevi-ated version of "Illegal Smile" over its opening credits. The show starred a grizzled Western character actor, Jack Elam, along with a couple of young unknowns, Gary Busey (as Truckie) and Mark Hamill (as Doo-bie). But *The Texas Wheelers* couldn't stand up against its detective-show competition on NBC, *The Rockford Files*, and was canceled after only four episodes. "Hearing 'Illegal Smile' come over the television was the aural equivalent of a Dali melting watch—really strange," Prine told Tucker. "Some executive at ABC must've lost his job over that choice."

"Paradise" continued to garner publicity for Prine three years after its release. In October *People* magazine ran an article titled "John Prine Goes Back to What's Left of Paradise," featuring a photo of him stand-ing in front of the world's largest shovel. "In talking to kin and other folks still around, Prine concluded that the laying waste of Paradise was perhaps more complex than his lyrics suggested, and that not the least of the culprits was the Tennessee Valley Authority, which has a power plant there," Frank Martin wrote.

Another Prine tune caught the ear of one of Prine's boyhood heroes that October. Baton Rouge native Duke Bardwell had begun playing bass in Elvis's TCB Band earlier in 1974. During a show at Lake Tahoe, the King was running out of steam and started calling out his band mem-bers to take turns behind the mike. "Everybody was doin' gospel music," Bardwell said in an interview posted on YouTube in 2010. One of his bandmates, Kathy Westmoreland, "sang this huge God song," he said. ". . . They had charts on it, and they were just kickin' ass on it." After several other people sang, drummer Ronnie Tutt suggested Bardwell get a turn, to which Elvis replied, "Yeah, right." But someone else seconded the motion. "I sang all the time," Bardwell said. "I always had my acous-tic guitar. Always workin' on a song."

Elvis finally relented—and gave Bardwell a sarcastic introduction: "My bass player's gonna sing a song—this oughtta be good." Bardwell was terror-stricken: "I was a deer in the headlights, man, I couldn't move. I was goin', 'No-no-no-no-no.' He just made a deal out of it, and I had to do it, I had no choice. And I didn't know what I was going to do—I was goin', 'How am I gonna follow all this God music?'" Finally singer Donnie Sumner bailed him out by suggesting, "Do the hurricane song." The song was Prine's "Please Don't Bury Me," the chorus of which contained the line "Throw my brain in a hurricane." "Boy, it was just perfect," Bardwell said. Eventually the band caught up with him. "By the second chorus, the whole band had it, and all the singers came in singin' on it," Bardwell said. Elvis, he says, "thought we just set him up big time. But I mean, they all had been hearin' me do it down in the dressing room and at the parties and stuff like that. I mean, talk about, 'Thank you, Jesus!' Bailed me out."

He was worried about the song's off-color ending, but it didn't faze Elvis. "We were going from 'my heavenly father' to 'kiss my ass good-bye,' and it just took everybody by surprise," Bardwell told Arjan Deelen in a 2008 interview for the website elvisnews.dk. "Elvis really got off on it. He really didn't know it—they didn't know who John Prine was." After the song ended, Elvis "was doin' all this dramatic crackin' up," Bardwell said. "He was down on one knee laughin'. All that stuff." After the show, Bardwell got word that Elvis's manager, Colonel Tom Parker, wanted to see him. "I looked at Ronnie and I said, 'I'm a fired sonofabitch for sayin' "kiss my ass goodbye" right after Kathy did the God song,'" Bardwell said. But Parker hadn't been fazed, either: Tutt told Bardwell, "The Colonel said to tell you that's one of the funniest things he's ever seen at an Elvis Presley concert." It was the only time Parker ever even acknowledged his presence.

The evening ended with Elvis calling Bardwell up to his room: "Elvis said, 'Bring your guitar, come upstairs.'" He asked Bardwell to sing "Please Don't Bury Me" again . . . and again . . . and again. "I don't have any idea how many times he told me to sing that song," Bardwell said. "Had to be twenty. I lost waaaaaay count. But I wasn't gonna quit. I wasn't gonna say, 'No, Elvis, I'm tired o' this shit, man.'"

CHAPTER 8

Tangled Up in Blue

▼

By the beginning of 1975, Prine was starting to get tired of his own shit. He told Kristofferson that when he wasn't performing, "he didn't want to *look* at his guitar." After years of free-flowing ideas, inspiration was starting to fail him. "I'd kind of run the gamut with writing either ballads or even thinking about putting a character in a song," Prine told William Ruhlmann. He decided it was time to shake things up: "I started writing anything different than I had before, just for the sake of trying to stay out of a rut."

The new songs were for his fourth album. Prine also wanted to try working with a different producer for the first time, and selected Steve Cropper. The Memphis guitarist and songwriter was a member of Booker T. & the M.G.'s and cowriter of some of the greatest soul songs in history: Wilson Pickett's "In the Midnight Hour," Eddie Floyd's "Knock on Wood," and Otis Redding's "(Sittin' on) The Dock of the Bay." He had begun to stretch out as a producer by the mid-seventies, taking the helm for records by Poco, José Feliciano, and others. "It wasn't like I didn't want to use Arif anymore, I just wanted to go somewhere different and try a different kind of recording with a different person," Prine told Ruhlmann. His record company, however, was not pleased. The powers that be at Atlantic, Prine said, "took it as kind of a slap in the face."

They recorded at Ardent Studios in Memphis, following in the footsteps of ZZ Top, Leon Russell, the Staple Singers, and James Taylor. "I went down to Memphis to cut a couple of tracks with Steve, just for us to feel each other out," Prine told Todd Everett in a 1975 interview with the *Los Angeles Free Press*. "We cut four songs with just a rhythm section and it sounded so great that I started writing in the studio." His backing band featured some familiar faces (Goodman, pedal steel player Leo LeBlanc) along with a number of new players: Al Bunetta's brother, Peter, on drums, and guitarist Rick Vito, who had played with Todd Rundgren, Delaney and Bonnie, and John Mayall. Cropper brought in some of his cronies, namely, the Memphis Horns and Donald "Duck" Dunn, bass player for Booker T. & the M.G.'s. Prine wanted a live sound without a lot of overdubs.

Several of his new songs were inscrutable abstractions—"Wedding Day in Funeralville" didn't sound like a song title; it sounded like a concept for a surrealistic Firesign Theater comedy sketch. "Forbidden Jimmy," an unusual detour into island rhythms, contained references to water skiing, Dorian Gray, and a mystery woman named Ginger Caputo. One of the more accessible songs was "Come Back to Us Barbara Lewis Hare Krishna Beauregard" (despite its cumbersome title), a comic portrait of a familiar character of the era, inspired by some aging hippies Prine met on his 1973 Colorado tour. "What I had in mind was this girl who left home, did drugs, did religion, did husbands, and ended up doing diddley," Prine wrote in the liner notes for 1988's *John Prine Live*.

The title track, "Common Sense," used the common I–IV–V chord progression, though Prine mixed it up with extra chords, as usual, stretching the music to fit his lyrics. "Saddle in the Rain" also kept his sidemen on their toes, seeming to modulate between D and E minor. "That Close to You" shifted from A to D in the bridge like a middle-period Beatles song.

As with "Mexican Home" on his previous album, Prine's father partially inspired "He Was in Heaven before He Died," the chorus of which began, "And I smiled on the Wabash / The last time I passed it." "I was thinking about the trips we used to take down to Paradise," Prine wrote in the liner notes to his 1993 *Great Days* anthology. "We'd cut through Indiana and cross the Wabash River; I wanted to make a specific reference to that." He refused to play it straight even on that song, however, opening with a line about "a rainbow of babies / Draped over the graveyard." "Where do you go from there?" Prine wrote. "I consider that a challenge, though, to paint myself into a corner and then get out. I figured out that what you're trying to do as a writer is go to places that aren't so comfortable, that you don't already know how to get out of." (The song's music, however, was a reassuring return to the comparatively conventional, pedal-steel-driven country rock of Prine's previous albums.) Instead of closing the album with another classic country cover, this time he went with a Chuck Berry rocker, "You Never Can Tell."

Prine was perfectly content with the record he cut in Memphis. But Cropper was moving into the rock 'n' roll big leagues as a producer, working on Rod Stewart's next record around the same time. He decided Prine's album needed fleshing out. Despite the singer's reservations, Cropper and Prine took the tapes to Los Angeles and added the kinds of overdubs Prine said he wanted to avoid, most notably backing vocals by the likes of Bonnie Raitt, Jackson Browne, and Glenn Frey of the Eagles. *Common Sense*, released in April 1975, ended up being Prine's hardest-rocking record to date, and very much of its time. With its funky rhythms, blaring horns, and oohing backup singers, it was an album that wore floppy hats and half-buttoned polyester print shirts, an album that snorted coke off the cover of an Ohio Players album while a Quinn-Martin cop show played on the console TV across the room. Prine was sure the album "was my most accessible stuff to date," he told Ken Tucker. Though still failing to qualify as a hit, *Common Sense* sold much better than its predecessors, coming within spitting distance of the Top 40. The album peaked at No. 66 and stayed on the charts for ten weeks.

Common Sense was no hit with critics. For the first time in his career, a new Prine album got mostly bad reviews. Greil Marcus, reviewing the record for the *Village Voice*, didn't mince words: "*Common Sense* is John Prine's latest, and worst, record." Robert Christgau gave it an A-minus despite calling it "the most genuinely miserable album I've heard in years." Stephen Holden liked it even less than he had liked *Diamonds*. "*Common Sense* is a confused, self-indulgent fourth album by a major songwriter gone downhill," he wrote in the opening sentence of his *Rolling Stone* review.

Prine assembled a full band for the first time to tour with him and promote the new record. Everett caught up with him and his "flowing new mustache" in the spring of '75 at a motel off Sunset Boulevard. "I'm now writing with a band in mind, which is considerably different from writing for just a voice and guitar," he said. The band featured drummer Peter Bunetta along with a bass player, keyboard player, and lead guitarist. "I imagine that it was awkward for both me and them at first," Prine said. "I've never worked with a band before. But we've done about 14 dates together already; they've come off pretty well." Chet Flippo was not impressed with Prine's 18 April performance at Avery Fisher Hall in New York, giving it a bad review in *Rolling Stone*: "Prine apparently wants to turn his energies toward rock but hasn't yet figured out how to do it. Meanwhile, his writing is suffering for it." Flippo also noted "a stagehand who delivered an unending series of what appeared to be small cups of beer." The alcohol, he wrote, "did little to lubricate Prine's rasp, but that mattered not a whit to the assembled fanatics."

The singer was unhappy with his label, and he thinks Atlantic may have done more to promote *Common Sense* because the label realized he might be thinking about jumping ship. "Atlantic just didn't know what I was," Prine told Ruhlmann. "They'd say, 'Hey, John, you're great, we can't wait until you break big.' And then they'd sit back and wait." The record company ignored his efforts to reach out and craft a promotional plan for the album, he said. "I said, 'Let me know what you think and what you want to do to promote this,'" Prine told Tucker. "Nobody ever got back to me." By that point Jerry Wexler played less of a day-to-day role in the record company's operations, and Prine found the label's chairman, Ahmet Ertegun, largely inaccessible, too busy jet-setting with the Rolling Stones and Led Zeppelin to give Prine the time of day. Prine asked to be released from his contract. In an ironic twist of fate, his Atlantic albums started making money around that time. "Just as I was getting ready to leave the company, all my records went in the black," he told Tucker. "I don't sell much, but I sell steady. And they wanted me to give 'em three or four more albums." The label milked the Prine material on hand for one final album, releasing the 1976 best-of *Prime Prine*, which culled the most obvious songs from Prine's first four records, drawing heavily on his debut. No one associated with Prine was involved in the release. "A friend of ours in the art department called us one night and snuck us into the place," he told Ruhlmann. They wandered through Atlantic's dark Manhattan offices "so we could at least look at the cover before it came out."

In the Bicentennial year, Prine declared his independence from Atlantic Records—and went back to performing solo. A photo from the era shows him posing in front of his 1951 Ford Custom Club Coupe, grinning like he just won a Burton Cummings lookalike contest. Freelance music journalist Bill Conrad, on assignment from a Texas magazine called *Buddy* (after Buddy Holly), caught up with him early in '76 at the Hall of Fame Motor Inn near the Country Music Hall of Fame in Nashville. Prine was wearing "threadbare jeans—pegged, patched, and rolled at the bottom—exposing olive sweat socks inside Converse sneakers," Conrad wrote. "The open-collar shirt and secondhand suit jacket were secondary attire." After Prine offered him a drink, Conrad asked if he had a band with him. Prine "smiled and shrugged" before saying, "Naw, ran out of money." He was playing a show with Raitt and Tom Waits at Opryland USA, a brand-new theme park in the suburbs and home to a new auditorium for the Grand Ole Opry nearly twice as large as the old Ryman Auditorium downtown.

Prine's former keyboard player, Alan Hand, now backed Raitt. "Love your shoes, John," Raitt told Prine. The two of them teamed up with Waits to rehearse a version of an old R&B song, "High Blood Pressure" by Huey "Piano" Smith and the Clowns. A ragged first attempt prompted Raitt to say, "That oughtta go down in the *anals* of history!" During a rehearsal break, Conrad asked Prine if he liked living in Chicago. "Naw, just too lazy to move," Prine said. He expressed enthusiasm for his recent full-band tour: "Loved it! I really got my kicks, man!" His solo set later that night leaned heavily on songs from his first album. When Raitt brought Prine and Waits onstage for "High Blood Pressure," she "had the house almost rocking for a few minutes," Conrad wrote. "Then it was over. The house lights came up. Bonnie, John, and Tom locked arms behind each other to bow as one, and left their audience feeling okay."

Concert reviewers continued to note Prine's heavy drinking. In June he played a benefit for a folk club in Ann Arbor, Michigan, along with David Bromberg, Jay Ungar, David Amram, Leon Redbone, and the National Recovery Act—Dave Prine's duo with Tyler Wilson. Writer Guerin Wilkinson, reviewing the show for the *Michigan Free Press*, said Dave's band played a couple of Carter Family spirituals, along with some original songs and tunes from "78 RPM records unearthed from attics across the country." John Prine "was the crowd-getting star performer of the day, although his music is certainly more pop than traditional folk." Wilkinson wrote that "something had to have happened" to Prine between sets, "because when he appeared for his second set, he was giggling, chain-smoking, and could hardly stand on his feet. Furthermore, no one was willing to believe that the four paper cups he had set to the side of the microphone stand really contained water." It got worse before it got better: "At least a quarter of the audience was too embarrassed to watch Prine complete his set in fear that he would fall on his face, pee in his pants, or start taking off his clothes. Fortunately, the worst that happened was that he kept forgetting his lyrics, and I found his second set even more brilliant than his first."

That fall Prine headed down to the Caribbean for his thirtieth birthday, vacationing on the island of Aruba. An unexpected opportunity brought him jetting back to the mainland. His old Second City pal John Belushi had become a breakout star on the late-night NBC sketch-comedy show *Saturday Night Live*, already famous for his portrayals of a Samurai warrior working mundane urban jobs, Captain Kirk from *Star Trek*, and Marlon Brando as the Godfather attending a group therapy session. Belushi had been lobbying for a Prine appearance as one of the show's weekly musical guests. "Every time some big musical act got booked and somebody got sick or they had to cancel, Belushi would always put my name in the hat and say, 'Ya gotta get John Prine,'" Prine told Craig Outhier of the *Phoenix New Times* in 2009. When the Beach Boys canceled at the last minute, Belushi finally got his wish. "I shot out to New York, and met all the original cast and did the show," Prine said in a 2008 interview with Dan Buckley of WRLT for *Music Business Radio*. "The show couldn't have been hotter at the time—it was a lot of fun." Actress Karen Black, known for her appearances in *Easy Rider*, *Five Easy Pieces*, *Airport 1975*, and *Nashville*, hosted the show that week.

A television studio was familiar turf for Al Bunetta—his father, Frank, had worked on such fifties TV shows as *The Honeymooners* and *Your Show of Shows*. Frank Bunetta joined them for Prine's *SNL* appearance—where Prine remembers *SNL* producer Lorne Michaels bragging about originating the concept of live TV, despite its having been a common phenomenon in the medium's early days. "At the time, they were fixing the newer studios at NBC, and so they were doing the shows in Brooklyn at the old studios," Prine told Buckley. "So Frank walked in there with us, and some of the old gaffers and cameramen that were still working there stopped what they were doing and turned around to say hello to him."

Prine had a funny new song he was eager to showcase, but *SNL* wanted time-tested material from his debut album. "I had just written 'The Bottomless Lake,' but the producer didn't want me to do it and I insisted on it," he said in an interview for a blog called *The College Crowd Digs Me*. "He wanted me to do two songs from my first album, and I said, 'I'll do one. I'll do "Hello in There," and that's it.'"

The new song was an amalgamation of old family stories. It was based in part on his grandfather Luther's tale about the family that missed the ferry in Kentucky and disappeared in the river; in part on Prine's memories of a couple of family trips. One day his family went fishing in Illinois and got caught on the pier in a thunderstorm. "We all headed out maybe fifteen miles west of Chicago," Prine told Jason Wilber. "It was wide-open country then—you didn't have to go far." Bill would back the car to the end of a narrow pier to make it easier to drive back after a day spent fishing and drinking beer. On one such trip, a big thunderstorm engulfed the family before Bill could get them back to dry land. "It just got more and more violent until it was striking the trees around us," Prine said. "We were on the lake, and my mother said, 'Bill, let's get out of here.' And as he was driving [on the pier], the rain was coming down so hard that those old windshield wipers—the rain was laughing at 'em. The wipers were just going back and forth and doing absolutely nothing." As Bill inched along, Verna panicked: "My God, Bill, you're gonna kill all of us." About halfway up the pier, a lightning bolt struck a big oak tree nearby "and shook the entire pier and everything around us as if it was the end of the world. My mother thought, with all the water falling around us, she thought we fell into the lake." Another family trip took the Prines to Baraboo, Wisconsin, the summer home of Ringling Brothers and Barnum and Bailey Circus, Prine told Wilber: "It was on Devil's Lake, and Devil's Lake was supposed to be a bottomless lake. There was a train that went around Devil's Lake back in the twenties, and it run off the tracks and fell in and they never did find the people. And so there was always that mystique about it. So I thought, 'Well, if it's bottomless, it must still be falling.'"

After a parody of a presidential debate between Gerald Ford (Chevy Chase) and Jimmy Carter (Dan Aykroyd), Black introduced the musical guest: "And now, one of the best singer-songwriters of today, John Prine." He stood alone in a stark spotlight, surrounded by darkness, wearing a loud shirt with a fashionably humongous collar. He finger-picked an acoustic guitar with a capo on the neck. Prine's thick black hair approached bouffant volume, his face all cheekbones and flowing mustache—offset by a tiny soul patch just under his lower lip. He cut his eyes around like a suspect under interrogation while singing "Hello in There," his tone harsh, his delivery tense. His eyelids fluttered a bit as he sang a guttural "hello in tharrrrrrrrrr" during the chorus. Prine ended the song with a quick "thank you," rewarded with enthusiastic applause, whistles, and whoops from the studio audience.

A stentorian introduction from announcer Don Pardo preceded his second song: "Now, once again, here's John Prine." The singer quickly set up the tune: "This is a song from a story my grandfather told me about a family that went out for a Sunday drive and, uh, they never came back. It's called 'The Bottomless Lake.'" The opening lines of the song rendered his spoken introduction almost superfluous: "Here's the story of a man and his family / And a big trip that they took." Though his voice still sounded harsh on the verses, his tone sounded more relaxed by the time he reached the chorus:

We are falling down
Down to the bottom of a hole in the ground
Smoke 'em if you got 'em
I'm so scared I can hardly breathe
I may never see my sweetheart again

As the car descended, the family went on about its business—eating chicken, telling stories, listening to the radio. When the baby got a bel-lyache, the mother rocked it to sleep. "Well, if the ferry been there at the end of the pier / We'd be halfway to Uncle Jake's," Prine sang, clearly amusing himself. "Instead of looking at fish out the window I wish / We'd hit the bottom of the Bottomless Lake."

The silver screen also beckoned. Prine crossed paths with a producer working with one of the era's biggest stars, Dustin Hoffman, who had two hit films in 1976: *All the President's Men* and *Marathon Man*. Now he was prepping for a forthcoming movie called *Straight Time*. "I was going to play an ex-con friend of his," Prine told Nick Krewen in a 1995 interview with the *Hamilton (Ontario) Spectator*. "This wasn't something I was pursuing. I talked to his producer, who thought I was just great for the part and thought I should meet with Dustin Hoffman." The actor tended to play down-to-earth characters, and his real-life persona took Prine by surprise: "He was totally movie star. He had a big pair of sunglasses and a white poodle in his lap that he was petting to death. So Dustin Hoffman is asking me if I'd ever had any acting experience, and I said, 'Nothing.' He said, 'You've never done anything?' And I said, 'Nothing—not even in high school.'" The singer clearly wasn't what Hoffman was expecting, either. "There was a long silence," Prine said. "We were out on the balcony, and he had me facing the sun. Finally he said, 'Well, how did you get here?' And I said, 'I don't know. Maybe somebody boinked your secretary.' Then he gave me the book that the movie was from, and I never heard from him again."

CHAPTER 9

Seeking Asylum

▼

Six years after David Geffen tried to buy Prine's management contract, he signed Prine to a three-album deal with Asylum Records in 1977—a much more modest commitment than the ten-album deal with Atlantic. Asylum was smaller than Atlantic and more oriented toward singer-songwriters. Steve Goodman had recorded for the label since 1975, and it was home to a squadron of mellow Southern California hit-makers: the Eagles, Linda Ronstadt, Orleans, Jackson Browne, and Andrew Gold. (Not every artist on the label fit that mold, however. The Everly Brothers' old piano player, the tough, literary-minded rocker Warren Zevon, had recently released a brilliant self-titled album for Asylum, produced by Browne. Dylan had also recorded briefly for Asylum, breaking from Columbia Records for the only time in his career to put out the two albums before *Blood on the Tracks.*)

Prine was not in a mellow mood. Ten years along, his marriage to Ann Carole had seen better days—Prine told William Ruhlmann it was "coming apart at the seams." He wanted a change of scenery, and he wanted to rock. In the summer of 1977 he headed south to Nashville for preliminary work on his next album. Prine sought a harder rockabilly sound, so he went to the source: Cowboy Jack Clement, who had been Sam Phillips's right-hand man at Sun Studios in the fifties. Clement had produced sessions for Jerry Lee Lewis, Johnny Cash, Charlie Rich, Charley Pride, Doc Watson, Townes Van Zandt, and Waylon Jennings, and written a string of memorable country songs: "Guess Things Happen That

Way," "Ballad of a Teenage Queen," "Dirty Old Egg-Suckin' Dog," and "Flushed from the Bathroom of Your Heart." Clement knew Elvis from Sun Studios, but never worked with him. Elvis died that summer, on 16 August.

Clement had signed with Asylum's sister label, Elektra, and he and Prine worked on both of their albums simultaneously—after a fashion. Clement "was a huge mentor to me and the reason why I moved to Nashville," Prine told Paul Zollo. "I moved there and we worked for three to four months, solid. And through all kinds of outside forces and things that shouldn't have been going on in the studio, we didn't get the record that we were playing every day. We really enjoyed making the record, but we didn't get it on tape the way we were hearing it in the studio. This was the first one I was doing for Asylum Records, and they kept spending money on it."

One of the distractions for Prine was the bass player on the sessions—an attractive young woman named Rachel Simpson. "I got involved with somebody, and it got to be a very sticky affair," Prine told Zollo. He wasn't the first singer with Muhlenberg County connections she had played with—Simpson had also backed Don Everly. "John is one of my favorite people, and it was a productive time for him," Clement told Lloyd Sachs in an interview for Prine's 2005 profile in *No Depression*. "We did a lot of experimenting and messing around, him and me playing guitars, which I thought was the direction to pursue. But he had things going on. We'd start working on a song and he'd start singing something else. He had a crush on the bass player, Rachel. . . . That was part of the distraction, but there were other things, too." A video from the sessions showed Prine harmonizing with Simpson, a thin-nosed redhead with bangs and a feathered Farrah Fawcett hairdo, wearing a strapless yellow sundress. The song? A new Prine tune with a chorus that went, "How lucky can one man get?"

As the summer wound down, Prine taped another national television appearance, heading to Texas at the end of August. This time he got to perform an entire set, backed by a band for part of his performance. The show was *Austin City Limits*, then in its third season, produced by KLRU and syndicated on PBS. Goodman appeared on the same show. *Austin City Limits* showcased the city's eclectic music scene, along with artists from across the nation, with leanings toward country, country rock, and folk music. Previous guests ranged from Willie Nelson and Townes Van Zandt to the Amazing Rhythm Aces and Jimmy Buffett.

Prine and Goodman split the hour of airtime. Goodman, a manic imp in a blue suit, gave his cowriter credit when introducing "You Never Even Called Me by My Name": "This is a song I wrote with John Prine, and we tried to put into one song [everything] that had ever been in any of the country and Western songs we'd ever heard. Good thing for a little Hebrew fellow from Chicago to do, you know what I mean?" Prine performed part of his set solo with an acoustic guitar. He repeated "Bottomless Lake" from his *SNL* performance, and sang an unrecorded number about an altar boy who got hit by a train in Maywood when he was a kid. Introducing a more upbeat new song, "That's the Way That the World Goes 'Round," Prine said, "The people I'm gonna bring out later on to play with me, they been playin' in Nashville with me all summer. Been tryin' to put a record together—one of those black things that goes around in a circle, you know? Sometimes you make 'em in two days, and sometimes it takes two years." For the rockers, Prine strapped on a Gibson electric guitar to front a band with Peter Bunetta on drums and Simpson on bass. "I been comin' down here since about '71," Prine told the audience, dropping the name of an Austin club. "Played at the Castle Creek and you people have always been real nice to me."

After the *ACL* taping, it was back to Nashville. Al Bunetta remembered a chaotic scene at the home studio, which Clement called the Cowboy Arms Hotel and Recording Spa. "I think there were four recordings going on at the same time," Bunetta told David Hooper. "I'm not sure, but there were a whole lotta people playing, people cooking. It was this party that went on, and whenever I'd go into town, I never knew when they were recording. It'd be like—one place, no, and they left here and the bus took them there, and they're on a houseboat now—can't get out there. It was just an incredible creative merry-go-round that just kept going on. And John, I guess, was having the fun of his life." Working with Clement renewed Prine's enthusiasm for his profession. "Jack got me really back into music as I'd never been before," Prine told Ruhlmann. "We'd play from 10 o'clock in the morning till 10 o'clock at night. Sometimes we'd record, and sometimes we'd just play music. We'd play any songs—some of mine, some of his, just some old country stuff, some rock and roll."

Prine especially appreciated the attention Clement paid to his sing-ing. "The other producers I'd worked with, nobody ever said nothin' about my singin' one way or the other," Prine said in an interview for the 2006 Clement DVD *Shakespeare Was a Big George Jones Fan.* "Whether they liked it, hated it, or if I should change it or try and do somethin' to it. And Jack was just trying to get me to sing as good as I possibly could. Not better than I possibly could, just as good as I possibly could." But the sessions never gelled, and Prine finally threw in the towel and started looking for other producers. He owed Asylum an album. "I went out to L.A. and I talked to, *Christ,* twenty different producers, really great guys, great producers," Prine told Zollo. "Big-time producers. And I just didn't want to do it. I just didn't have the heart to do the record again." He finally turned to Goodman to bail him out. "Well, just don't look to me to approve or disapprove," Prine told Goodman. "I'm just to-tally . . . numb." He gave his old friend creative control over the project.

That fall Ken Tucker interviewed Prine for *Rolling Stone* while the singer was in New York to perform for the Dr. Pepper Music Festival in Central Park, playing with an "eight-piece, just-some-pals pickup band." Prine talked with Tucker about leaving Atlantic, signing with Asylum, and planning for his next album: "Latter-day rockabilly is the mood I'm aiming for." In January 1978 he joined Goodman at Chicago Recording Company, a new studio founded three years earlier, to make an album on his home turf for the first time. Besides Goodman, steel guitarist Leo LeBlanc was one of the few familiar faces from previous Prine sessions. Mike Utley from Jimmy Buffett's Coral Reefer Band played keyboards. Sid Sims, who had recorded with Goodman, played bass. Several friends from Chicago sat in: singer Bonnie Koloc; mando-lin player Jethro Burns from the veteran comic country duo Homer and Jethro; and Burns's guitar-playing son, Johnny.

After the failed experiment of his previous record, Prine fell back to his proven strengths as a songwriter. "The direction I'd gone in *Com-mon Sense* worked out fine for one album's worth, but it wasn't lead-ing anywhere for me," he told Ruhlmann. "So, I went back to what I thought I was best at." The result was the finest collection of songs since his debut album, a winning mix of humor and pathos, hummable folk songs, churning rockers, and somber musings recorded over a three-month stretch. Prine in this album ignored prevailing musical winds, unlike fellow "new Dylan" Bruce Springsteen, who released an intense, stripped-down album around the same time, *Darkness on the Edge of Town*, that reflected the influence of punk rock. Neither did Prine and Goodman aim for the kind of slick, heavily produced California-rock sound that had made Fleetwood Mac a household name in 1977 and helped James Taylor's *JT* album become the biggest seller of his career that same year. (There also appeared to be little risk of Prine going disco.)

Lyrically, he surveyed his life in the Chicago suburbs just before leaving them behind. The album opened with "Fish and Whistle," a sing-along march with a trilling pennywhistle that could have played over the opening credits of *The Andy Griffith Show*—if not for the song's happily irreverent chorus:

> Father forgive us for what we must do
> You forgive us; we'll forgive you
> We'll forgive each other till we both turn blue
> Then we'll whistle and go fishing in heaven

Prine had gotten his first taste of paid labor in Melrose Park, just north of Maywood. "My first job, when I was twelve or thirteen, was at Skip's Fiesta Drive-In, which was the big place for the hot rods to hang out," he told David Fricke for the *Great Days* liner notes. The restaurant was just across the street from Kiddieland, a local amusement park. "I worked there during the daytime and helped this old Swedish janitor with his chores," Prine said. "The carhops wore hula skirts, and kids would buy the cheapest thing, a cup of custard, so they could watch the carhops and stuff. And then they'd take the custard and throw it on the ground. The next day, I'd be out there on my knees with hot boiling water with ammonia, trying to scrape this custard off. I thought, 'This is what it's all about, all my jobs are going to be like this.'"

The lyrics to "Fish and Whistle" looked back first to Prine's service in the army motor pool ("I was in the army but I never dug a trench / I used to bust my knuckles on a monkey wrench"), then all the way back to his Skip's Fiesta days: "On my very first job I said thank you and please / They made me scrub a parking lot down on my knees / Then I got fired for being scared of bees / And they only give me fifty cents an hour." The similarly bouncy "That's the Way That the World Goes

'Round," introduced on *Austin City Limits*, walked a lyrical tightrope between pleasure and pain. (A husband beat his wife with a rubber hose, then—following the classic cycle of an abuser—"takes her out to dinner and buys her new clothes.") But the production was so lively (featuring Travis picking and the instrument of choice for elementary school music lessons, the recorder) that it was hard to hear the song as anything but upbeat. "I was kind of fed up with a lot of cynicism that I saw in people, even in myself at the time," Prine said. "I wanted to find a way to get back to a better world, more childlike." Prine also resurrected the rambunctious "Aw Heck," written in West Germany more than a decade before. A vintage photo on the back cover of the album shows Prine in his army days, playing guitar in the barracks for his fellow GIs. "There She Goes" was a deceptively jaunty country song that Merle Travis himself could have written, with lyrics that sounded inspired by Prine's crumbling marriage:

> Well, I seen her on down at the courthouse
> I was sober as the judge
> We'd tried to talk things over
> But the grudge just wouldn't budge

"Sabu Visits the Twin Cities Alone" commented indirectly on the music business while recalling movie promotions of Prine's youth, when minor stars (action heroes, Western cowboys) made personal appearances at theaters. "I was flying out of Minneapolis–St. Paul, toward the end of a tour," Prine wrote in the *Great Days* liner notes. "I had this vision of the look on Sabu the Elephant Boy's face in the old jungle movies; he always had this dazed and confused look. And I saw myself like that in the mirror. I just looked like, 'What am I doing here?'" In the song, a movie producer sent Sabu on a winter promotional tour "in the land of the wind-chill factor." Prine accompanied himself on guitar, with a bit of clarinet and accordion added for color. Bonnie Koloc added ghostly harmonies. Prine used humor to balance off a lonely, depressing scenario: "Sabu was sad; the whole tour stunk / The airlines lost the elephant's trunk." Writing "Sam Stone," Prine said, had convinced him that no subject was off-limits, but even he acknowledged that his song about Sabu "was very odd."

For the first time since his debut, Prine released no covers. He did cowrite one song, however, teaming up with Phil Spector, the legendary Wall of Sound producer of everything from early sixties girl-group records to albums by the Beatles and John Lennon. Longtime Prine booster Robert Hilburn of the *Los Angeles Times* had introduced them while Prine was on the West Coast interviewing prospective producers. Hilburn told Prine that Spector was a fan of his work. "You're kidding me," Prine replied. "Oh, no," Hilburn said. "He was quoting 'Donald and Lydia' to me the other night." Spector lived up to his eccentric reputation: "The first six hours I was at the place, he's the craziest person I'd ever met," Prine told Zollo. At one point Spector pulled out a pistol, as was his wont. "You'd always see it before the end of the evening," Prine said. But Spector settled down when they started playing together. "From the moment he started playing music, he became like Joe Normal!" Prine told Ruhlmann. "I guess it soothed him." They completed "If You Don't Want My Love" before Prine left, a melancholy tune about a relationship on the wane.

For the album's title track, also introduced on *Austin City Limits*, Prine used the name of the fake musical he had invented years before as a cheap way to copyright a large batch of songs: "Bruised Orange" (to which he appended the parenthetical "Chain of Sorrow"). The moody, ominous, slow-building waltz stood in stark contrast to the album's jaunty folk songs, dredging up Prine's memories of "a long-ago Sunday" in Maywood:

> An altar boy's been hit by a local commuter
> Just from walking with his back turned
> To the train that was coming so slow

He was singing about an incident that happened one morning during the period when he was shoveling snow for the Episcopal Church of the Holy Communion in Maywood. As Prine trudged about twelve blocks north through the snow, he gradually realized something had happened. "I heard a bunch o' sirens over on the North Western tracks over there," he told the *Soundstage* camera. "The only people that was out that time of morning was newsboys and, you know, guys just doin' a job like me, or else altar boys. A lot of churches around here. Some kid had been walkin' along, I guess his head was just in a cloud, kinda daydreamin', and a train hit him."

Prine arrived in time to see the aftermath on the faces of a group of mothers as they waited for the remains to be identified. "Right where this park bench sat close to the railroad tracks this kid got hit, and he got hit pretty bad—nobody could recognize him," Prine said. The body was so mangled the pieces had to be hauled off in bushel baskets: "There was about ten or eleven mothers standin' around in a circle, didn't know whose altar boy it was. They was all grievin', and then they told this one woman it was her son. I'll never forget the looks on those other women's faces."

"Bruised Orange" captured the mood of that grim day, the only distraction coming from the song's intrusive sax solo. Prine could have been singing to himself, offering priceless advice to anyone going through a divorce or similarly gut-wrenching experience:

> For a heart stained in anger grows weak and grows bitter
> You become your own prisoner as you watch yourself sit there
> Wrapped up in a trap of your very own chain of sorrow

Throughout the album, Prine's vocals were more relaxed and confident than ever before. Like Clement, Goodman pushed him harder than previous producers. "It wasn't a time period I liked being around Steve," Prine told Sachs. "He was like Edward G. Robinson as your producer. He wouldn't mind if I argued every day, but I didn't have it in me. We made a deal we'd go in and do this, though, so I listened to him." They got into a heated argument after a session one night at the Earl of Old Town as a singer covered "Hello in There." According to Clay Eals, Goodman grabbed Prine's shoulders and Prine shouted, "Goddamn it, I don't want to do it that way! Why can't you fuckin' understand?" The doorman eventually intervened. "Oh, sorry," Prine said. "We're just working out something here."

An all-star chorus sang behind Prine on the closing number, "The Hobo Song," as if the entire Chicago folk music community (and beyond) were giving him an affectionate send-off before his move to Nashville. Most of the musicians who played on *Bruised Orange* sang on the track—young bluegrass hotshot (and Kentucky native) Sam Bush, along with Jackson Browne, Ramblin' Jack Elliott, Al Bunetta, Dave Prine, and John Cowan. Additional Chicago voices chiming in were Fred and Eddie Holstein and the Earl of Old Town himself, Earl Pionke. Even Prine's road manager and the recording engineers joined the fun.

On *Bruised Orange*, Steve Goodman badgered Prine into making his most Goodman-like album—and one of Prine's finest. Prine had generally darker musical and lyrical inclinations than his friend, sometimes playing John Lennon to Goodman's Paul McCartney. The tension between the men gave the album a healthy balance, with Prine veering off into some oddly visionary ("Sabu"), darkly cautionary (the title track), and churning rockabilly ("Iron Ore Betty") directions before Goodman pulled him back into the good day sunshine ("Fish and Whistle," "That's the Way That the World Goes 'Round"). It may not have been the album Prine wanted to make, and Prine clearly had more fun dicking around with Cowboy Jack in Nashville for a few months than he did working his ass off with his old pal Stevie in Chicago for a few weeks.

But Goodman rescued him from making a self-indulgent, critically and commercially unpopular rockabilly indulgence . . . at least temporarily. *Bruised Orange* contained what would prove to be the most enduring collection of Prine songs since his first album, with more than half of them earning a semipermanent place in his live show. It was an album gleefully and defiantly removed from its era, almost punk in its refusal to conform to commercial or cultural norms—if little more punk sonically than Raffi's *Singable Songs for the Very Young*. At the time, Prine was undoubtedly happy just to get it over with and get a break from the taskmaster. But producing *Bruised Orange* was one of the biggest favors Goodman ever did for Prine, career-wise, ranking with the night Goodman badgered Kristofferson and Anka into giving Prine his most important audition.

A stark black-and-white photo of Prine and his hair helmet adorned the front cover of *Bruised Orange*. On the back he singled out Browne for thanks, along with "Jack Clement for the Summer of '77." He and Goodman ended up with a spare, acoustic-guitar-driven pop-folk rock record that occasionally veered uncomfortably close to Buffett-style whimsy, but generally stayed on track. Despite the strength of its songs,

Goodman's sympathetic production, and a new label, *Bruised Orange* once again found Prine struggling to find a larger audience. The album stayed in the Top 200 longer than any of its predecessors, thirteen weeks, but never climbed higher than No. 116.

Critics loved it, however—clearly forgiving Prine for *Common Sense*. Several magazines named *Bruised Orange* one of the Top 10 records of the year. *Time* magazine critic Jay Cocks wrote the *Rolling Stone* critique—with Prine and the English hard-rock band Foreigner sharing the lead review slot for the magazine's 7 September 1978 issue. The headline: "John Prine's best album." Cocks began by likening Prine to novelist Larry McMurtry, who once had a T-shirt made for himself that read "MINOR REGIONAL NOVELIST." He suggested equivalents for Prine: "FADED FOLKIE" and "BARD WITHOUT A BEAT." But times had changed, Cocks wrote: "This is a peak record. It has a whole lifetime in it. *Bruised Orange* is about getting lost, and being in love, and staying a stray in a world of fixed fates." The literary comparisons continued when Cocks likened "Sabu" to a short story by *Winesburg, Ohio* author Sherwood Anderson. He praised Prine for his "funny and ironic" love songs, and called Goodman "the best and certainly the most congenial producer Prine has ever had." Frequent contrarian Robert Christgau offered a more modest appraisal, acknowledging the album's strengths while finding fault with Goodman's "harmless and corny" production work. He gave it a B-plus.

Not long after they finished making *Bruised Orange*, comedy superstar Steve Martin gave Goodman a big break, tapping him to open a tour of coliseums. Prine, meanwhile, was seven years into his recording career and tired of being praised as an unheralded genius. He had been hearing it for years by that point, "goin' straight from bein' a mailman to folks saying, 'God, you're a genius!'" he told Peter J. Boyer in a 1978 interview syndicated by the Associated Press. "I used to say, 'If I'm a genius, how come it took me five years to get out of high school? If I'm a genius, how come I don't have three Cadillacs?'" He was starting to think about forging his own path in the music business: "If I can get a hit record, I'm gonna start my own record company called Oh Boy Records, and I'm gonna make nothing but records that pop outta your dashboard and make you tap your foot." Paul Nelson reviewed a live Prine show at New York's Bottom Line for *Rolling Stone* in the summer of '78, damning him with faint praise: "In many ways, it was the *nicest* music I'd heard in months." The singer would deliver more substance by embracing his darker material, Nelson wrote: "John Prine still seems to want to be liked rather than respected."

The photo accompanying the review showed a smiling, clean-shaven Prine strumming an electric guitar, a Fender Stratocaster. He had put together a band for the *Bruised Orange* tour, and it boasted some of the musicians from the recording sessions, led by guitarist Johnny Burns, who helped him recruit some other Chicago players. They called themselves the Famous Potatoes. "John was into this band," drummer Angie Varias told Sachs in 2005. "He was playing with new enthusiasm. He wanted to do Elvis songs and Johnny Cash and rockabilly and rootsy stuff. He couldn't get enough of that music."

Prine was still determined to make a rockabilly album, and this time he wouldn't keep his fans waiting for three years. He told Ruhlmann he had a very specific sound in mind: "I still like the idea of a recording sounding like you walk into somebody's house, and they've got equipment down in the basement, and the band is playing, and you open up the door, and that's what your hear. So, I wanted a record that sounded like that." He hadn't pulled it off at Clement's home studio, so he decided to return to Clement's old stomping grounds, Memphis. Sun Studios had closed down a decade before (despite a common misconception that Prine recorded there), but Sam Phillips Recording Studio, located a few blocks north, was open for business.

"When Asylum asked for another record, I said, 'Well, I'm gonna give them a record,'" Prine told Sachs. "'I'll give them the record I was gonna make before I made *Bruised Orange*.'" He lined up Sam Phillips's sons, Knox and Jerry, to produce the album. They got started in January 1979. "We got an apartment not far from there, Johnny Burns and all the guys, and we recorded six nights a week," Prine said. "We'd go in at six at night and leave at six in the morning." Longtime Prine sideman Leo LeBlanc showed up for some of the sessions, and rockabilly veteran Billy Lee Riley ("Flyin' Saucers Rock and Roll," "Red Hot") guested on "No Name Girl," a song Riley cowrote with Clement. Sam Phillips hadn't produced a record in years, but the recording sessions lured him out of retirement. "Once Sam heard what was going on, he'd be in there at 4 a.m., his devil eyes flashing," Prine said.

The Vietnam War and its veterans had gotten a lot of attention the previous couple of years. The war had finally ended in 1975, two years after U.S. troops withdrew. President Carter pardoned U.S. draft dodgers in 1977. A series of popular movies in 1978 and '79 addressed the war (*The Deer Hunter, Apocalypse Now*) and its lingering effects on veterans (*Coming Home*). During his summer with Clement, Prine had written his first Vietnam-related song in several years, "Saigon," a stripped-down rocker about a veteran still suffering from the war's aftershocks: "All the static in my attic getting ready to blow." "That pretty much sums up the Vietnam guy that comes back and is just flippin', you know?" Jerry Phillips said in an interview for a 2000 profile of his father that aired on the A&E TV series *Biography*. By 1979 Prine was ready to record the song. "It was written—and we always performed it—to really pump like a Jerry Lee Lewis thing," he told Bill Flanagan. "The whole idea of it was this guy's in a bar and he just goes bonkers."

This was as close to punk rock as Prine was going to get. "Sam put my guitar player's amp in the echo chamber, turned it up so it'd blow the tubes out in it," Prine told the A&E cameras. "'Cause he wanted to have pieces of hot metal flyin' through the air—that's what he said." But Sam didn't stop here. "We were doin' it at like about 130 miles an hour," Knox told A&E. "He said, 'Hey look, you guys: Do you know what half of that speed is?' And they said, 'Yes sir, we know.' He said, 'Well, can you play it half of half?' And he looked at John and he scooted his chair over to him in his face and says, 'And John, can you put some sex into it?'" They nailed the song on the very next take. "I was in the studio with Sam Phillips, you know?" Prine said. "If Sam told me to stand on my head and sing that night, I would've."

Sam ultimately got credit for producing two of the album's ten songs. "Sam thought my voice sounded so awful that he would stick around and see if he could maybe help fix it," Prine told A&E. The sessions, which stretched across five months, ended up being about as loose as the Clement sessions. "We ended up with something like five hundred hours of tape—and took the best of what we had, and Asylum just about had a heart attack," Prine told Sachs. "They called me out to L.A., and one of the heads there said, 'John, what you've got here is not what I think you want.'" Drummer Angie Varias wasn't surprised at the label's reaction to such a raw record, given that "everyone in the office dressed like the Cars, with skinny ties and shiny suits." It was a new experience for Prine. "This was the first time, in all the years, that I'd ever gotten even a raised eyebrow from a record exec," he told Ruhlmann. He insisted that the recordings were exactly what he wanted, he told Sachs: "I said, 'That's expensive noise on there. We did a lot of things to get the noise on those tapes.' At the time, Steely Dan and the Eagles were the kinds of records out there, and the sounds were highly digital. That was the popular sound for the records that sold, and this was not that at all."

Pink Cadillac was named for a line associated with Elvis from one of its rockabilly covers, "Baby Let's Play House": "You may drive a pink Cadillac but don't you be nobody's fool." The album wound up being a radical departure for Prine, a 180-degree turn from *Bruised Orange*. (Only that album's "Iron Ore Betty," a throwaway rocker, had given fans the slightest hint at Prine's subsequent direction.) For the first time in his recording career, lyrics were clearly a secondary concern; he was now focused much more on rhythm and the raw feel of the tracks. No one hearing this album would accuse him of trying to be "nice." "Automobile" was Prine's answer to Elvis's "That's All Right, Mama," a shuffling acoustic rocker. Half the songs were covers. The record was divided about evenly between rockers ("Chinatown," "No Name Girl") and slower blues songs and ballads ("Cold War," "Down by the Side of the Road"). Prine tied up various career threads on the closing song, the oft-covered "Ubangi Stomp." Warren Smith recorded the original for Sun in 1956. His guitarist was Chips Moman, who would later found American Sound Studio in Memphis, where Prine recorded his first album. "To me, *Pink Cadillac* was a total success," Prine told Ruhlmann. "I loved it. I thought, 'That's what I'm out doin' every night; that's what we sound like at clubs.'"

In the liner notes, Prine once again "thanks Jack Clement for the summer of '77." "Our only criteria for what we wanted on this album," Prine wrote, "[were] that (1) it didn't bore Knox Phillips, who is a highly opinionated, basically fair and honest person, (2) it made Jerry Phillips' leg shake; Jerry is an ex-professional, most perfectly formed midget wrestler, and has a very honest and opinionated leg, (3) that I would hear something on tape that made me feel half as good as I do when I play the music in the first place." Sam Phillips told Prine "that what we had here was basically good and honest and that I had met the song and the song had met me." The album wouldn't help Prine meet any new fans, though; sales slipped back to the level of his first three records. *Pink Cadillac* peaked at No. 152 on the album charts, dropping out of the Top 200 after seven weeks.

Reviews were all over the map. Robert Palmer praised the album in the *New York Times*, calling it "Prine's masterpiece to date." At the other extreme, Dave Marsh called *Pink Cadillac* "an almost unqualified disaster" in a *Rolling Stone* review. The album, he wrote, "mars the reputation of everyone involved. Prine has never sung such a half-assed grab bag of songs, partly because he wrote so few of them (and is in no way a classic interpreter of any material except his own), partly because the outside stuff he chose is so thoroughly mediocre." Marsh also took issue with a mix that buried Prine's vocals, while Christgau, in his review, seemed relieved not to have to hear them: "Prine has never rocked harder. But he's slurring his vocals like some toothless cartoon bluesman emulating an Elvis throwaway—related to the Sun sound, I guess, but perversely. Are the new songs any good? Hard to tell." He gave the record a B-minus.

Prine's slow record sales didn't interfere with his ability to land high-profile TV appearances. In 1980 he appeared on *Soundstage*, a concert show produced by WTTW in Chicago and broadcast on PBS stations across the country: "John Prine, one of the most original and likable personalities in American music, comes back home." The show's producers made a minidocumentary about the hometown hero, sending a camera crew along as Prine, now thirty-three, accompanied by Johnny Burns, drove the singer's '51 Ford with wide whitewall tires out to the suburbs. "Maywood!" Prine said. "This is it, Maywood, Illinois, where I was born and raised." The show alternated between concert and documentary footage. "That bank over there—my grandfather helped build that bank," Prine said. "[You know, the] one who was a carpenter?"

Backed by the Famous Potatoes, Prine sang "Automobile," "Spanish Pipedream," and "Fish and Whistle." Introducing "Angel from Montgomery," he said, "I wrote this about a forty-seven-year-old housewife from Montgomery, Alabama—except she's about fifty-seven now." Before "The Accident," there was footage of Prine and Burns driving to a nondescript intersection in a residential area. "This lady lives on Third and Green and she don't even know it!" Prine half-yelled out the open car window. "This is more famous than the Grand Canyon!"

After "Hello in There," the show cut to footage of Prine and Burns sitting on the back steps of the singer's boyhood home. The paint was peeling off the side of the house, and the porch door leaned left while the house leaned right. A sign for a Freeway gas station was visible in the distance over Prine's shoulder. He talked about his father listening to WJJD, and the audience heard a brief clip of Randy Blake introducing the *Suppertime Frolic* radio show. Prine took a moment to introduce Burns before they sang "Paradise" together.

"John plays guitar with me and he's my number one partner in crime," Prine said. "We're bound to become stars someday, or else we're gonna go to jail—right, John?"

"Or come back to Maywood," Burns said.

"Well, that wouldn't be so bad."

In a cut back to the concert, Billy Lee Riley joined Prine and the band on stage. "He's knockin' 'em dead in Europe these days," Prine said. They teamed up for "No Name Girl" and one of Riley's Sun hits. "For all of y'all who is over thirty-five years old, you might remember this song," Prine said, introducing "Red Hot." Back in Maywood, Prine—a cigarette hanging from his lips—pointed out the church that inspired "Bruised Orange" and told the story of the boy hit by the train. The band played that song and "Saigon." During the rocker Prine twitched, Elvis-style, and strutted around the stage. Before the show closed with "How Lucky," Prine got reflective with Burns about easing into middle age: "Did you ever have a whole lotta growin' pains when you got somewhere around the age of thirty? Well, I never thought that age mattered much. I just thought that age was something that just was there every year, like Christmas, you know? I never thought it mattered a whole lot. But I guess it mattered a whole lot to me. Seemed like I started going back over everything I'd ever done and wondered if I wanted to do that for the next thirty [years] or not, you know? I finally decided, 'What the heck. I might as well.'"

Prine and Burns were thick as thieves in those days. Prine called Burns "Carl Fire," while Burns called Prine "Johnny Trouble," according to a 2013 Facebook post by Burns: "You used to untune my guitar when I was soloing . . . and unplug it when we sang in the same mic . . . and turn your back to the audience so they thought YOU were playing the hot guitar solos. And when you told those girls at the Goldrush that I was gay. . . . And how we'd sneak off to Nashville to 'have our necks straightened' and somehow it was always MY idea. And hitting all the late night bars, shit faced and obnoxious, demanding to take over the stage from the unlucky performer, and generally leaving a wake and an impression that John Prine kept questionable company."

Having finally purged his rockabilly urge with *Pink Cadillac*, Prine wasted no time in completing his three-album obligation to Asylum. A decade after telling Studs Terkel he hoped he ended up recording his first album in Muscle Shoals, he headed down to the northwest corner of Alabama to record his seventh album. He ended up in neighboring Sheffield, Alabama, home of Muscle Shoals Sound Studio—founded in 1969 when the house band splintered off from Rick Hall's FAME Studios (located in Muscle Shoals proper). They had backed a parade of soul legends at FAME: Aretha Franklin, Wilson Pickett, and Otis Redding. At Muscle Shoals Sound, the band dubbed the Swampers by Lynyrd Skynyrd front man Ronnie Van Zant—keyboard player Barry Beckett, bassist David Hood, guitarist Jimmy Johnson, and drummer Roger Hawkins—had also done well for themselves. The Rolling Stones were one of the first major acts to record at Muscle Shoals Sound, cutting "Brown Sugar" and "Wild Horses" there during their 1969 American tour, though the songs weren't released until two years later. Other recordings at the studio: the Staple Singers' "I'll Take You There," Paul Simon's "Kodachrome" and "Loves Me Like a Rock," Rod Stewart's *Atlantic Crossing* album (produced by Steve Cropper around the same time he produced Prine's *Common Sense* in Memphis), half of Bob Seger's breakthrough *Night Moves* album in 1976, the Sanford-Townsend Band's "Smoke from a Distant Fire," Lynyrd Skynyrd's final *Street Survivors*, and Bob Dylan's gospel move, *Slow Train Coming*, in 1979.

Beckett produced *Slow Train Coming* and its 1980 follow-up, *Saved*. He signed on to produce Prine's album, recorded with Prine's road band, the Famous Potatoes. "I just more or less picked stuff I didn't record on *Pink Cadillac*," Prine told Sachs. His bass-playing girlfriend, Rachel (who had stopped going by Simpson and reverted to her maiden name, Peer), sang harmony on a couple of tunes. The result, *Storm Windows*, was a return to a relatively polished, full-band sound closer to *Sweet Revenge* or *Common Sense* than the acoustic folk-pop of *Bruised Orange* or the murky rockabilly of *Pink Cadillac*. (Prine continued to keep his lyrics pared back, though, the dense, convoluted wordplay of *Common Sense* receding further into the background.) Burns cowrote two of the new songs with Prine, and the album contained two covers: "All Night Blue," a wistful, pedal-steel-saturated ballad written by Muscle Shoals songwriters Ava Aldridge and Cindy Richardson, and "Baby Ruth," a greasy rocker written by John Wyker for his band Sailcat, which recorded the slower, funkier original version of the song at Muscle Shoals in the early seventies.

Both of Prine's covers were standouts, and *Storm Windows* contained a number of strong originals. "One Red Rose" was a lovely acoustic ballad closer in spirit to Prine's early albums, while the title track was a resigned epic in the vein of the Band, Dylan, and Van Morrison—and extraordinarily rare for a Prine song in being built around the piano (courtesy of Beckett, emerging from the control room to play on this one song). "Silence is golden / Till it screams / Right through your bones," Prine sang. He let his goofy side out to play on just one song, "Living in the Future," which mocked pop-culture attempts to predict the future:

> We're all driving rocket ships
> And talking with our minds
> And wearing turquoise jewelry
> And standing in soup lines

"I was thinking about, like, *Parade* magazine," Prine told Flanagan. "When I was a kid they'd run articles on 'How Your Hometown Will Look in Twenty Years—in 1980!' I kept thinking about that. The only city that looks halfway like those illustrations is Seattle, with the monorail they left up after the World's Fair." The song also contained some of the strangest lyrics about sex ever recorded by Prine—or anyone else, for that matter. The sweet self-pleasure of "Donald and Lydia" had given way to "Jake the barber's lonely daughter," who got intimate with her father's barber pole: "Pressure on the left, pressure on the right / Pressure in the middle of the hole." Then there's "old Sarah Brown," who sold tickets at a porn theater

Where they grind out sex
And they rate it with an "X"
Just to make a young man's pants grow
No tops no bottoms just hands and feet
Screaming the posters out on the street

The album closed on an upbeat note with "I Had a Dream," a stomping rocker with rousing interplay between the piano and organ. Prine's lyrics are often cinematic, and quite literally so in this song, where he seemed to have a drive-in theater in mind: "Birds were flying left and right / Through the light of a movie screen." In the year of such platinum-selling albums as the *Urban Cowboy* soundtrack and Bob Seger's *Against the Wind* (also partially recorded at Muscle Shoals), Prine's album meshed with its times better than any he had ever made. The cover even featured a slick, airbrushed portrait of Prine, his flowing black mane parted in the middle, his head tilted seductively. But seven albums into his recording career, he simply couldn't buy a hit: The record peaked only slightly higher than *Pink Cadillac* at No. 144, staying in the Top 200 for an identical seven weeks. Critics liked it much better than its predecessor, though: Ken Tucker, reviewing *Storm Windows* for *Rolling Stone*, said the album struck a "stunning balance" between *Bruised Orange* and *Pink Cadillac*. "*Storm Windows* shuffles between these extremes with a sly deftness . . . producer Barry Beckett always makes sure that the singer's old-tomcat mewl dominates the mix." Christgau gave the album an A-minus: "Finally Prine has fun in the studio without falling bang on his face like he did at Sun [*sic*]. . . . Not stunning, but real smart, real relaxed—one to play." A *People* magazine review praised the singer's "wry humor" and "homespun artistry" while speculating on his failure to make a dent on the charts: "Faded-denim folksiness and a Midwestern twang that makes 'Bible' sound like 'babble' rarely find their way into Top 40 play lists."

CHAPTER 10

Oh Boy

▽

In 1980, just after the Me Decade wrapped up and just before the Rea-
gan era dawned, Prine finally settled for good in Music City. A year later,
Asylum dropped him and Goodman on the same day. "They got rid of
my whole roster in one five-minute morning," Al Bunetta told Clay Eals.
For the first time in ten years, Prine had no record deal. Asylum let him
go after releasing three albums that sold poorly—by major-label standards, at least. "I kinda saw that coming down the pike," Prine told me
in 1988. "Lotsa labels dropped lotsa people because they weren't selling 100,000-plus records." He didn't start looking for another record
deal immediately: "I just totally put on the brakes," he told William
Ruhlmann. "I wanted to separate everything, 'cause I was really tired of
mainly the business end of it. I was wondering where the fun was with
the music, this thing that I took on as a hobby years earlier that I used to
get so much out of long before I ever sang a song for anybody else except
myself."

He didn't rule out starting an entirely new career, leaving the music
business behind. It was a period of major changes in his life. Though
his marriage had started "coming apart at the seams" years before, his
divorce didn't become official until 1981. He and Rachel Peer got married not long afterward. She had recently extended her Muhlenberg
County connections by joining Don Everly in a band he called the Dead
Cowboys.

Prine's friends in Nashville tended to be fellow songwriters, and soon he started doing what comes naturally. Among his collaborators were Bobby Braddock, who wrote the country classics "D-I-V-O-R-C-E," "He Stopped Loving Her Today," and "We're Not the Jet Set"; Prine's old buddy from Kristofferson's band by way of Muscle Shoals, Donnie Fritts, who wrote "Breakfast in Bed," which Dusty Springfield put on the B side of "Son of a Preacher Man," as well as "We Had It All," a 1973 hit for Waylon Jennings; and Roger Cook, who wrote "Here Comes That Rainy Day Feeling Again," "I'd Like to Teach the World to Sing (in Perfect Harmony)," and "Long Cool Woman in a Black Dress" in his native England before moving to the United States.

Prine and Bunetta started talking to independent labels, looking for a friendlier home for his music. One of those labels was Sugar Hill Records in Durham, North Carolina. Founded by Duke University graduate Barry Poss in 1978 following his apprenticeship with the tiny bluegrass label County Sales in Floyd, Virginia, Sugar Hill had established itself as a home for country music that didn't fit the slick Nashville formula. Ricky Skaggs was the label's breakout star, and the intimate, artist-friendly label seemed like a natural fit for Prine. He made no secret of his flirtation: an October 1982 concert review in the University of Virginia's student paper said, "Prine is currently working on new songs for an album which may appear by the end of the year on the Sugar Hill Records label." Goodman produced a couple of Prine songs as he gradually pieced together a follow-up to *Storm Windows* while figuring out who would release it.

Poss ended up being a little too helpful. He "explained how an independent label worked so well that I called him back and told him I was starting my own," Prine told me. Starting Oh Boy also meant passing up a shot at recording for Dylan's label. "Columbia, at the time, wanted John to be on their label," Bunetta told David Hooper. ". . . I said, 'Well, John, you don't seem happy about it.' He said, 'Well, I'm not.' 'As your manager, this is a good deal.' But he decided to stay and make Oh Boy work. You don't look back. He always said, 'Labels will tell you what to do, but they can never tell you how to do it, how to make that hit.' And he made a lotta common sense. He has a lotta common sense." (One presumes Bunetta was not merely referring to unsold copies of Prine's final album for Atlantic.)

Starting a record company is a simple process, Prine told *Music Row Magazine* in the mid-1980s: "You go out into the desert, you put your hand on a rock, and you say, 'I am a record company.'" For Oh Boy, Prine started modestly toward the end of 1981: a Christmas 45 on red vinyl. In January 1982 Prine and Goodman taped a second *Austin City Limits* performance. Jethro Burns joined Goodman for several songs, and Prine and Goodman performed "Souvenirs" together, with lovely guitar interplay. "He played a back melody, so that you could barely hear the difference of who was playing, on tape or when we did it live," Prine told Paul Zollo. "And I realized a large part of what he was doing was making it sound like I was playing the good part. And that's basically the kind of guy he was. The kind of guy who wouldn't need to shine the light on him, even though he could ham it up with the best of them."

The move to Music City would soon pay off for Prine in a big way. "In Nashville it's hard to avoid co-songwriting," he told Greg Kot. "If you have a beer with someone, the next thing you know they're calling you up to cowrite." Roger Cook enlisted Prine to help him finish a song called "Love Is on a Roll." "I like to cowrite," Cook said during a 1983 appearance on The Nashville Network show *Bobby Bare and Friends*. "It creates a certain kind of chemistry sometimes. If you write with someone, you come up with something you just wouldn't have come up with—not in quite the same way." In this case, Prine says, the song was essentially complete before he even got involved. He ended up writing the bridge and one of the verses. "I couldn't understand why Roger just didn't sit down and finish the song right there in front of me, because I thought the whole song was there," Prine told Peter Cooper at the Country Music Hall of Fame. Smooth-voiced Texan Don Williams had hit No. 1 on the country charts in 1980 with "I Believe in You," a song Cook cowrote with another songwriter. Williams recorded "Love Is on a Roll" with identical results: The song hit No. 1 on the country charts in 1983.

That same year, Prine appeared on a special "Songwriters Showcase" episode of *Austin City Limits* with Rodney Crowell, Billy Joe Shaver, Bill Caswell, and Keith Sykes. Prine didn't think he could write a country hit without a collaborator. "You have to have a certain structure, and the Nashville guys I cowrite with know it's gonna be barking up a wrong tree to pitch a six-minute song to a producer looking for a single," he told Kot. "If you can write a really good song in three minutes, get to the point, it's pretty neat. By myself, if I stumbled across a 'hit,' I don't think I'd know it." Prine joined Cook to sing "Love Is on a Roll" on *Bobby Bare and Friends* after walking in as a "surprise" guest. "John, what are you doin' around here?" Bare asked. Prine replied, "Oh man, I was walkin' east on Music Square West tryin' to sell some songs, and I seen a car parked in front of here that looked familiar, so I walked in to try and bum a cigarette. I'd like to stick around, but Rachel's got dinner on the stove."

Prine also collaborated with a fellow Midwesterner, Indiana rocker John Cougar, in the wake of Cougar's No. 1 album *American Fool*, released in 1982. Working with Prine may have been part of Cougar's efforts to mature artistically beyond such wildly popular but lunkheaded hits as "Hurts So Good" and "Jack & Diane." For his next album, 1983's *Uh-Huh*, Cougar reclaimed his real surname, Mellencamp, and wrote some of the best roots-rock songs of the decade, such as "Crumblin' Down" and "Pink Houses." One song on *Uh-Huh* is credited to Mellencamp and Prine, a throwaway ballad called "Jackie O" with muddled lyrics about superficial social climbers: "So you went to a party with Jacqueline Onassis / If you're so smart, why don't you wear glasses?" Despite getting nowhere with Dustin Hoffman and his poodle years earlier, Prine still had the acting bug. He talked to Mellencamp about how he would like to be able to take a break from the road and make some movies. "I said I had just never found the right vehicle," Prine told Jack Hurst in a 1990 interview with the *Chicago Tribune*. "All I'd been offered was convicts and ex-junkies."

Prine said Oh Boy was named after the Buddy Holly song—except when he gave an alternate explanation. He claimed to have originally floated the idea with Rachel. "I was kinda kiddin' around with my wife, who was my girlfriend then," Prine told Justin Mitchell in a 1985 newspaper interview. "I said, 'I'd like to start my own record company and call it Oh Boy.' And she said, 'Why?' and I said, 'Well, when things are goin' real good, we can just go, 'Oh boy, oh boy, oh boy, what a year we've had!' And when things ain't so good, you get all [morosely] 'Oh, boy.'"

But the dream didn't end there. "I also want to distribute this orange soda pop," Prine told Mitchell. "It's called Whoopee Orange Soda. I wanna get it distributed in the South so I can watch little kids drinking Whoopee Orange Soda. If I can get that and Oh Boy Records, then that'll be success." It may sound like a joke, but Prine wasn't kidding about his love for orange soda: For years his concert rider included a requirement for a case of Orange Crush, along with such other necessities as a fifth of Stoli Vodka, a carton of Marlboro cigarettes, and two complete dinners consisting of nothing but steak and potatoes—one preshow, one postshow. ("I don't eat vegetables," Prine told Bill Flanagan, though he clearly made an exception for spuds.) One promoter said the requirement for a fifth of vodka before the show "made me very nervous, so I struck through it and I put 'a *pint* of vodka *after* the show.' And so I think he was a little irritated with me as a result of that."

Steve Goodman rolled out Red Pajamas Records in 1982 after his health took a turn for the worse. He went beyond Prine's Christmas single to release an entire LP, *Artistic Hair*, a live album consisting of songs from tapes Bunetta had confiscated from bootleggers at concerts over the years. "He had to put a record out so he could work and feed his family," Bunetta told Hooper. "It was his idea to start the label, not mine, and not John's—it was his idea." Once Prine was set on the idea of recording for his own label, he returned to Cowboy Jack Clement's home studio. With Goodman's health declining, Prine hired Jim Rooney to coproduce his next album.

The pair met at a music festival in Maine in 1976. "We were there three or four days and had some quality time in the bar where we got acquainted," Rooney wrote in his 2014 memoir *In It for the Long Run: A Musical Odyssey*. "Much later he told me that after meeting me he went and told his guitar player that he thought he had just met Huckleberry Finn! I had a motor home instead of a raft, but I was certainly floating freely down the river of life, and I had red hair and freckles, so maybe he was partly right." Rooney had a long history in the music business. He managed a folk club in Boston, his hometown, in the sixties; served as director of the Newport Folk Festival; and ran Bearsville Studios in Woodstock for Albert Grossman. He played guitar and sang on records by Clement, and others, while Rachel Peer played bass on Rooney's 1980 album *Ready for the Times to Get Better*. Rooney was starting to make a name for himself as a producer, as well, taking the helm for two albums by up-and-coming Texas folkie Nanci Griffith. He had already worked with Prine on his 1981 Christmas single.

Together Rooney and Prine crafted an organic, gently rocking sound featuring a parade of accomplished musicians. Leo LeBlanc showed up with his pedal steel, of course. Prine wrote three songs with some of his old Muscle Shoals buddies—two with Donnie Fritts and one with Dan Penn and Spooner Oldham, and Fritts and Oldham joined Prine in the studio. A cofounder of Derek and the Dominos and a former George Harrison sideman, Memphis native Bobby Whitlock, sat in on keys. Joining all the Nashville cats was former Lovin' Spoonful front man John Sebastian, who played harmonica on one song and autoharp on another.

The resulting album, *Aimless Love*, struck a balance between contemporary Nashville production standards and Prine's rough-hewn style, like a more laid-back *Sweet Revenge*. The vocals were the best of his career to date by a wide margin: on-key, relaxed, and slightly submerged in the mix to smooth out the ragged edges. Playing with session pros tamped down some of Prine's idiosyncrasies—there would be no *Common Sense*–style elastic song structures or wild key changes here. For the first time ever in the studio, Prine—now pushing forty—sounded like he was having a ball. The album opened with the jaunty "Be My Friend Tonight," about a loser's amiable attempt to get laid. Prine wrote it with Cook and an old Chicago character, Shel Silverstein: *Playboy* cartoonist, poet, screenwriter, children's book author (*The Giving Tree*), and, of course, songwriter. Among his best-known songs are "A Boy Named Sue" (as performed by Johnny Cash) and the 1973 Dr. Hook and the Medicine Show hit "The Cover of the *Rolling Stone*." The protagonist of "Be My Friend Tonight" had had a run of bad luck ("I threw a party; nobody came / I bought all the tickets; they canceled the game"); now he was ready to get lucky: "I'll sleep on the couch; you can leave on that light / Well, I won't do nothing wrong till you say it's right."

One song survived from Prine's sessions with Goodman, "People Puttin' People Down," a "misery loves company"–themed weeper. The songs Prine cowrote with Fritts, "Somewhere Someone's Falling in Love" and "The Oldest Baby in the World," were sweet and funny—despite the fact that the latter was inspired by a *National Enquirer* headline about the victim of a horrible premature-aging disease. The song was a sequel of sorts to Dylan's "Just Like a Woman," a lighthearted portrait of a woman with "the mind of a child / And a body peaking over the hill." She'd been looking for love in all the wrong places and coming up empty. "She would if she could," Prine sang, "and she should—but nobody will." Eight years after debuting "The Bottomless Lake" on *Saturday Night Live*, Prine finally got around to recording a lively, spare studio version of that song.

A few tunes took a darker turn. The doomy "Maureen, Maureen" was a character study sung in the first person by an outrageously unreliable narrator: "I shot a doctor last night on the airplane / Well, they said he wouldn't hurt us / But he got me real nervous and mean." Rachel harmonized on a couple of dreamy ballads (the title track and "Slow Boat to China"), and turned "Unwed Fathers" into a full-blown duet. The song, cowritten by Braddock, may have been Prine's best since his debut album, a character song that held its own with "Sam Stone," "Hello in There," "Angel from Montgomery," and "Donald and Lydia." Over the course of the song, a girl went "from a teenage lover to an unwed mother / Kept undercover like some bad dream."

> In a cold and gray town, a nurse says, "Lay down
> "This ain't no playground, and this ain't home"
> Someone's children, out having children
> In a gray stone building, all alone

"Unwed Fathers" inspired a run of Prine covers not seen in more than a decade. A young country star, Gail Davies, released it as a single, with Dolly Parton singing harmony. More country royalty followed suit, with Johnny Cash and Tammy Wynette both recording versions of the song. (Cash had also covered "Paradise" in 1981, using it as a recurring theme for *The Pride of Jesse Hallam*, a made-for-TV movie he starred in.) *Newsweek* magazine hailed "Unwed Fathers" as the best country song of 1984.

Prine released *Aimless Love* in the spring of '84, two years after the Sugar Hill rumors. The front cover featured a simple, classy black-and-white portrait of a seated Prine, his thick black hair the shortest it had been since his mailman days. The back cover and lyric sheet featured shots of the singer trading glances with a friendly-looking dog and strumming his guitar before an army of Big Boy restaurant mascots, a character used at Bob's, Shoney's, and other chain diners found across the country at Interstate exits. The label's logo used a simple drawing of the Big Boy's head, his mouth forming the "O" in Oh Boy.

It was the longest gap between albums for him since the three-year span between *Common Sense* and *Bruised Orange*. (Not counting the *Prime Prine* anthology.) But his fans hadn't forgotten him: They followed him into the indie-label wilderness, buying more than fifty thousand copies of *Aimless Love*—still low by major-label standards, but a home run for a fledgling independent. "I went into this label not as a thing against major labels or because we were struggling to find a major deal," Prine told Peter Cronin in a 1995 *Billboard* interview. "I just didn't want to continue recording unless it was in a manner that seemed to make more sense to what I actually did, which was pack my suitcase and go on the road to make a living." He used his former employer—the U.S. Postal Service—to distribute the record. "The first album was almost totally mail order," Prine told Jeremy Tepper. "Specialty stores took it in, and people helped us and gave our address out over the air and stuff." The mailing address was a post office box in Los Angeles—Goodman and Bunetta had both moved to Southern California.

Without a push from a major label, it took a while for *Rolling Stone* to notice *Aimless Love*, but the magazine finally got around to reviewing it in the middle of 1985. Don Shewey called it "a friendly, human-sized collection of typically low-tech country-folk tunes." Robert Christgau gave the album a B-plus, giving the singer little credit for growth since *Storm Windows*: "Prine's reappearance on his own label suggests that the reasons for his absence were more corporate than personal." Stephen Holden, reviewing *Aimless Love* for the *New York Times*, said Prine "has returned triumphantly to the ultra-spare country-folk idiom of his earliest and finest records."

In April Prine and Goodman hit the road for a brief tour together, a six-day, seven-show outing. Though kept at a distance by life on the road and homes nearly a continent apart, the old friends remained close. They cowrote a boozer's lament called "How Much Tequila (Did I Drink Last Night)?" that appeared on Goodman's 1983 album *Affordable Art*. "He called me every time he got an idea for a song," Prine said in the Goodman DVD interview. "Usually it wasn't a long period of time between Steve gettin' an idea for a song and it becoming an actual song. And he'd just call up in the middle of the night or the morning or whatever, wherever he was on the road, and he'd just go, 'Johnny!' And I'd go, 'Steve?' And he'd set the phone down and sing the song to me. And I'd go, 'Hey, that's great!' And he'd hang up. Like that was it, but he wanted me to know that a new song existed." Even before chemotherapy and his decline in the early eighties, leukemia was never far from Goodman's mind. "It was something he always talked about, a dark-humor thing," Prine wrote in the *Great Days* liner notes. "We'd go to airports, and he'd look up at the word 'Terminal,' shake his head, and go, 'Why do they have to have that sign up there?' It was like that for years."

Prine visited Goodman in the hospital as the summer of 1984 came to a close, but he wasn't there on 20 September, the day Goodman died. "You'd think you'd be halfway prepared for it when it came," Prine wrote. "But he might as well have gotten hit by a train. It was a big loss for me." Six weeks after Goodman's death, fifty-four artists converged at the Pacific Amphitheater in Costa Mesa, California, for a tribute concert, among them Prine, Kristofferson, Jimmy Buffett, Rosanne Cash, Randy Newman, and Willie Nelson, whose cover of "City of New Orleans" hit No. 1 on the *Billboard* country singles chart 3 November 1984—the day of the concert. Prine and Emmylou Harris sang "Souvenirs" as a duet.

To accommodate Goodman's hometown fans, Bunetta put together a second tribute that took place 26 January 1985 at Chicago's Arie Crown Theater. Prine and Johnny Burns also played at the Chicago show, joined by such nationally known acts as Arlo Guthrie, Bonnie Raitt, David Bromberg, and the Nitty Gritty Dirt Band, along with such Windy City mainstays as Bonnie Koloc and Fred and Ed Holstein. Prine played last, singing "Angel from Montgomery" with Raitt and closing with a cover of Goodman's tribute to his car-dealer father, "My Old Man." Bunetta and his cohort Dan Einstein kept Red Pajamas Records going after Goodman's death, releasing live recordings from the Chicago concert as a double album called *Tribute to Steve Goodman*. The album featured Prine's duet with Raitt, along with his performances of "My Old Man," "Souvenirs," and "Please Don't Bury Me."

Oh Boy geared up for a follow-up to *Aimless Love*. To generate interest, the label served notice to its mailing list, compiled from people who ordered the first album. By doing so, the label stumbled into Kickstarter-style crowd funding decades before the fact. "We sent out that I was going into the studio and recording the second album," Prine told Tepper. "They, in turn—we wasn't asking for it—they sent checks in to pay for the album that hadn't even been recorded yet. That's when I knew Oh Boy was working." He clearly saw no need to deviate dramatically from the *Aimless Love* formula, recording once again at Clement's studio with a crew of Nashville musicians. Rooney coproduced for a second time and played guitar and sang on several songs, while Rachel

Peer-Prine played bass on one song and sang harmony on several others. "John and Rachel were having a very up-and-down time of it, but the resulting songs might have been worth all the trouble," Rooney wrote in his memoir. "Perhaps the best song to come out of the turmoil generated by Rachel and John's relationship was the aptly titled 'Speed of the Sound of Loneliness.'" Prine's acoustic guitar picking played a more prominent role than on the previous album.

The resulting mix had a stronger bluegrass feel than *Aimless Love*, a more polished take on the kind of sound Prine got with Mardin on *Diamonds in the Rough*. Where the 1972 album ended with a Carter Family song, the 1986 album, *German Afternoons*, opened with one: "Lulu Walls," a rollicking tale of unrequited love about an "aggravatin' beauty." A second cover also drew from Prine's earliest influences: "They'll Never Take Her Love from Me," a Leon Payne weeper recorded by Hank Williams. Prine wrote about half of the songs by himself, including "Speed of the Sound of Loneliness," a wistful tale of love gone awry; "Bad Boy," about a straying lover ("I was your best friend / Now I'm a real dog"); and "Linda Goes to Mars," a comic variation on "Angel from Montgomery" about a woman who mentally checked out of her marriage from time to time, told from her husband's point of view:

> Now I ain't seen no saucers 'cept the ones upon the shelf
> And if I ever seen one, I'd keep it to myself
> For if there's life out there somewhere beyond this life on earth
> Then Linda must have gone out there and got her money's worth

Several songs had cowriters. Prine unveiled a song he wrote with Goodman, "If She Were You," a country classic worthy of Hank Williams about a man blinded to his new lover by an old flame: "When she speaks to me I hear your sweet voice calling / When I close my eyes your face comes into view." A different slant on romantic disconnection came in "Love, Love, Love," cowritten with Keith Sykes, who opened for Prine at the Bitter End years before and had since played in Jimmy Buffett's Coral Reefer Band. Rodney Crowell protégé Bill Caswell teamed up with Prine to write "Out of Love," a corny tune full of references to beer commercials: "If you've got the time, we've got the beer," a Miller High

Life slogan, became "So if you got the time / We got the tears." (The song was inspired by a morning beer run he and Caswell made when they got together to write, Prine told a concert audience in 1986.) Far better is "I Just Want to Dance with You," an easy-rolling collaboration with Roger Cook and a worthy successor to "Love Is on a Roll": "If this was a movie then we're right on cue / I just want to dance with you."

Prine closed *German Afternoons* with a fiddle-driven remake of "Paradise," finally giving the song the pure bluegrass feel it always called for. "The song over the years had turned into such a bluegrass standard," Prine told Ruhlmann. ". . . the first version of 'Paradise,' in order to get a fiddle part on it, we had to ask a guy from the Memphis symphony to come in and play the violin like a fiddle, and I always remember that, and I wanted to make a more of a bluegrass version of it." A small choir sang harmony: Peer-Prine, Sykes, and country comer Marty Stuart, a native of Philadelphia, Mississippi, born in 1958, who played with bluegrass legend Lester Flatt as a teenager and had recently left Johnny Cash's band to start a solo career.

While neither groundbreaking nor terribly ambitious, *German Afternoons* was a lively, enjoyable, and well-written album by a pro hitting his stride in middle age. The album title sounded like a throwback to Prine's army service, but its origin lay elsewhere: "I had this guy explain to me once that a German afternoon is like you go into town with some errands to run and stuff to do but then you run into an old buddy you haven't seen. And you drop into a bar for just a minute and start to talk. And next thing you know it's already evening and you've just spent a German afternoon." The cover featured a whimsically surreal photo of Prine outdoors just after sunset in a treeless landscape, seated and strumming a guitar, illuminated only by the light emerging from a slightly ajar refrigerator door. *German Afternoons* would sell almost as well as *Aimless Love*, more than forty thousand copies, and reviews were positive. "True, this is probably the worst album title in pop music history," a reviewer for *People* wrote. "But Prine, the '70s folkie who hasn't recorded on a major label in six years, makes up for it with 11 affable, lively tunes that are full of tradition yet never sound dated." Christgau gave Prine another B-plus: "Just in case you were wondering, this relaxed, confident album is where Prine comes out and admits he's a folkie, opening with an A. P. Carter tune he's been performing for a quarter century and commandeering sidemen from New Grass Revival and suchlike." *German Afternoons* also earned Prine his first Grammy nomination in fifteen years in the Contemporary Folk Recording category. He ended up beating himself this time—the award went to *Tribute to Steve Goodman*.

After the *German Afternoons* sessions wrapped up, Rooney and photographer Jim McGuire accompanied the singer to Muhlenberg County. "We rode up in John's 1949 red Ford coupe and got into the Rambling Rose Motel in Central City," Rooney wrote. "After a couple of vodkas John said, 'Okay, fellas, how would you like to take a ride to Paradise?'" It was a cold night, but Prine parked the coupe near the Green River and they got out to look around. Soon they were confronted by security guards from the power plant. Prine told the guards, "We just drove up from Nashville, and I was showing my friends where things used to be."

Benefit concerts reached epic scale in the mid-1980s with the intercontinental Live Aid, and Prine played the second Farm Aid, staged at a racetrack just east of Austin on 4 July 1986. Other acts on the bill: Dylan, Tom Petty and the Heartbreakers, the Beach Boys, Waylon Jennings, and, of course, Farm Aid organizers Willie Nelson, John Mellencamp, and Neil Young. Prine wore a red coat he borrowed from James Dean—or could have, by the *Rebel without a Cause* looks of it. If not for Rachel backing him on bass, his brief daytime set could have come from a decade and a half earlier, featuring "Sam Stone," "Paradise," and a duet with Raitt on "Angel from Montgomery" (Kristofferson dashing out from the wings from time to time to add harmony vocals). Prine jumped the gun on the final verse, flashing a sheepish grin at Raitt. He looked trim and happy at thirty-nine, his mullet showing a hint of gray at the temples, the hot Texas wind blowing his hair back occasionally to reveal a forehead just beginning to creep north.

In 1987 Oh Boy issued a second Prine single—this time on green vinyl: The A-side was a delightful, politically incorrect novelty number cowritten with frequent Shel Silverstein collaborator Fred Koller, a Chicago native whose songs were covered by Jerry Lee Lewis, Conway Twitty, Loretta Lynn, and many others. It was called "Let's Talk Dirty in Hawaiian":

Wacka, wacka, nooka likka
Wacka, wacka, nooka likka
Would you like a lei?

Prine wrote the B-side, "Kokomo," continuing the Pacific Islands theme with a tune about a man "in a small fishing village northeast of Guam" who longs to be in Kokomo . . . Indiana: "As the fish swim by / So does Joe / For his body is in Guam / But his mind is in Kokomo." Prine seemed to be having fun keeping his expectations modest, no longer chasing after hits in an era of unprecedented record sales. The singer told *Musician* magazine in 1987 that he was earning more with his own label than he would have gotten from a major.

After fifteen years and nine albums (ten if you count *Prime Prine*), Prine and Bunetta started planning something most artists would have gotten around to much earlier: a live album. At first they tried to cull performances from throughout his career, but eventually abandoned the idea because different venues and recording techniques made them hard to blend together. A few random tracks from different venues made the final cut: the performance of "Souvenirs" with Goodman from *Austin City Limits* and a gorgeous duet with Raitt on "Angel from Montgomery" in Chicago (transposed from Prine's original key, G, to the key Raitt recorded it in, where she plays in D with a capo on the second fret to put it in E). But most of the songs were crisp new recordings made during a three-night solo acoustic stand in California. "About 80 percent of this new thing is taken from shows at the Coach House in Capistrano the weekend the swallows came back," Prine told me. He produced the album with Rooney and Dan Einstein. The entire room was miked to capture the feel of being at the show, from the laughter of the crowd to the clink of ice cubes in glasses. "Everything seemed to click right in and it sounded like a good time to put it out," Prine said.

John Prine Live, released in 1988, leaned heavily on Prine's first three albums and *Bruised Orange*, largely bypassing *Common Sense* (though it kicked off with "Come Back to Us Barbara Lewis Hare Krishna Beauregard"), *Pink Cadillac*, and *Storm Windows*, and containing only one cut apiece from his other Oh Boy albums. The emphasis was on Prine as storyteller, balladeer, and comedian, with extensive liner notes on the lyric sheets and long introductions for many of the songs. The story he told about "Funky" Donnie Fritts ("the leanin' man from Alabam'") to introduce "The Oldest Baby in the World" was a masterpiece of comic phrasing and timing, rivaling a young Andy Griffith. Prine told how Fritts earned big money taking minor roles in Kristofferson movies, which his wife used to build a mansion in Nashville: "When you'd go into the front door there'd be a foyer there, and Donnie'd never even heard of a foyer—now he owned one."

In his written notes about "Grandpa Was a Carpenter," Prine told how relatives corrected him on some of the song's details. The lyrics said Empson "chain-smoked Camel cigarettes," "Except he smoked Kools, as my Aunt Alice reminds me, and Mema didn't school at Bowling Green," Prine wrote. "Ah, such is the mind of a minor poet." (He exacerbated the errors by misspelling his grandfather's middle name, adding a superfluous "H" after the "C" in "Scobie.") In his spoken introduction to "Sam Stone," Prine talked about going with Bunetta to visit the Vietnam Veterans Memorial on the Mall in Washington, D.C., completed in 1982: "We looked up our friends in there and went and found their names on the wall. And when you stand there lookin' at their names, there's black marble, and you can see your reflection in the wall." In the notes for "Sabu Visits the Twin Cities Alone," Prine wrote that after recording the song he learned Sabu "retired from show business," and he and his wife became successful restaurateurs in San Francisco: "I should be so lucky."

The album cover featured a cartoonish outsider-art painting by Linda Smith showing Prine from behind as he stood onstage, a diverse audience (some of the people had pink and green skin) facing him. The back cover showed an early sixties Prine family photo of John playing guitar, Billy playing bass, and Dave playing fiddle while Bill and Verna looked on. "This record is for my mother, Verna Prine," the back cover said. "Thanks Mom." Verna now lived one town over from Maywood, in Melrose Park. Two decades into his adulthood, she still kept her third boy well fed on visits home to Illinois, sending him back to Nashville "with Tupperware on the airplanes—big Tupperware things of hash," Prine told Ronni Lundy. "She asks me what I want for birthdays and Christmas. I say, 'Ten pounds of hash.'"

Though not widely reviewed (neither *Rolling Stone* nor Christgau deemed it worthy of critique), *John Prine Live* became Oh Boy's biggest hit to date, selling more than sixty thousand copies. The album was packaged with a postcard addressed to Oh Boy soliciting comments and questions, along with a four-page catalog split between Oh Boy and Red Pajamas Records. Bunetta and Einstein had released five albums by Goodman as of 1988, along with the live album from the 1985 Chicago tribute show. *John Prine Live* earned the singer another Grammy nomination, once again in the Best Contemporary Folk Recording category. This time Prine lost to newcomer Tracy Chapman.

Prine's career was just getting started when the Nitty Gritty Dirt Band released their legendary 1972 album *Will the Circle Be Unbroken*, which featured the proto-Americana band backing enough country music legends to fill the Opry stage, including such Prine heroes as Mother Maybelle Carter, Merle Travis, and Doc Watson. The album was recorded in August 1971—the same month Prine's debut album was released. But he was a veteran Nashville presence himself by the time the band got around to recording a sequel toward the end of 1988, and they invited him to join them in the studio. They recorded a rousing, fiddle-and-mandolin-driven version of "Grandpa Was a Carpenter," sweetening Prine's vocals with nice group harmonies.

Prine made yet another appearance on *Austin City Limits* in 1988 and finally played a bona fide concert in Muhlenberg County. In August the Everly Brothers—who had reunited five years earlier after a decade apart—organized a concert in Central City to fund scholarships and community needs. They invited Prine to join them, and he put his handprints in cement before the show. The concert closed with everyone onstage singing "Paradise." During a press conference that afternoon, the Everlys had said they wanted to honor Kentucky's musical heritage. "The coal mines bred an awful lot of poets," Don Everly said. "Just listen to John Prine's 'Paradise.'"

Divorce bred an awful lot of poets, too (consider, for example, Dylan's *Blood on the Tracks*, Paul Simon's *Still Crazy after All These Years*, Fleetwood Mac's *Rumours*, Marvin Gaye's *Here, My Dear*, Richard and Linda Thompson's *Shoot Out the Lights*, Springsteen's *Tunnel of Love*, and Beck's *Sea Change*). As the eighties came to a close, so did Prine's marriage to Rachel.

CHAPTER 11

Tunnel of Love

▼

John Prine stood before a funky orange painting, addressing the audience in a TV studio. "Country songs and country songwriters are a strange lot," he said, fiddling idly with the capo clamped to the neck of his acoustic guitar. "Seems like some of the best country songs over the years have come from some of the sadder situations in life—like divorce." He wore black jeans, a black shirt, and a red tie that his guitar had pulled slightly askew. A few dabs of gray dotted his black mullet. "Having recently acquired my second divorce, about a month later the song truck pulled up and dumped a buncha great songs on my lawn. This song is called 'I Guess I Wish You All the Best.'" His voice rose when he got to the song title, and he stretched out "all" in his trademark Muhlenberg–meets–Maywood–in–Music City drawl.

After tapping out a rhythm with the heel of a cowboy boot, Prine picked out a lilting intro on guitar. The lyrics were an artfully plainspoken look at the wreckage of a failed romance:

If you fell just like I did
You'd probably walk around the block like a little kid
But kids don't know; they can only guess
How hard it is to wish you happiness

The performance was from *Route 90*, a TV show Prine hosted for a week in 1990 for Channel 4 Television in the United Kingdom. Joining him were the likes of Nanci Griffith, George Strait, Rodney Crowell, Rosanne Cash, and k. d. lang. Hosting the TV show was one of several notable firsts for Prine that year, he joked to the *Chicago Tribune*: "Well, it's the first time I've ever gone through a second divorce."

The split with Rachel left Prine floundering for a while. "I went out and bought this electric train, 'cause I never had one before," Prine told an audience. "I brought it back home and nailed it to the dining room table. Just 'cause I could." Now in his mid-forties, he thought about becoming a professional fisherman or resuming his academic career. "I've never gone to college for a day, so I was thinking about maybe going to school," he told Dan DeLuca in an interview for the *Philadelphia Inquirer*. "It kinda looks fun, y'know?" The world of academia had been good to his brother Dave, who was earning a reputation as a national expert on bridges as a structural engineer at Northwestern University, located just up the coast of Lake Michigan from Chicago in Evanston, Illinois. (Who can forget Dave's lecture "Early Detection of Steel Rebar Corrosion by Acoustic Emission Monitoring"?)

In April Prine played at Farm Aid IV, held this time at the Hoosier Dome in Indianapolis, John Mellencamp's home court. Mellencamp was about to start shooting his first movie (whose title would ultimately be *Falling from Grace*), as both director and star. He requested permission from Prine to use "Souvenirs" as the title song, and asked him for a new song to use elsewhere on the soundtrack. Texas novelist Larry McMurtry, fresh from his success with the adaptation of *Lonesome Dove* into a hit TV miniseries in 1989, wrote the screenplay. Eventually Mellencamp offered Prine a small acting part. "It was a principal character, the apologetic brother-in-law," Prine told Jack Hurst. "I wouldn't have that many lines; the rest of the time I would just kind of be there, and when I wasn't there they would be talking about me. You couldn't beat it. I said, 'Sure,' and jumped in with both feet." He was impressed with McMurtry's script: "The dialogue seems realistic, like something an actual family might say to each other." That summer, Prine spent four days of the week filming around Mellencamp's hometown—Seymour, Indiana, located about halfway between Indianapolis and Louisville, Kentucky—and three days on weekends playing concerts around the country. "I always love playing the music, but the traveling has gotten to me over the years," he told Hurst. "Used to be, they could put me in the middle of anywhere and I'd just go, 'Gee, I've never been in this part of Iowa before,' and be out buying postcards and everything. But the traveling gets old, no matter how you do it."

Oh Boy reissued Prine's three Asylum records around 1990. Four years after *German Afternoons*, Prine was overdue for a new studio album. He had struggled with writer's block in the late eighties, but going through a divorce had broken the logjam. And he didn't suffer in solitude for long—Prine met a raven-haired beauty fifteen years his junior named Fiona Whelan while on tour in Ireland, and they hit it off immediately. She was the oldest of six sisters and worked at Windmill Lane Recording Studios in Dublin. The new songs he was writing were sprinkled with references to his new love in addition to his divorce, and he went into the studio in Memphis with his old buddy Keith Sykes behind the board to flesh them out, looking for a different kind of sound than the laid-back country feel of *Aimless Love* and *German Afternoons*. "Al and I had decided that we were going to make a record that nobody could look at and go, 'Oh sure, you've got your little independent label so you can sell cassettes at gigs,'" Prine told David Wild in a 1992 *Rolling Stone* interview. "I was thinking it might be my last album, so it was important it be a good one." The recordings with Sykes sounded fine, but they weren't quite what Prine was looking for: "They almost sounded like really great demos."

There was no shortage of people hoping to work with Prine, Bunetta told Peter Cronin: "We had producers from [Pink Floyd's] Roger Waters to Michael Kamen breathing down our neck." (Kamen was a former member of the New York Rock Ensemble who had worked on film scores and arrangements for rockers such as Queen and David Bowie.) Meanwhile, the bass player for one of the biggest rock bands in the world, Tom Petty and the Heartbreakers, was looking to raise his profile as a producer. Milwaukee native Howie Epstein had replaced the band's original bassist, Ron Blair, in 1982, and toured and recorded with them in the intervening years—including a 1986 world tour in which Petty and his band backed Dylan, one of their primary influences. In 1990 Epstein produced a series of demos that became *I Fell in Love*, a lively, sparkling album by a daughter of June Carter Cash, Carlene Carter—who also happened to be Epstein's girlfriend. Carter straddled the line between country and a pop-rock sound akin to that of her ex-husband, English rocker Nick Lowe. The Oh Boy team initially tried to get Petty's guitar player, Mike Campbell, to produce, but they were quite happy to settle for Epstein when Campbell showed no interest in the project. Bunetta and Prine liked Epstein's ideas. "He came up, and he stayed all day long and didn't stop talking with ideas and everything," Prine told Cronin. "Nothing seemed off the wall. It all seemed like just great stuff."

In November they started recording at a twenty-four-track studio, Huh Sound Theatre—aka the guest bedroom of the home Epstein and Carter shared on Laurelcrest Drive in Los Angeles. They intended to see how things sounded after a couple of days. "I knew how I wanted his voice to sound," Epstein told Joe F. Compton in a 1992 interview for *Dirty Linen* magazine. "I did not want to detract from that thing he has by himself—the fingerpicking thing and his voice—so the idea was to build everything around that. I thought that some of the other records buried his voice a little too much." This would be no repeat of the three-day sessions that produced *Diamonds in the Rough* and *German Afternoons*: Prine and Epstein wound up working in the studio for the better part of a year.

With Epstein's help, Prine assembled a team of major-league musicians. Epstein played some of the bass parts himself, and two of his fellow Heartbreakers contributed to the sessions: guitarist Mike Campbell and keyboard player Benmont Tench. Veteran L.A. session musicians also joined in, such as bassist Bob Glaub and multi-instrumentalist David Lindley (member of a brilliant sixties psychedelic band, Kaleidoscope, and Jackson Browne's right-hand man for years), who played guitar, bouzouki, fiddle, and something called a harplex, seemingly never heard before or since. Ubiquitous English guitarist Albert Lee played on some tracks. He had served as musical director for the Everly Brothers' 1983 reunion concert at the Royal Albert Hall and subsequent tours; contributed guitar to the Epstein-produced Carter album; and recorded with Browne, Bo Diddley, Rosanne Cash, Rodney Crowell, Foster and Lloyd, and countless others in the seventies and eighties. Leo LeBlanc ended his long unbroken string of appearances on Prine albums, replaced on pedal steel by Jay Dee Maness, a member of the Desert Rose Band in the eighties with Chris Hillman, founding member of both the

Byrds and the Flying Burrito Brothers. Maness had played on two seminal country-rock records in 1968, the Byrds' *Sweetheart of the Rodeo* and *Safe at Home* by Gram Parsons's International Submarine Band, as well as records in subsequent years by Phil Everly, Herb Alpert, Tanya Tucker, Arlo Guthrie, Bonnie Raitt, and Dwight Yoakam.

"Howie has one of those houses that looks like it's going to fall off the cliff," Prine told Robert Baird in a 1991 interview for the *Phoenix New Times*. "But it was great. All we paid for was the musicians, the tape and the engineer. I recorded most of it in a hallway. I mean a hallway—we're talkin' three-and-a-half feet wide." Epstein was burning the candle at both ends, playing bass by day on a follow-up to Petty's smash *Full Moon Fever* album and producing Prine by night. Over a nine-month stretch, the musicians gestated the "great songs" Prine said the song truck had dumped on his lawn, ultimately giving birth to his first full-blown rock 'n' roll album since 1980's *Storm Windows*. The title of the song he had debuted on English television was shortened to "All the Best," and it was joined by a number of other commentaries on Prine's divorce and new romance. The chorus of "Everything Is Cool" focused on the divorce . . .

> Everything is cool
> Everything's okay
> Why just before last Christmas
> My baby went away

. . . while the verses focused on Fiona:

> I was walking down the road, man
> Just looking at my shoes
> When God sent me an angel
> Just to chase away my blues

The song's intro found Prine playing a rare diminished chord. He also played in drop D tuning with a capo on the third fret, putting the song in F.

Prine wrote most of the new songs by himself, but teamed up on a handful of others. He worked with Roger Cook again to write "Unlonely," an exquisitely simple love song: "Once I was lonely / Nobody but me / My heart in a prison / Love set me free." Campbell wrote hard blues music to accompany Prine's bleak lyrics on "Great Rain," while Prine's old buddy Pat McLaughlin (who sang harmony on the *Bruised Orange* album) helped craft a very different sort of blues on the salacious "Daddy's Little Pumpkin":

> I can see the fire burning
> Burning right behind your eyes
> You must of swallowed a candle
> Or some other kind of surprise

The song was thrown together after McLaughlin reintroduced Prine to one of his early inspirations, Mississippi John Hurt. Epstein overheard Prine messing around with the unfinished song and insisted he complete it for the record. Prine and McLaughlin finished the song over the phone, and Prine recorded it that same day. "John came up with 'Daddy's Little Pumpkin' on the day we were mixing the album in Nashville," Epstein told Compton. "I heard it and we recorded it as a demo and that first take was the one that ended up on the record."

Keith Sykes cowrote "You Got Gold," a bouncy love song: "Life is a blessing, it's a delicatessen / Of all the little favors you do." Prine recorded one cover, the jaunty "I Want to Be with You Always," a No. 1 country hit for Lefty Frizzell in 1951. The song's full-bodied feel came from a well-balanced combination of Dobro, sax, and clarinet—all played by John Jorgenson, another Desert Rose Band vet—and accordion, played by Phil "Mister Squeeze" Parlapiano of the Brothers Figaro. Elsewhere Parlapiano played mandolin and, further broadening Prine's musical palette, harmonium—aka pump organ. Prine name checked Parlapiano in the lyrics to "The Sins of Memphisto," where a daydreaming character was "looking at the babies and the factories / And listening to the music of Mister Squeeze." Prine Travis-picked over a modified calypso beat that gave the song a feel similar to the Harry Nilsson hit "Coconut" from two decades earlier.

It was a casually visionary song about loss of innocence, relationships, sex, aging, and the passage of time, one of the most remarkable in Prine's catalog, effortlessly tying together various lyrical threads from throughout his career as a songwriter. There was cinematic imagery ("The hands on his watch spin slowly around / With his mind on a bus that goes all over town"), as well as overt references to movies (*The Bells of St. Mary's, The Count of Monte Cristo*), characters ("Esmeralda and the Hunchback of Notre Dame / They humped each other like they had no shame"), and Hollywood stars (Lucy and Ricky). The character in the first verse sounded like the latest incarnation of Barbara Lewis Hare Krishna Beauregard or the oldest baby in the world: "Sally used to play with her hula hoops / Now she tells her problems to therapy groups." There were also references to a character who sounded very much like Prine at various stages of his life. The middle-aged version "is sitting on the front steps drinking Orange Crush / Wondering if it's possible for me to still blush." The child sounded as though he was down in Paradise having one of those out-of-body experiences that led a mystified Bill and Verna to take their peculiar boy to an optometrist:

> A boy on a bike with corduroy slacks
> Sleeps in the river by the railroad tracks
> He waits for the whistle on the train to scream
> So he can close his eyes and begin to dream

True to form, Prine ended the song with a goofy joke, Esmeralda whispering in the Hunchback's ear, "Exactly odo, Quasimodo."

"I'm convinced I was just working the whole song to get around to the punch line . . . ," Prine wrote in the *Great Days* liner notes. "It's just hip lingo, kind of like 'No shit, Sherlock.' I'd had it for about four years, trying to work it into [a] song." The song's title stemmed from Prine's mistaken belief that Memphis, Tennessee, was named after an ancient Egyptian city called Memphisto. (Later he learned the Egyptian city, like its modern counterpart, was just plain old Memphis.) "I also got it confused with Mephisto, Mephistopheles, the devil," he wrote. "But I thought, that's okay, it's kind of like the devil going to Memphis, Tennessee." Remarkably, the song was something of an afterthought—written when Epstein demanded two more songs as work on the album wound down. Prine thought the well was dry: "I went and locked myself in a hotel room and went, 'If he wants a song, he'll get a song.' I tried to write one from as far in left field as I could." It's an old producer's trick ("We gotta have another song!") that had also borne fruit with other songwriters over the years, from the Turtles ("Elenore") to Bruce Springsteen ("Dancing in the Dark").

Prine had stopped for dinner at his favorite Italian restaurant in Southern California the day he arrived to start work on the record, and bumped into Springsteen. "He gave me a bunch of phone numbers and said, 'When you guys get into the record and have something to play, please invite me over. I'd just love to play guitar or harmonica or sing or whatever,'" Prine told Baird. Simply making a full record in Los Angeles for the first time gave Prine access to a large new cast of characters on a looser timetable than the Nashville pros. "Lindley, who I've known for years but never worked with, drove up in a van full of 18 instruments, unpacked and stayed for a week," he said. "If I'd have made this record in Nashville, I would have had to sit down and seriously plot it out with people like him." Springsteen, in town working on his follow-up to *Tunnel of Love*, dropped by the sessions to sing backup on "Take a Look at My Heart," a lusty rocker left over from Prine's long-ago songwriting session with Mellencamp—and a far better song than "Jackie O." Bonnie Raitt sang harmony on "Unlonely," while the sultry front woman for Australia's Divinyls, Christina Amphlett, sang backup on the Frizzell cover. (Her band's recent hit, "I Touch Myself," showed that Amphlett knew her way around a masturbation song as well as Prine did.) "By the time we brought Christina down to sing on a Lefty Frizzell song, Howie and I were looking at each other saying, 'Hell, we'll try anything,'" Prine told DeLuca. Phil Everly sang on "You Got Gold," while Epstein's boss, Tom Petty, added the distinctive grain of his voice to the song that would end up leading off the album, the deceptively upbeat "Picture Show."

Parlapiano's accordion kicked the song off, racing along as if already in midstream, bobbing and weaving around organ, piano, and a twangy electric guitar repeating a hooky riff. Like "The Sins of Memphisto," "Picture Show" reveled in Prine's lifelong love for classic movies—while acknowledging stardom's toll, likening it to the old American Indian legend about a photograph stealing its subject's soul. Recording only a couple of miles (as the crow flies) across the 101 from the Hollywood sign, he was on the brink of his own silver-screen debut—Mellencamp's movie was now in the final stages of production. Prine sang about three stars from his boyhood who all came to bad ends: John Garfield, Montgomery Clift, and James Dean, characterizing the latter as "A young man from a small town / With a very large imagination." (Or was that another bit of autobiography?) Prine had been kicking the song around since the early eighties, when a movie studio approached him about a possible musical showcasing "charismatic figures." He chose James Dean. "They sent me a bunch of neat clippings, things I'd never seen before, and I started writing 'Picture Show,'" he told Compton. When Prine asked for money to keep working on the project, the studio declined, and the singer set the song aside for a few years.

Prine delivered strong, confident, and relaxed vocals throughout the Epstein sessions. On "Unlonely," he practically crooned. He tracked most of his vocals in that three-and-a-half-foot hallway. "Towards the end we put John in the bathroom," Epstein told Compton. "He seemed to like it there." Epstein pushed Prine even harder than Goodman did on the *Bruised Orange* sessions. "Howie and me, we'd argue about the most minute things, until we got what we wanted," Prine told William Ruhlmann. The demand for more material caught him off guard: "It was a total surprise to me when he asked me to do that. And it turned the record around and put a different shine on it." Epstein told David Wild he thought it was a perfectly reasonable request. "My attitude was that he's this great songwriter, so it shouldn't be a big deal for him to write some more songs. I didn't want to sell John short. He is way too good for that."

For the other song he cranked out on command, Prine drew inspiration from Verna. In "It's a Big Old Goofy World," Prine—singing over warm, atmospheric backing via some of the album's most exotic instrumentation—has fun seeing how many classic similes he can string together:

> Why it's clear as a bell
> I should have gone to school
> I'd be wise as an owl
> 'Stead of stubborn as a mule

"I was over visiting my mother, and she liked to work crossword puzzles, and she would buy the easy ones," Prine told Ted Kooser. "She liked to work by quantity. And sometimes in these crossword-puzzle books they would have other games in there, you know? And one of 'em was these similes. We were sitting on the couch together one day and my mother was telling me some that she used when she was a little girl in Kentucky. Some of 'em were just hilarious. They'd have to do with somebody's name down the street. Anyway, I got to thinkin' about 'em and I decided to try to put them all together in a song and see if it would work."

The song that would become the album's sort-of title track was a combination of two unrelated ideas. The first stemmed from a guy at a party who told Prine the middle of Jesus's life was a complete mystery. "I said, 'You mean, like, nobody knew where he was?' And he said, 'Nobody,'" Prine told Jason Wilber. "So that kinda stuck in the back of my mind. I thought, 'Nobody. One of the most influential and controversial figures in the history of mankind, and nobody knew where he was for 18 years.' I snuck away on a fishing trip once with this waitress for a couple of days, and by the time we got back to Nashville, everybody knew where we were." Prine spoke the verses and sang the chorus, which came from an unfinished tune: "It was a whole other song I was writing that had no home, had no place to go. And it was about a guy that—everything was the same in his life, nothing changed. His address was 23 Skidoo." (In the 1920s, the phrase "23 skidoo" was popular slang for getting out while the getting was good.)

Prine had been making unconventional allusions to Jesus since his early days as a songwriter, in "Sam Stone" ("Jesus Christ died for nothing, I suppose"), "Spanish Pipedream" ("Try and find Jesus on your own"), "Your Flag Decal Won't Get You into Heaven Anymore" ("Now Jesus don't like killin' / No matter what the reason's for"), and "Everybody" ("I said, 'Jesus, you look tired' / He said, 'Jesus, so do you'"). "Jesus the Missing Years" went way beyond those offhand mentions, filling in a large historical gap in Christ's life story as only Prine could imagine: "He discovered the Beatles, and he recorded with the Stones / Once he even opened up a three-way package for old George Jones." (Jones spent much of the early nineties on the road with Merle Haggard and Conway Twitty.) Jesus also went to see *Rebel without a Cause*, providing a nice bookend to the James Dean references in the album's opening song. Like a sixties dropout two millennia ahead of schedule, Jesus wandered across Europe, married an Italian girl, invented Santa Claus, drank, and took drugs before ultimately realizing what fate had in store for him. The song—like the life of its protagonist—took a dark turn toward the end:

Oh my God, what have I gotten myself into?
I'm a human corkscrew and all my wine is blood
They're gonna kill me, Mama. They don't like me, bud.

As the recording sessions dragged out, money got tight. Where *German Afternoons* had cost about thirty thousand dollars, its studio follow-up was now approaching six figures. Bunetta ended up betting his family's home on his client. "We were kind of running low on funds for recording, so I just got some money by putting my house up as collateral just to have operating capital and to do a few more things with the record," he told David Hooper. "But it was an easy [decision]—to be around that, it wasn't as chancy as one might think. But my wife said, 'If you don't do it, you're not gonna ever be happy. So just do it.'"

Dylan also gave Prine a small nod around that time. Twenty years down the road, the version of "Donald and Lydia" he reportedly recorded still hadn't surfaced. But Dylan played a measured, heartfelt version of Prine's "People Puttin' People Down" from *Aimless Love* at shows in Italy and Brazil in the summer of 1991. Bonnie Raitt, meanwhile, had reached the pinnacle of her career with two quadruple-platinum albums, 1989's *Nick of Time* and 1991's *Luck of the Draw*. That summer she invited Prine to open for her on a tour of outdoor amphitheaters, putting him in front of some of his biggest crowds. He toured with a band for the first time since the Famous Potatoes era, backed by Parlapiano and his Brothers Figaro partner Bill Bonk, along with bass player Roly Salley from Chris Isaak's band, who wrote the *Pink Cadillac* song "Killing the Blues." Prine road tested songs from his new album, such as "The Sins of Memphisto" (also the name of his band) and "All the Best." "The truth is it gets lonely out there on the road," Prine told Wild. "It's nice to have a new band to tell all my old jokes to." That year's Gulf War in Iraq and the nationalistic fervor it spawned (L.A. riot grrrl band L7 dubbed it a "Wargasm") inspired Prine to pull "Your Flag Decal Won't Get You into Heaven Anymore" out of retirement, telling audiences, "Unfortunately, some things never change, and this song is one of 'em." He resurrected the song "mostly in reaction to the Desert Storm victory celebrations that went on for six or seven times as long as the war," he told Compton.

The Missing Years—the first new Prine record released primarily on compact disc—came out the same day the Raitt tour began. It had a big, expansive rock sound, timeless but radio-ready. Never before had the singer, now on the brink of his forty-fifth birthday, achieved such an ideal combination of sound, singing, and songs. The cover of his big rock album was a photo of Prine leaning against a big rock, a confident smile lighting up his face. In the liner notes, he acknowledged Verna "for the inspiration," thanked Epstein "for a great record," and offered "lots of love to Fiona." (The CD booklet also featured a snapshot of Prine leaning in to share a moment with Fiona, seated in a convertible.)

Twenty years removed from his debut album, the singer sounded like a completely different performer than the awkward Chicago kid who made *John Prine*. Now he was a seasoned Nashville pro taking his show on the road to L.A., rubbing shoulders with the likes of Bruce Springsteen and Tom Petty and more than holding his own. As a cohesive sonic and thematic statement, *The Missing Years* ranked with *Sweet Revenge* and *Bruised Orange*—and probably went them one better. It was Prine's *Born to Run* or *Damn the Torpedoes*, a swaggering rock statement that fully realized his potential.

Threads run from his debut through *The Missing Years*: "The Sins of Memphisto" captures the tenor of its times just as "Spanish Pipedream" had two decades before, hippie-era utopian fantasy having given way to characters who found a way to live in society (with a little help from therapy groups) rather than running away from it. "All the Best" stands up as a song of crumbled romance every bit the equal to "Far from Me." "Jesus the Missing Years" is a character study as audacious and unforgettable as "Sam Stone" or "Donald and Lydia."

Epstein brought out the best in Prine, pushing him to a peak performance as a songwriter and vocalist at an age when most singers are well past their prime. The producer also assembled a supporting cast of backing musicians and singers that guaranteed Prine's stellar work would be matched note for note, his hard work buoyed by some of the most accomplished pros in the music business. Together they came up with an endlessly listenable album full of the strongest songs Prine had written since the seventies—some of them as good as any he had ever written.

Critics ate the album up, making it a watershed moment in Prine's career. Robert Christgau gave it an A-minus and a glowing write-up: "He says he put a lot into his first album in five years because he figured it might be his last ever, which it won't be; I attribute its undeviating quality, gratifying variety, and amazing grace to talent, leisure time, and just enough all-star input. I wouldn't swear there's a stone classic here—just nothing I wouldn't be happy to hear again." Alanna Nash, reviewing the album for *Entertainment Weekly*, also gave it an A-minus: "While little here is stunning—except for the Dylanesque 'Take a Look at My Heart,' a 'dear sucker' letter to Prine's ex–old lady's boyfriend, with a subdued cameo vocal by Bruce Springsteen—all the songs are keepers, perfectly relaxed and wry. And so what if a lot of them start out to be about one thing and end up being about another? Doesn't life?" John Milward gave it four stars in *Rolling Stone*, declaring it Prine's best album since *Bruised Orange* and one "filled with idiosyncratic delights." Epstein's "subtle production," Milward wrote, "keeps the emphasis on arrangements framed by Prine's acoustic guitar and sandy vocals."

Prine and the Oh Boy team were accustomed to good press, but *The Missing Years* finally made the singer more than just a critics' darling: It sold in unprecedented numbers. *Prime Prine* eventually went gold, selling more than half a million copies, but it took well over a decade to do so. *The Missing Years* did good business right out of the gate, selling a quarter of a million copies within months, four or five times the rate of his previous Oh Boy releases. It may not have been *Thriller*, but in Prine's world it was a smash hit. Bunetta's bet had paid off; he wouldn't lose his house.

The album earned Prine another Grammy Award nomination, for Best Contemporary Folk Album. It got his music on the radio for the first time since he walked away from major labels. He even made his first music video to promote *The Missing Years*, a decade after MTV hit the airwaves. The clip for "Picture Show" was shot around Southern California in film noirish black and white to match the subject matter of the song, and got airplay on what was then MTV's sister station aimed at adult music fans, VH1. Rock photographer Jim Shea directed. Tom Petty lip-synced his harmonies and strummed a guitar alongside Prine, while in other scenes the Brothers Figaro did their thing, Mister Squeeze squeezing his squeezebox. There were shots of a 1940s car driving through the desert, and several shots of Prine roaming the exterior of Griffith Observatory above Hollywood, an iconic building also featured in the climactic final scene of *Rebel without a Cause*.

Petty sang Prine's praises in *Rolling Stone*. "It goes beyond just craft," he told Wild. "The guy is instinctively good. Anybody who writes songs is a fan of John Prine." Roger Waters, a longtime Prine fan, borrowed from the melody of "Sam Stone" in writing the 1983 Pink Floyd song "The Post War Dream," which opened with the lines: "Tell me true, tell me why, was Jesus crucified? / Is it for this that Daddy died?" Waters asked Prine to record a duet with him. "His is just extraordinarily eloquent music—and he lives on that plane with Neil Young and Lennon," Waters told *World Magazine*. When the new Dylan bumped into the old one on a return trip to L.A., Dylan told Prine how much he liked *The Missing Years*. "At an age when so many of his contemporaries are trading on nostalgia, Prine is just hitting his creative peak," Wild wrote. The album's reception reinvigorated Prine and ended all talk of him retiring from the music business. "Meeting Howie was a giant step," Prine told Wild. "I always knew what to do with an audience, but the studio was a different story. So for me to be proud of a record is something, and I couldn't be prouder of this one. And hey, it's only taken me twenty years to get it right." He expressed gratitude that success had found him at an age when he was mature and stable enough to handle it: "If my first couple of albums would have sold well, I would have ended up in a fucking institution. Now I can enjoy it."

The same week the *Rolling Stone* article appeared, in late February 1992, Prine finally won a Grammy Award. *The Missing Years* earned him a statuette over competing albums by Indigo Girls, Beausoleil, Rosanne Cash, and Jerry Garcia and David Grisman.

CHAPTER 12

Into the Great
Wide Open

▼

The Mellencamp movie came out the same month Prine won his Grammy, but "Souvenirs" was no longer the title song. It had been renamed *Falling from Grace*, and told the story of a philandering country star, Bud Parks—played by Mellencamp—home from L.A. in his Indiana hometown and wrestling with his demons. (Not to mention his domineering father, played by Claude Akins.) Prine played Mitch, Bud's bespectacled, depressed, debt-ridden brother-in-law. In the movie's first extended scene, he traded dialogue with Bud's wife, Alice, played by Mariel Hemingway (whose grandfather, Ernest, grew up in Oak Park, Illinois, next door to Prine's hometown).

> *Alice:* C'mon, Mitch. Tell me who's mad at whom over what.
> Start with the old folks and work down.
> *Mitch:* Mainly they're all mad at me. Especially Sally.
> Only I don't know what I done, Alice.

In an interview for the *Nashville Banner*, Prine told Dan DeLuca he was playing a character "with low self-esteem, who can't hold his liquor," adding, "It's typecasting." Mitch never really emerged from the background, and the character's most dramatic moment in the movie happened offscreen, when he wrecked his new pickup truck and broke his collarbone. It wasn't exactly a star-making role for Prine, and *Falling from Grace* didn't do much for Mellencamp, either: The movie got mixed reviews, and failed by a wide margin to recoup its modest $3 million budget at the box office. Roger Ebert, who had helped launch Prine's professional career two decades earlier, neglected to mention the singer in his review, but he loved the movie: "Mellencamp turns out to have a real filmmaking gift. His film is perceptive and subtle, and doesn't make the mistake of thinking that because something is real, it makes good fiction. The characters created here with McMurtry are three-dimensional and fully realized."

"Souvenirs" didn't even make the final cut for the movie's soundtrack, but the movie did feature a scene set to a rocked-up version of "All the Best." The soundtrack also had Prine singing with an all-star band, the Buzzin' Cousins, for a mid-tempo rocker called "Sweet Suzanne." He traded lines with Mellencamp, Dwight Yoakam, Joe Ely, and James McMurtry, the singer-songwriter son of the film's screenwriter, who released his debut album in 1989. Supergroups were all the rage in the early nineties, following in the wake of the Highwaymen (Johnny Cash, Willie Nelson, Waylon Jennings, and Kris Kristofferson) and the Traveling Wilburys (Dylan, Petty, Roy Orbison, George Harrison, and Jeff Lynne). Other supergroups of the era were Little Village (John Hiatt, Ry Cooder, Nick Lowe, Jim Keltner) and the Texas Tornados (Freddy Fender, Flaco Jiménez, Augie Meyers, Doug Sahm).

These were the salad days for Prine and Oh Boy. "Things are going really, really great right now," he told DeLuca. "It's like a dream or something. We're even gonna put out one or two records by other artists this year. We couldn't afford that before." Oh Boy would release It's About Time by Prine's old friend Keith Sykes later that year. A slightly revamped version of the Sins of Memphisto backed Prine on a tour of theaters in 1992, with bassist Roly Salley exiting and guitarist Duane Jarvis entering. Prine and the Cowboy Junkies took turns opening the shows, and the young Canadian band backed Prine and the group's lead singer, Margo Timmins, when they recorded a duet version of "If You Were the Woman and I Was the Man." In a rare concession to modernity, Prine and the band would play along to a drum machine on "The Sins of Memphisto," the singer looking about as ill at ease as a dog trying to send a fax. Prine made his fifth appearance on Austin City Limits, splitting the hour with Jimmie Dale Gilmore.

The celebrity gossip magazine People deemed Prine ascendant enough to merit a profile, written by Cynthia Sanz, in the summer of

1992: "This year, with about 150 performance dates on his schedule, he will spend as much time on the road as in the three-bedroom Nashville home he shares with two cats, a miniature Doberman and an artificial Christmas tree that he keeps up year-round." "A couple of years ago, I was going through my divorce and was real depressed," Prine told Sanz. "I thought the lights and decorations were so nice, I just decided to let it stay up." Off the road Prine would spend his time checking out friends' shows, fishing, or hanging out at home alone, Sanz wrote: "I can just sit by myself and have this vivid imagination." Prine and Fiona saw each other about six times a year. "I'm not praying for marriage," Prine told Sanz, "but I got a feeling I will."

Prine wanted to keep the momentum from *The Missing Years* going. *Goldmine* published a comprehensive career retrospective in a December 1992 issue, and the singer told William Ruhlmann he planned to go back into the studio with Epstein in early 1993 and get another record out that fall: "I'm gonna start in February regardless of how few or how many songs I got by that time. I'd rather make this next one an ongoing process, just go in with Howie and start working." In March Prine got another boost when Nanci Griffith released her widely acclaimed *Other Voices, Other Rooms*, an album of covers—many of them duets—produced by Jim Rooney. She sang Townes Van Zandt's "Tecumseh Valley" with Arlo Guthrie, Tom Paxton's "Can't Help But Wonder Where I'm Bound" with Carolyn Hester, and "Speed of the Sound of Loneliness" with the songwriter himself. (She and Prine had previously performed the song together when Prine hosted the *Route 90* TV show in the UK.) Prine and Griffith played angels in the video for the song. "I still have my wings at home," he told Kara Manning in a 1995 *Rolling Stone* interview. "We spent the day filming in a cemetery with angel wings on, and it was about 13 degrees. Every time a little wind came under me and Nanci, we'd begin to take off."

Plans for a sequel to *The Missing Years* got sidetracked in 1993. Taking advantage of Prine's newfound momentum, Oh Boy teamed up with Rhino Records, reissue-label extraordinaire, to put together a comprehensive two-CD collection of his work. Unlike with the release of *Prime Prine*, when the singer had to sneak into Atlantic Records' offices after hours just to get a look at the cover art, the artist and his team had full control over *Great Days: The John Prine Anthology*. Released in August, the forty-one-track set contained songs from all of his previous albums, including six from his debut, three from *Diamonds in the Rough*, five from *Sweet Revenge*, four apiece from *Common Sense* and *Bruised Orange*, three from *Pink Cadillac*, four apiece from *Storm Windows* and *Aimless Love*, two from *German Afternoons*, one from *John Prine Live*, and two from the still-fresh *The Missing Years*. The collection also contained a duet with Goodman on "Souvenirs," previously released on Goodman's 1983 album *Affordable Art*, as well as the Raitt duet on "Angel from Montgomery" from *Tribute to Steve Goodman*. Finally, there was a live version of "It's a Big Old Goofy World" from the syndicated radio show *Mountain Stage* that had been released in 1991 on *Best of Mountain Stage, Vol. 2*. The fifty-page booklet packaged with *Great Days* had liner notes by *Rolling Stone* writer David Fricke, who selected the tracks, along with Ruhlmann, author of the *Goldmine* story the year before. There were notes about each song by Prine and a wealth of photos, dating back to the singer's childhood in Maywood. "Writing is about a blank piece of paper and leaving out what's not supposed to be there," Prine wrote for an introduction. "Here's forty-one songs collected under the title *Great Days*. There were many great days and many not so great days. I tried to turn them all into great songs." This anthology was dedicated—without explanation—to Gloria Stavers, "the founder of *16* magazine." He also gave credit to his business team: "I'd still be singing these songs to the walls if it hadn't been for Al Bunetta and Dan Einstein."

The collection inspired Robert Christgau to give Prine his first full A grade since *Sweet Revenge*: "There aren't forty-one best Prine songs. There are fifty, sixty, maybe more; the only way to resolve quibbles would be a bigger box than commerce or decorum permits. And his catalogue's out there, with *John Prine*, *Sweet Revenge*, and *Storm Windows* durable favorites. But this is just the place to access his kind, comic, unassumingly surreal humanism. Prine's a lot friendlier than your average thriving old singer-songwriter ([Neil] Young, [Richard] Thompson, [Leonard] Cohen), and his disinclination to downplay his natural warmth or his folk-rock retro may make him impenetrable to victims of irony proficiency amnesia. But no one writing has a better feel for the American colloquial—its language, its culture, its life. Except maybe [novelist] Bobbie Ann Mason." Bob Cannon, reviewing the collection for *Entertainment Weekly*, went Christgau one better and gave it an A-plus: "Easily one of the most distinctive lyricists of the singer-songwriter school,

John Prine excels at wry portraits of lovable losers ("Donald and Lydia") and life's absurdities ("That's the Way That the World Goes 'Round"), all of which have only improved since his stunning 1971 debut. To the unconverted, his rudimentary melodies and wheezy voice may get tiresome, but that would be missing the point. It's *Great Days: The John Prine Anthology* and no one writes songs as succinctly poignant and occasionally goofy as Prine."

As for Prine's "rudimentary melodies and wheezy voice," he had never claimed to be a great singer or musician. "In the past six, seven years, I realized that I am very limited in my strumming," Prine told Joe F. Compton in an interview for *Acoustic Guitar*. "I was talking to Carlene Carter. She and I both have three types of strumming: fast, slow, and calypso. That's it, the only rhythms we know! So if I'm writing and strumming, the song is going to come out with one of those three. That's why my most memorable melodies—such as 'That's the Way That the World Goes 'Round' and 'Hello in There'—come from single-note fingerpicking."

Mick Jagger and Keith Richards turned fifty in 1993, and the national UK newspaper the *Independent* asked a slew of celebrities to name their favorite Rolling Stones song. Prine had a couple: "At my favourite bar, Brown's in Nashville, there's a jukebox. It has one Stones song, 'Waiting on a Friend,' and the rest is all country music. It's got great lyrics and a cheesy keyboard thing in it, and it just sounds so good beside George Jones. Otherwise I go for 'Stupid Girl,' again because it's got great lyrics. Jagger and Richards are great writers because they've got a sense of humour." Brown's, established in Nashville's Hillsboro Village neighborhood in 1927, is a greasy spoon known for its cheeseburgers. Another favorite Prine hangout was in the Green Hills neighborhood: Joe's Village Inn, a pool hall with a sleazy reputation. One observer described it as "an old-fashioned, smoky, sticky-floored, red-leather-seat joint."

Many of the people closest to Prine converged in Nashville in the early nineties. Bunetta moved the offices for Oh Boy, Red Pajamas, and his management company east from Los Angeles. Fiona and her school-aged son, Jody, immigrated from Ireland in 1993. In September the two of them accompanied Prine, Verna, and Billy to a Hamm family reunion in Muhlenberg County. The *Central City Leader-News* documented the occasion, publishing a picture of a beaming Prine with his arm around his "longtime friend, Fiona." A month later Verna moved back south, to Music City, more than half a century after she married Bill and left Muhlenberg County for Maywood. Baby boy Billy (now forty years old and six foot eight in his stocking feet) soon followed suit. He had led a series of bar bands since the late seventies, from Whiplash and the Lawsuits in Northern California to Billy and the Bangers back home in Chicago. Remaining in Illinois with their families were Doug, who would rise to the rank of lieutenant before retiring from the Chicago Police Department, and Dave, still doing structural engineering work on the faculty at Northwestern.

For the 1993 holiday season Oh Boy released *A John Prine Christmas*, which contained the two songs from the first Oh Boy single twelve years before and a random assortment of other seasonal tunes—not all of them celebratory. Two songs repeated from *The Missing Years*: an alternate take of "Everything Is Cool" ("Just before last Christmas / My baby went away") and a live version of "All the Best":

> I guess that love is like a Christmas card
> You decorate a tree, you throw it in the yard
> It decays and dies, and the snowmen melt
> Well I once knew love, I knew how love felt

The eight-song CD had a live version of "Christmas in Prison" and closed with "A John Prine Christmas," a spoken-word track in which the singer told holiday stories from his childhood, one about the time he ate an ornament from the family Christmas tree.

Prine started a family of his own in 1994. On 1 December Fiona gave birth to her second child, an eight-pound son, John Patrick Whalen "Jack" Prine. His father was there for the birth—and Prine's manager was off in the waiting room while his wife, Dawn, assisted in the delivery room. "The baby's so beautiful," Bunetta told the *Nashville Banner*. "This is the first time I've seen John Prine walking three feet off the ground."

While Fiona was growing a baby, Prine and Epstein had been busy gestating the follow-up to his hit album. "I think my writing did open up because of what Howie brought back to me with *The Missing Years*," Prine told Peter Cronin. "I was willing to try more stuff, and I told Howie from the beginning that I wouldn't nix any of his ideas up front. If I didn't like it when we got down to the final mix, *then* it would go."

Epstein told Cronin he offered a similar hands-off attitude to the singer: "I initially approached Prine pretty much letting him do his thing. We built everything around the song, the guitar, and his vocal, and then embellished from there. There are elements of *The Missing Years* on this new record, but this time we took it to another level."

Prine started the process intending to write all the songs by himself, but eventually hit a wall. "At first I kept holding off, saying, 'I'll be better next month' and, 'Let's go to the movies,'" he told Compton. "One night I go to the movies and the kid selling the popcorn says, 'I am Nathan Nicholson, and my dad really likes your writing and would love to write with you.'" His dad was Gary Nicholson, a Texas-born country songwriter who had written songs for George Jones, Willie Nelson, Reba McEntire, and many other artists. "I walked out of that theater so ashamed, because I had told Gary that we would get together someday and write and I hadn't called," Prine said. They quickly made up for lost time, cowriting several songs Prine subsequently recorded with Epstein.

The recording sessions took place at Epstein's home studio again, and most of the musicians from *The Missing Years* returned—David Lindley and Mike Campbell being notable exceptions. A new guitarist, Waddy Wachtel, offset Campbell's absence to some degree, though his playing on Prine's rockers injected considerably more bombast than anything Campbell was likely to have played. Like bassist Bob Glaub, Wachtel was a veteran of countless L.A. sessions and tours backing artists such as Linda Ronstadt, Jackson Browne, and James Taylor. Some guest vocalists showed up, as well, though with the exception of British rock veteran Marianne Faithfull they were minor leaguers (Sass Jordan, Carlene Carter) compared to the heavy hitters who sang with Prine on *The Missing Years*. Epstein and Prine decided to invite Faithfull to the party after the producer read her 1994 autobiography. "Well, it turns out that Marianne was a big fan of *The Missing Years*, and when she was writing the book, she said that every time she wrote about Mick Jagger, she'd play the song 'All the Best' over and over," Prine told *Rolling Stone*. (Faithfull would end up covering "All the Best" in concert, calling it "a lovely, sarcastic little song written by John Prine.")

Prine's new songs exhibited his customary range of stylistic diversity, from the tough, bluesy rocker "Ain't Hurtin' Nobody" to the delicate ballad "Day Is Done." Though he had largely left behind his more outrageous, surreal lyrical experiments of the seventies, some of the new songs offered a skewed perspective on life, such as the oddly named "Humidity Built the Snowman," a vague commentary on the impermanence of relationships: "You won't find me walking 'round your part of town / Humidity built the snowman; sunshine brought him down." "New Train," which would become the album's opening track, kicked things off on a bright, optimistic note, with bouncy music and "be here now" lyrics that seemed inspired by Prine's new musical lease on life:

> No faded photographs of yesterdays
> Are in the books that I read these days
> To fly away from that memory town
> You must keep both your feet on the ground

Epstein and Prine largely stuck with the warm, spacious sound of *The Missing Years*, though the new album slid into commercial-rock territory here and there, such as on "We Are the Lonely" and "Quit Hollerin' at Me."

Unfortunately, several of the songs Prine wrote with Nicholson detracted more than they added. The clunky "We Are the Lonely" sounded dated the day they recorded it, filled with lame jokes inspired by personal ads: "SWF with a Ph.D. / Seeks TLC at the A&P / GWM, nice and trim / Seeks S-E-X at the G-Y-M." "Quit Hollerin' at Me" was a cranky-old-man anthem, filled with complaints about everything from loud TV commercials to fast-food register clerks pushing super-sized orders of French fries. A lyrical twist at the end—"there ain't no voice that's louder / Than the one inside my brain"—did little to redeem the song. The stomping rocker "Big Fat Love" (Epstein called it "the Aerosmith number") is a one-dimensional song about a two-dimensional girl—a "skinny little thing" who made up for her lack of curves with (you guessed it) "big fat love." If they had recorded "Day Is Done" and the slinky, easy-rolling "Same Thing Happened to Me" (both also credited to Prine and Nicholson) and left it there, the album would have avoided several major pitfalls. But Nicholson had no hand in the worst song, "Leave the Lights On," credited to Prine, Epstein, Parlapiano, and drummer Joe Romersa. Prine seemed to be aiming at Cowboy Jack Clement–style whimsy, but it's a wonder no one convinced him it was a terrible mistake to rhyme "telephoney" with "Rice-A-Roni" and "forty-two-inch Sony" with "Twilight Zoney."

After the success of *The Missing Years*, Prine and Epstein may have thought they could do no wrong, and the cheesier songs sound like calculated attempts to get Prine on the radio. "People tend to associate independent business with el cheapo records," Bunetta told Cronin. "But this album took a lot of time and cost a lot of money to make, and the campaign behind it is going to be equal to what the record cost, at least." Not every song was a swing for the rock-radio fences. The lovely closing track, a cover of Floyd Tillman's "I Love You So Much It Hurts," wouldn't have sounded out of place on a Randy Newman album. It was like nothing Prine had ever recorded, a naked cover of a 1948 country hit with Prine accompanied only by Benmont Tench on piano.

Even more daring was "Lake Marie," an epic tale that, on a surface level, repeated the formula of "Jesus the Missing Years": spoken verses, sung chorus. "I had this idea for a song that was going to have half talking, half singing in it," Prine told Mark Guarino in a 1999 interview for the *Chicago Daily Herald*. "It was going to have a strong chorus to it and it was going to start out with something that had a historical nature to it. I had nothing else. I just had an idea for a song like that. I just waited for something to come along that I thought I could fit into that." A show in Woodstock, Illinois, northwest of Chicago, led to the rest of the story. "I was soundcheckin' for a song at the Woodstock Opera House," Prine said. "The monitor guy mentioned something to another guy about Lake Marie. And I said, 'Lake Marie, is that around here?' And he said, 'Yeah, about 20 minutes down the road.' I said, 'I haven't been there in years.'" He and a high school girlfriend had picnicked in the area.

Prine and his brother Billy drove up around the Wisconsin state line to check it out. The librarian at a one-room library connected him with a local historian, who sent Prine some clippings about the history of the area. "And one of them was talking about the two sisters that the lakes were named after, Elizabeth and Mary," Prine told Guarino. "And the little story about the Indians that were around the area when they found the girl. And I said, 'That's that; that's the song right there.'" Prine blended in a few more images (sausages sizzling on an outdoor grill, a breeze through a woman's hair, memories of unsolved murders in the Chicago suburbs from his childhood) and "Lake Marie" was born:

Saw it on the news
The TV news
In a black-and-white video
Do you know what blood looks like in a black-and-white video?
Shadows! Shadows!
That's what it looks like

After much trial and error, Epstein and Prine decided they would have to record "Lake Marie" live to get the sound they were after. The only overdubs were the female backing vocalists. "The encouraging thing for me about 'Lake Marie' is that the bigger the chances you take, the bigger the rewards you might receive," Prine told Compton. As he had done throughout his career, the singer evoked intense emotion by focusing on adeptly chosen minutiae. Christgau would call the song "the surreal history of a wrecked marriage."

Lost Dogs and Mixed Blessings took two years to record, finally coming out in the spring of 1995. "I didn't want to try to come up with *The Missing Years II*," Prine told the *Fort Lauderdale Sun-Sentinel*. "Sure, it came out big and shiny, but it won't help if you put horns on it if the songs aren't good. Steve Cropper *did* put horns on *Common Sense*, and we still couldn't get it played." Prine and Epstein were ready for a break. "We kinda overextended ourselves on *Lost Dogs*," Prine said. ". . . I think we were pretty tired of each other. At the end of it, we shook hands and said, 'OK, we did it.'"

The cover of the album, by John Callahan, was a cartoonish painting of a hillbilly devil playing a squeezebox on the front porch of his shack while an angel claps along. Winged dogs fly over a graveyard in the distance. Elsewhere in the CD package there were a couple of black-and-white photos of Prine. On the back cover of the booklet he wasn't merely whistling *past* a graveyard—he was whistling *in* a graveyard, leaning against a cast-iron fence. The picture printed on the CD itself re-created the front cover of *Sweet Revenge* twenty-two years later, right down to the aviator sunglasses. Only the middle-aged Prine no longer sported a beard, and this time a pale-eyed dog wearing a bow tie shared the seat of a convertible with him.

Reviews for *Lost Dogs* were generally positive, but decidedly more mixed than the ones for its predecessor. Al Kaufman, assessing the album for the *Austin Chronicle*, called it "Prine's most self-assured and greatest work to date" and gave it four out of four stars. Christgau liked it even better than *The Missing Years*, giving it an A: "Although ex-Heart-breaker Howie Epstein gets more hooks out of his acoustic warrior than his old boss is tossing off, his idea of radio-ready does leave one waiting for the guitarist to shut up already. But usually that's because you're impatient for the next line, and usually it's a winner—if anything, Prine's waggish pathos and lip-smacking Americanese have been whetted by the divorce that keeps nosing in where it's not wanted."

Bob Cannon, reviewing the album for *Entertainment Weekly*, liked it considerably less than he had liked *The Missing Years*. He gave *Lost Dogs* only a B, declaring that Nicholson's "slick skills push Prine toward empty pop product." Jeff Salamon, critiquing the record for *Spin*, gave it a six on a scale of ten: "For the first time, Prine's nursery-rhyme stream-of-consciousness seems not like a sideways engagement, but an evasion—he's the funny guy who can't stop spouting one-liners even as his one true love is walking out the door."

Prine made his second video to promote *Lost Dogs*, with Jim Shea directing again. The song was "Ain't Hurtin' Nobody," and this time Shea traded the black-and-white footage of "Picture Show" for muted, doctored color footage. In the video, Prine cruised nighttime streets in a vintage Cadillac through the cheatin' side of town, shots of him rolling dice and flipping a coin alternating with shots of a prisoner lifting weights and a tattooed woman shooting pool. The album earned Prine another Grammy nomination. Despite the confidence expressed by Prine and Bunetta and Oh Boy's big promotional push, the album was not a huge hit. While it put him in the *Billboard* Top 200 for the first time since *Storm Windows*, *Lost Dogs* peaked at No. 159 and dropped off the charts after only nine weeks, the initial burst of sales tapering off quickly.

For his *Lost Dogs* tour, Prine assembled the Lost Dogs Band, his first full-scale touring rock band since the Famous Potatoes. Parlapiano served as the band's musical director and utility infielder, playing keyboards and mandolin in addition to accordion. Former Mellencamp guitarist (and *Falling from Grace* costar) Larry Crane provided the same driving energy he had given to his former employer. Bass player Dave Jacques (pronounced "jakes"), a native of Worcester, Massachusetts, had been an in-demand Nashville session player since the late eighties. Young drummer Ed Gaus was a product of the Chicago suburbs like Prine, growing up north of the city in the village of Northbrook, Illinois.

He had taken private lessons from Mellencamp's legendary drummer, Kenny Aronoff, while attending the Indiana University School of Music. "The roughest thing is coming up with a set list," Prine told the *Sun-Sentinel*. "I'm used to playing whatever I feel like. But now I've got the band and even my own lights. The lighting guy likes to know what you're going to play next."

Fiona, meanwhile, barely made it home from the hospital with Jack before Prine got her pregnant again. Tommy Whelan Prine was born ten months after his brother on 4 October 1995, six days before his father turned forty-nine. Prine called them his "Irish twins."

Soon Prine added a lead guitarist to the Lost Dogs Band. "I got a guy on electric guitar who can play the blues like crazy, but his real love is bluegrass," Prine told the *Sun-Sentinel*. "His name is David Steele, and he can play steel licks on the electric guitar. So we can get pretty country, too." The affection was mutual. "I love John so much, and he was so nice to me," Steele told Jason Wilber in an interview for his *In Search of a Song* radio show. "And he bent over backwards to have me in his band. It was changing the budget to have another player. So he really went out of his way for me. And he gave me incredible freedom onstage—too much freedom, sometimes." The band toured with the singer for months and backed him on his sixth *Austin City Limits* appearance. Prine had started to get pudgy and his hair had mostly gone gray, but he played with as much energy and good humor as ever. He split the hour with a brilliant, funny young songwriter, Todd Snider, who had clearly learned a great deal from Prine.

Steele recalled a memorable appearance on the NBC talk show *Late Night with Conan O'Brien*: "Conan is a huuuuuge fan, so he was around, like all day. Hangin' around the dressing room, talking to John, and asking John about this song and that song. Brought a guitar in at one point and had him sign it. I mean, we'd already done *The Tonight Show*. But now we're doing *Conan*, it was like, 'Man, I'm in show business.' It was so damn exciting, and we're all wearing suits, and we're in New York City. It was just everything." All the excitement led Steele to go a little overboard when they taped a performance of "Quit Hollerin' at Me" for the show. "The next day, we were leaving New York, and we all met in the lobby," Steele said. "I hadn't seen John, and I walked up to him, and I said, 'Did you see the show last night?' And he said, 'Yeah, I thought it was pretty good.' And I could tell by the way he said it that he wasn't sure. So I kind of offered up a little, 'I didn't realize—I kinda played a lot, really, at the ending.' And he said, 'Yeah, I felt like Eric Clapton's vocalist.'"

Later Steele jumped ship in the middle of the tour to join Steve Earle's road band, calling it "the craziest-hardest decision I've ever made in my life." "I called Steve back and I told him I would take the gig, and I said, 'I need to tell John, so just keep it between you and me for now,' and he was cool with that," Steele told Wilber. ". . . He said, 'Man, that's no problem. I love John. You ever seen me pick an acoustic guitar? I play with two fingers because of John Prine. That's where I learned how to play acoustic-style fingerpicking.'" Steele's replacement was none other than Jason Wilber, a young Indiana native who had been studying music since age five and played with other country and folk artists: Hal Ketchum, Carrie Newcomer, and one of Prine's favorites, Iris DeMent.

Oh Boy documented Prine's work with the Lost Dogs Band on his second concert album, *Live on Tour*, released in 1997. The song selection drew heavily from his most recent, rock-oriented studio albums, with a few cherry-picked songs from earlier in his career: an unadorned "Unwed Fathers," a dramatic "Storm Windows," and a gorgeous reading of "The Late John Garfield Blues," which opened with a delicate accordion intro before Parlapiano switched to piano. At the end of "Illegal Smile," Prine reflected his new family situation by updating the campy ending he had been using for years: "Well done, son of a gun, hot dog bun, Attila the Hun, my sister-in-law—my sister-in-law—my sister-in-law is an *Irish nun!*" (Prine and Fiona had finally made it official, tying the knot in 1996. "A large Irish contingent came over, and the wedding went on for days," Rooney wrote. "Maura O'Connell, Roger Cook, Sandy Mason, and I sang 'Only Love' in the church. There wasn't a dry eye in the house.")

The songs were recorded at various locales around the country: the Boulder Theater in Colorado, the Navy Pier Skyline Stage in sweet home Chicago, and the home church of country music, the Ryman Auditorium in Nashville. West Coast singer-songwriter Peter Case cowrote a new song, "Space Monkey," which Prine could barely get through without laughing. It was a tragicomedy about a primate cosmonaut launched into orbit by the Soviet Union, then forgotten for decades: "One day he slipped on a banana peel and the ship lost control / It spun out of orbit and shot out the black hole." The chorus sneaked in a new twist on an old Merle Travis line: "Space monkey, space monkey / What you doing out there? Why, it's dark as a dungeon way up in the air." (The monkey eventually ended up back home in post-Soviet Moscow, drowning his sorrows at a karaoke bar with other ex–lab animals, "drinking American vodka imported all the way from Paducah, Kentucky.") The album closed with three new studio recordings: "If I Could," a fast, wordy country song written by Tim Carroll in the vein of "I've Been Everywhere"; a catchy, boozy lament called "Stick a Needle in My Eye," cowritten with Pat McLaughlin; and "You Mean So Much to Me," cowritten with Donnie Fritts, Prine closing his second album in a row by singing a lovely ballad accompanied only by Benmont Tench on piano.

Einstein shared production credit with Prine on *Live on Tour*. "Thanks to Al Bunetta and Dan Einstein," Prine wrote in the liner notes. "Without their encouragement, this record would still be tapes in a box." Greg Kot, reviewing the album for the *Chicago Tribune*, gave *Live on Tour* three and a half out of four stars.

Johnny Cash gave Prine and Goodman props in his 1997 autobiography, *Cash*: "I don't listen to music much at the farm, unless I'm going into songwriting mode and looking for inspiration. Then I'll put on something by the writers I've admired and used for years (Rodney Crowell, John Prine, Guy Clark, and the late Steve Goodman are my Big Four), or any music in any field that has real artistry, or something that promises a connection to what's essential in my own music: old blues, old country, old gospel."

While he never recorded "You Never Even Called Me by My Name," Cash liked another Prine-Goodman collaboration so much he recorded it twice. He cut "The Twentieth Century Is Almost Over," a bouncy, funny, gospel-flavored song ("Did anybody see them linoleum floors / Petroleum jelly and the two world wars? / They went around in revolvin' doors"), first for his 1980 album *Rockabilly Blues*, then again for the 1985 debut album by the Highwaymen—which happened to be produced by Chips Moman, founder of American Studio in Memphis, where Prine recorded his first album.

CHAPTER 13

A Close Shave

▼

What's everybody whispering about? I've got cancer!
For Christ's sake, it's not a venereal disease.

HUMPHREY BOGART

One day in 1997 Prine was shaving and felt a lump on the right side of his neck. Eventually he got it checked by a doctor, who took a tissue sample and had it tested. The test came back positive for cancer.

Squamous cell carcinoma begins in the moist surfaces inside the head and neck. Tobacco and alcohol use are major risk factors, and Prine had consumed plenty of both in his day. Concert reviewers and interviewers commented on his drinking many times during the seventies. He holds or smokes a cigarette in the photos on half of his early album covers, and smoked heavily even during concerts.

"The doctor who had to tell me had a harder time than I did with it initially," Prine told Greg Kot in a 1999 *Chicago Tribune* interview. "I could tell he hadn't done this sort of thing much before, and after he got done telling me, I felt like I should take him to the circus just to cheer him up." Things got more difficult for Prine when it came time to figure out how to treat it: "There were so many options, and each doctor had a different plan. It was like, should I take Door No. 1, 2 or 3?" As he weighed his options, word got to Knox Phillips, whom Prine had remained friends with since making *Pink Cadillac* nearly twenty years before. Knox called to tell him he "had the exact same thing I did, [had] done all the research and finally gone to a hospital in Houston to get treatment," Prine told Kot. "We're great friends, but he and I knock heads a lot, so I was like, 'Who's Knox to tell me my doctor's wrong and his doctor's right?'" Prine had already decided to go with nonsurgical treatment at a Memphis clinic and stuck to his guns.

Knox believed that same clinic almost killed him, so he sicced his father on Prine to persuade him to change his plans. It was the first time Prine had spoken to Sam since they had worked together in 1979. "It took Sam an hour on the phone to convince me," Prine told Roddy Campbell in a 2005 interview for *Penguin Eggs* magazine. "Finally he just told me if I didn't he'd come to Nashville and kick my ass every inch of the way. And it's hard to say no to Sam Phillips. Sam had a religious fervor to everything he talked about, whether it was women, music, or religion, it still sounded religious. And when he told me he was going to do that if I didn't go see this doctor, I said, 'Mr. Phillips, I will.' And I went, and as soon as I met this doctor I knew he was the right guy." Prine scheduled an appointment at the University of Texas M. D. Anderson Cancer Center and headed south. "They practically have a welcoming committee to greet me," he told Kot. "It took a load off my shoulders, because the scary part is not knowing who the doctor is going to be, what the treatment is going to be. So I can thank Sam Phillips for stepping in."

His medical team recommended surgery to remove the lump, followed by about six weeks of radiation treatments. Which raised the concern of how the treatment might affect Prine's singing voice—or so his doctors thought. "I said, 'Have you guys heard me sing before?'" Prine told Kot with a laugh. "The radiation guy wanted to put some lead shields in front of my vocal cords to protect them during the treatments, and I told him I wish he could go in there and sweep the whole area. Why not just start over?" The treatments would cost a great deal of money, but Prine now had a wife, children, and "a great little band" to consider, so he forged ahead.

Oh Boy continued to expand its roster in the nineties, releasing records by the Bis-Quits, Heather Eatman, R. B. Morris, and Donnie Fritts. For Prine's next record, he revisited an idea for a "pet project" he had been kicking around since the eighties, "something I've talked about more than I did the last fifteen years," he told John Hiatt. "In fact, I cornered some people—I'd end up saying, 'I've got this great idea for a record with all cheating songs, with about ten different women singing with me.' People would usually go, 'That sounds good,' then they'd change the subject.'" But the producer of *Aimless Love* and *German Afternoons*, Jim Rooney, actively encouraged him: "He said, 'You know that sounds like a good idea.' That's all it takes—just a little encouragement. He said, 'If you want to do it, I'll be glad to do it with you.' Jim got me to sit down and write a list of the girls I wanted to sing with and a list of the songs I wanted to do."

Rooney had shepherded two duet albums for Nanci Griffith, both of which Prine sang on. On the most recent, 1998's *Other Voices, Too (A Trip Back to Bountiful)*, Prine had teamed up with Griffith on a cover of "The Streets of Baltimore," a 1966 song by Tompall Glaser and Harlan Howard covered by many artists, but probably best known to rock fans from versions Gram Parsons recorded both with the Flying Burrito Brothers and on his own. Where Griffith concentrated on standards such as "Who Knows Where the Time Goes?" and "Hard Times (Come Again No More)," Prine had something kinkier in mind—and no shortage of material. Duets and cheating songs had been Nashville's bread and butter for decades.

"At first my idea was to record all cheatin' songs, but the problem with that was that it started becoming a contest, like which was the best cheatin' song?" he told Bob Edwards in a 1999 interview for NPR's *Morning Edition*. "Should I do 'A Cheatin' Situation' or 'Lovin' on Backstreets and Livin' on Main,' or what should I do?" His solution would give the collection of songs an operatic sweep: "I started figurin', well, you can't have cheatin' if they didn't get together and meet in the first place. And then again, you'd have to have a breakup song after they found out they'd been cheatin' on each other, and after they break up you'd have to have a song about gossip—about everybody in town talkin' about the whole thing. So it came down to meetin', cheatin', and retreatin'.'"

Then there was the issue of securing duet partners. "I made a list of my favorite girl country singers, and I actually expected about two out of every three to tell me that they were going to China for two years, or say, 'That's a nice idea, John, I'll get back to you,'" he told Edwards. "But everybody that I asked—the first nine off the list—said, 'Yeah, when do you want me, and what song are you gonna send me?' I was pretty bowled over. But I figured if I could get those nine girls I'd have the record I was lookin' for." The final lineup was a mix of traditional and outsider country and folk artists, old school and new school. Melba Montgomery, who preceded Tammy Wynette in the early sixties as George Jones's duet partner, would team up with Prine on her own "We Must Have Been out of Our Minds." Connie Smith, another big country star from the sixties, would sing two duets, one of which was Don Everly's gorgeous "So Sad (to Watch Good Love Go Bad)." Emmylou Harris, who had been pushing country music boundaries since singing with Parsons in the early seventies, would join Prine on a Cowboy Jack Clement song, "I Know One." Other foils for Prine: alt-country pioneer Lucinda Williams; Dolores Keane, founder of the traditional Irish band De Dannan; and Patty Loveless and Trisha Yearwood, two of the biggest country stars of the nineties. Not to mention Iris DeMent, the Arkansas-born, Los Angeles–bred daughter of Pentecostal parents, youngest of fourteen children—and one of the few singers around who could out-drawl Prine.

Around the same time Prine and Rooney were making plans to record the duets album, Hollywood came calling again. This time it came in the form of Billy Bob Thornton, an Arkansas native like DeMent who had earned his reputation by writing, directing, and starring in the 1996 indie hit *Sling Blade*. A mutual friend introduced Prine to Thornton. "We became phone pals for about six months, and he asked me to come out to L.A. and just knock around with him," Prine told Hiatt. ". . . me and him went to a Chinese restaurant with Andy Griffith." The singer called Griffith "the consummate American" in a 2005 interview with Richard Harrington of the *Washington Post*. "Like if Abraham Lincoln was alive and I saw him on TV, he'd be Andy Griffith. You know, Will Rogers or the character Andy Griffith plays on 'Mayberry' [*sic*] always appealed to me from the time I could crawl—the folksy sort." (*The Andy Griffith Show*, which aired through most of the sixties, was set in the fictional North Carolina town of Mayberry, and the show's post-Griffith sequel was called *Mayberry RFD*.) Having dinner with Griffith "was the pinnacle of my career," Prine told Harrington. Or so he thought. Thornton didn't just take Prine to dinner with Griffith—he asked Prine to star in a movie with him and write a song to play behind the end credits. The song Prine ended up writing, "In Spite of Ourselves," was loosely based on the characters played by Thornton (Claude) and the movie's female lead, Laura Dern (Ruby). "I said, 'When you write a song about a movie, are you supposed to talk about 'em, or not talk about 'em?'" Prine told the *Sessions at West 54th* audience. "Because sometimes I go to movies and a song comes on, and it's like your alarm radio went off in your hotel room. 'What the heck's that song doing in here?' So Billy Bob just said, 'Mmmph.'"

"In Spite of Ourselves," as sung with DeMent, would become the title track of the duets album, which was recorded primarily at Jack's Tracks in Nashville. Prine used the movie characters as inspiration, but didn't get too literal. "They're obviously in love, and they argue all the time," he told Hiatt. "They're real jealous of each other. I just kinda took off from there, had these people saying stuff that doesn't sound very complimentary about each other, but they mean it in a nice way." The song was an instant classic, one of Prine's very best, with the singers accompanied only by Prine's buoyant Travis picking. But it took some doing convincing DeMent to accompany him. Among the couplets he wrote for the female character were "He's got more balls than a big brass monkey / He's a whacked-out weirdo and a lovebug junkie" and "He ain't got laid in a month of Sundays / I caught him once and he was sniffin' my undies."

"I called Iris," Prine told Campbell. "I said, 'Iris, I've got a song with some questionable material in it. I really believe strongly that you are the person to sing it. Would you at least listen to it a couple of times and then call and let me know?'" He didn't hear back from her for two weeks. "So finally I call her," Prine said. "I said, 'What's it going to be?' She said, 'Not while my mother's still living,' and we both start laughing." DeMent recorded it anyway, along with three other songs: Bobby Braddock's lighthearted working-class anthem "(We're Not) The Jet Set," originally recorded by Jones and Wynette in 1974; Felice Bryant's "We Could"; and an obscure country song by Onie Wheeler called "Let's Invite Them Over," with lyrics that may be even more perverse than the ones Prine wrote for "In Spite of Ourselves." "Melba Montgomery told me the guy that wrote that song, 'Let's Invite Them Over Again'—she thinks it was the only song the guy ever wrote," Prine told Meg Griffin.

"It's about wife-swappin'. It was a Top 20 hit in the mid- to early sixties. They're in love with their next-door neighbors; they're not in love with each other." Covering the song was Rooney's idea: "Jim more or less just said, 'It's your idea, whatever you want to do—but there's one song that I insist you and Iris sing.' And I said, 'What's that?' And he said, 'Let's Invite Them Over Again.' And I had forgotten about the song. I said, 'You're right—that oughtta be on this collection.'"

Prine's cancer treatment disrupted work on the album. "I found out some people don't like to say the word 'cancer,'" Prine told music journalist and musician Peter Cooper in a 2005 interview for the *Nashville Tennessean*. "One person said, 'How's your, uh, situation?' I said, 'Oh, it's got cancer, too.'" In January 1998 he went under the knife in Houston. "The doctors removed a small tumor, taking a portion of my neck with it," Prine wrote in an April 1999 letter to his fans. "I had six weeks of radiation therapy following the surgery." While recuperating, he told Edwards, "I put everything on the shelf. I just took it easy. I stayed around the house, read Archie comics, and trimmed my toenails and stuff like that." In the letter to his fans, Prine thanked everyone for allowing him the space to deal with the issue under the radar. "Until now I had decided to remain private about this matter so my family and I could concentrate on me getting better. Now I want to make a public statement to let you all know what has been happening." Prine told fans he was "looking forward to getting back on the road and singing my songs. Hopefully my neck is looking forward to its job of holding my head up above my shoulders."

Work resumed on *In Spite of Ourselves* that spring. There are brief moments where it was clear Prine's voice had changed in the wake of his cancer treatment, moments where it sounded harsher, more gravelly. But they hardly leapt out of the speakers—by and large, Prine and Rooney managed a seamless transition between the vocals recorded before and after his medical procedures. Prine's duets with Dolores Keane, on Moe Bandy's "It's a Cheating Situation" and Kieran Kane's "In a Town This Size," were among the post-op songs. "Dolores's voice had a beautiful smoky, slightly world-weary quality, which worked great with John's lower, grittier, new voice," Rooney wrote.

Keane wasn't the only singer on the album with Irish roots: On one of the more-recent-vintage songs, "'Til a Tear Becomes a Rose" (written by Sharon Vaughn and Bill Rice, and a hit duet for Keith Whitley and Lorrie Morgan in 1990), Prine teamed up with none other than his wife, Fiona. Her warm, heartfelt delivery stood up among stiff competition. "I knew that this was the capstone to all that had gone on in John and Fiona's life for the last four years," Rooney wrote. "They'd had the great joy of getting married and having Jack and Tommy and then having to deal with John's diagnosis and treatment of cancer. They'd come through it and were stronger than ever." Of course, all the romantic turmoil on the album couldn't go down without someone getting a "Dear John" breakup letter. Prine closed the set without a duet partner, whooping it up all by his lonesome on an old country song recorded by Hank Williams, "Dear John (I Sent Your Saddle Home)." Instrumentally, the spare production on *In Spite of Ourselves* never strayed from a traditional country sound, as befit its material. Built around acoustic guitar, mandolin, pedal steel, and honky-tonk piano, the album was Prine's most traditional country set since *German Afternoons*.

Most of the group formerly known as the Lost Dogs Band backed Prine and his duet partners, accompanied by such repeat Prine sidemen as Sam Bush and Glen D. Hardin. A couple of venerable studio musicians played pedal steel: Dan Dugmore, veteran of countless L.A. sessions before moving to Nashville, and legendary country pedal-steel player Buddy Emmons. They weren't merely recording old songs—Prine's coproducer ran the sessions in old-school Nashville assembly line fashion. "Rooney, God bless him, he stood there and, after we did two takes of a song, he'd go, 'That's it,'" Prine told Bill Friskics-Warren in a 1999 interview for the *Nashville Scene*. "Everybody, even the musicians, would look at him funny. But he'd be like, 'What else are you gonna do to this?'" It was not the first time Emmons had played on a studio recording of "We Must Have Been out of Our Minds." "I knew Buddy from his playing with the Everlys," Prine said. "But I didn't know that he had played on Melba and George's original. Melba walked in and she sees Buddy Emmons and turns around and says to me, 'You know, Buddy was there when George and I cut this.' So the band kicks in, 1-2-3-4, and I'm thinking, 'I'm singing George Jones's part with George Jones's duet partner and the steel player from the session. What am I doing here?'" In the liner notes Rooney wrote about growing up in Massachusetts listening to the *Louisiana Hayride* and the *WWVA Jamboree* out of Wheeling, West Virginia: "The country music I love speaks to me about real people living real lives. It speaks with a simple sympathy and understanding, often with a bit of humor. This is where John Prine comes from. It is the source of his strength as a writer and a performer."

Reviewers gave the album the usual boost. Robert Christgau, never free and loose with his A ratings, gave Prine his fifth. (After having relegated *Live on Tour* to "honorable mention" status.) "After two years of cancer treatments . . . the cheating songs and Nashville novelties on this duet album are a perfect way for Prine to keep his hand in until his muse feels as glad to be alive as he does," Christgau wrote. Longtime Prine fan Greg Kot reviewed the album for *Rolling Stone*, giving it three and a half stars: "Though his sidekicks are more technically gifted, Prine sounds like he knows the people in these songs personally: As he celebrates wife-swapping on Onie Wheeler's 'Let's Invite Them Over' and white-trash romance on Bobby Braddock's '(We're Not) The Jet Set,' he fairly twinkles with mischief."

DeMent explained that personal connection to the characters in the songs. "There's something about hearing a man and a woman singing together, and singing about such intimate stuff," she told Friskics-Warren after the album's release. "You feel like you're getting inside of somebody's private lives a bit." As strong as the album was, it would not prove to be a big hit: Its time in the Top 200 amounted to a one-week blip at No. 197, though the record spent thirty-two weeks on *Billboard*'s country charts. Fortunately, Prine didn't need a big hit to pay for his cancer treatments: George Strait got one for him. In 1998, the Texas-born Strait—one of the biggest country stars of the eighties and nineties—recorded a version of "I Just Want to Dance with You," the Prine-Cook song from *German Afternoons*. It hit No. 1 on the country charts, and Prine's songwriting royalties took care of his hospital bills.

"For a while there I just couldn't sing at all because I just didn't have any energy," Prine said in an interview for a 2005 *Austin City Limits* appearance. But he emerged from his two-year cancer ordeal with a new lease on life. "To me, it was like the army, in a way," he told Ted Kooser.

"It was something I hated when I was going through it, but I wouldn't want to have missed it for the world. It really was an experience that taught me a few lessons that I needed to be taught." Fiona stood beside him every step of the way, he said: "My wife and I went through it totally together." Once he had the energy to sing and play again, the first thing he had to do was relearn his songs. "It takes you a while to get back on your feet," Prine told the *Austin City Limits* camera. "And once I did, I couldn't sing the songs—especially the old ones—I couldn't sing 'em where I'd always sang 'em. I could just pick up a guitar and I knew right where to go to, where I thought I should go to to sing 'em, and I couldn't get up there anymore. I just figured out my voice had dropped. So I changed the key on everything, and when I did, a lot of the old songs became brand-new for me. It was really interesting to me. It was like I was hearin' 'em for the first time, almost."

He decided to rerecord a batch of his old songs in order to give his voice a trial run—and "because I have always wanted to be popular in Germany," Prine wrote in the liner notes for his next album, released in 2000. Oh Boy had distribution problems in Europe and signed a deal with a German label. "The guy said Germans were just starting to get interested in American roots music and if he had any collection of my old, classic songs, it would do well," Prine told Alex Rawls in a 2002 interview for *Offbeat*. Rerecording the songs would also allow Prine and his label to own master recordings of some of his best songs, since Atlantic and Asylum owned the original tapes for everything recorded through 1980. With Rooney helping produce again, Prine and many of the musicians from the *In Spite of Ourselves* sessions went to the Cowboy Arms Hotel and Recording Spa for a whirlwind three-day session in April 2000. "I went into the studio with my band and we laid them down the way we do them live," Prine said. "We didn't have to have any talks about arrangements. They sounded better when I recorded them than I thought they would." They cut versions of many of his best early songs ("Angel from Montgomery," "Sam Stone," "Blue Umbrella"), along with a select few from more recent times, such as "Fish and Whistle" and "Storm Windows." They even recut one song from the Oh Boy era, "People Puttin' People Down," giving it more of an organ-drenched rock feel than the *Aimless Love* original.

Fans may love the recordings from the beginning of his career, but they held no special place in Prine's heart. "I was still trying to find my voice then," Prine told Rawls. "I don't want to complain, but I started in this business before I meant to. It was just a hobby—songwriting—and I didn't sing for anybody. . . . I don't feel in retrospect like I was ready to go into a studio and make records. I would rather have just kept on writing and had a whole lot of material." Regarding *John Prine*, he says, "I can hear how nervous I was when I listen to that record and it makes me uncomfortable to hear my voice on it." He liked the versions on *Souvenirs* so much he decided it merited release on this side of the pond, as well. "We recorded the album for over there, but when we got done recording it, it sounded pretty good so we went ahead and put it out over here," Prine said.

The nondescript *Souvenirs* album cover featured a somewhat misleading, hand-tinted photo of a much younger Prine—appropriate to the era when the singer wrote most of the songs, but not the age when he recorded the current versions. The album didn't make much of a splash with fans or critics. "Songs like 'Hello in There' and 'Angel from Montgomery,' which both deal with aging, now fit even more naturally with his vocals," Michael Berick wrote in a review for *Country Standard Time*. "Perhaps it's the knowledge that Prine recently survived a cancer scare, but these new renditions also seem to exude more wistful and poignant qualities. Many tracks (such as 'Storm Windows') project an increased emotional depth, while 'Fish and Whistle' now lacks its original playfulness."

In February 2000 Prine returned home to play a benefit concert at his old high school, Proviso East, for the Maywood Fine Arts Association. The sellout show raised about forty thousand dollars. Brother Dave rejoined Tyler Wilson for a National Recovery Act reunion to open the concert. Organizers presented Prine with a blue glass vase inscribed "The First Ever Really Cool Guy from Proviso East 1964."

The singer reduced his backing band to a three-piece for a European tour. "A lot of the gigs over there we were playing for chump change," he told Peter Cooper in a 2010 interview for the *Tennessean*. ". . . I liked the way it sounded with just one guitar, a bass, and my all-around man, Phil Parlapiano, who played piano, organ, squeezebox, and mandolin."

When Parlapiano left for an extended jazz gig, the group was down to Dave Jacques on bass and Jason Wilber on guitar. With Parlapiano out, Prine said, "our band sound with Jason and Dave didn't get smaller, it got bigger. We didn't know why. But for some reason less is more." It also costs the man with his name on the marquee less to pay two backing musicians than it does to pay five or six, of course.

Around the turn of the twenty-first century the trio traveled to New York to perform on *Sessions at West 54th*, a music series syndicated on public television (the singer having survived the Y2K scare without serious incident). Indiana-born rocker John Hiatt hosted the show and taped interview clips with Prine. "John Prine has been known as a shrewd reporter of the human condition for almost thirty years," Hiatt said in his introduction. "His straightforward, romantic, and often humorous songs tell the stories of men and women getting by, getting lost, getting together, and falling apart." Prine dressed like a negative image of Colonel Sanders for the appearance, wearing a black suit and a Kentucky bow tie, his longish gray mullet curling behind his ears and spiked up on top into a near faux-hawk.

The singer and his band performed sparkling versions of songs from throughout Prine's career for an intimate crowd—"Souvenirs," "All the Best," "Sam Stone," and "Lake Marie." Iris DeMent joined them for a series of songs from *In Spite of Ourselves*, and the energy level skyrocketed. "Since most of these songs were hits, they're only about a minute and forty-five seconds long, you know?" Prine told the crowd. "So I had to record about half a million of 'em in order to make a record out of it." Before singing the title song, Prine told the audience about writing it for the Billy Bob Thornton movie—which had yet to be released. "Andy Griffith is our dad," Prine said. "That makes me like Opie's stepbrother." During an interview segment, Hiatt talked about seeing Prine in Nashville at the beginning of his career three decades earlier: "I remember you coming to the Exit/In in, like, '71, I think it was—Kris Kristofferson in the audience. I think Arif Mardin or one of the Atlantic bigwigs was along with you. It was sort of like [whispering], 'This is the new Dylan!'" Oh Boy released a DVD of the *Sessions at West 54th* performance on 11 September 2001—the day of the terrorist attacks that destroyed the World Trade Center.

Verna "Cotton" Hamm Prine died 22 September 2002 at age eighty-two, almost ten years after she moved to Nashville. Five months later, Howie Epstein died at age forty-seven of a suspected drug overdose. He and Carlene Carter had been arrested in a stolen car and charged with heroin possession two years earlier.

The Oh Boy roster remained modest through the new century's first decade. Todd Snider signed to the label after leaving MCA, releasing his first Oh Boy album, *Happy to Be Here*, in 2000. That same year Oh Boy started an "Oh Boy Classics" series, releasing collections by Roger Miller, Willie Nelson, Merle Haggard, and others. In 2003 the label released live albums by a couple of veteran singer-songwriters, Janis Ian and Kris Kristofferson—Prine returning an old favor by signing the singer who had given him his big break more than thirty years before. In 2003 Oh Boy VP Dan Einstein quit the music business after twenty-two years with Prine and Bunetta to open a Nashville bakery, Sweet 16th, with his wife, Ellen—whom he had met years before in L.A. in a Chinese-food cooking class. "My wife had a baking business independently, and she did catering and food styling," Einstein told Nashville's *City Paper* in 2007. "It got to the point where it was only going to grow so far without a storefront. We needed to make a conscious decision to make it a full-fledged business or move on and do something else. . . . I had always said that when the music business stops being fun, I am getting out and it was a time for me to go. This was a good opportunity to take a break and get away from it."

There was no danger of Prine quitting the music business for Hollywood. The Billy Bob Thornton movie, *Daddy and Them*, never made it to the big screen, but gradually trickled out for public consumption via cable network screenings and a DVD release. "It went straight to Blockbuster," Prine told a crowd in a song introduction on his 2010 live album *In Person & On Stage*. As in *Falling from Grace*, another small-town comedy-drama about a dysfunctional family, he played a quiet, hard-drinking secondary character, Alvin. He was the brother of Claude, Thornton's character, and usually had his head buried in a book. But Prine got considerably more screen time and dialogue in his second movie. "I stay nervous just about all the time," Alvin told Claude early on, as the family converged to deal with their Uncle Hazel (Jim Varney) getting arrested on an attempted-murder charge. Andy Griffith played the family patriarch, and he was surrounded by a talented cast that also featured Jamie Lee Curtis, Ben Affleck, and veteran British character actor Brenda Blethyn. In one of Prine's most memorable scenes, he sat on the front porch of the family home, hearing confession from Uncle Hazel's accuser (Tommy Christian, played by Walton Goggins) as he came out of the closet. Prine said very little in the scene, but his reactions and body language spoke volumes. When Tommy put his hand on Alvin's leg, Prine crossed his leg away from Tommy and discreetly leaned back. "I love Prine's face in this," Thornton said in the DVD special commentary. "He's tryin' to be polite, but he just don't understand this guy." One of the movie's producers added: "John is not normally an actor, but he's doing a really fine job of just reacting here, and just acting without words."

Prine has written many songs about missed personal connections, from "Donald and Lydia" to "Everybody Wants to Feel Like You." Toward the end of the movie, the previously reticent Alvin became the communicator, attempting to knit together the family's frayed connections, bursting through closed doors to explain feelings and motivations he thought others had failed to grasp. "Here's where Prine's character starts to show what he knows," Thornton said. "Because he's been the observer the whole time—doesn't say much, sits in the corner, reads his book. He's based on an uncle of mine who used to read books. The rest of the family would say, 'He's always got his nose stuck in a book,' like that was a bad thing." In the scene where Alvin confronted Claude about his relationship to Ruby (Laura Dern), Claude was sitting on the toilet, reading an issue of *Men's Health* magazine.

> *Claude:* Brothers oughten to see each other on the shitter.
>   I don't even let Ruby see me take a shit.
> *Alvin:* Maybe you ought to sometime.

In the DVD extras, Thornton also talked about a scene where Prine kept flubbing his lines. "John, for some reason, couldn't say 'chlamydia.' It was some kinda mental block he had—he couldn't say the word. And I told him every damn take, I said, 'It's "kluh-MID-ee-uh," John.' And every time he said 'chime-uh-dee-uh.'" The extras featured "The Return of Carl," a just-for-fun outtake in which Alvin had an exceedingly random conversation about muffins and psychology with Thornton's intellectually disabled, French fried–potato–loving character from *Sling Blade*. After the scene ended, Prine could barely contain his glee, laughing and slapping his leg repeatedly with a flyswatter before bursting into applause. Thornton, for his part, was delighted with Prine's performance in *Daddy and Them*: "John Prine was wonderful in this movie. I think he steals the movie. . . . John had just had an operation not too long before this movie was shot, on his throat—he had throat cancer, which he beat, God bless him. And he had kind of a messed-up throat at the time. And Jim Varney, who passed away a couple of years later, had found out that he had cancer before we started shooting. The whole time he was making the movie, he knew that he was going to have an operation right when he left there. So it's weird to look at John and Jim both in the same shape, kind of, when we were making the movie."

CHAPTER 14

Your Flag Decal Still Won't
Get You into Heaven

▼

The Prine family traveled to Ireland every summer, giving the boys plenty of face time with their "cousins, aunts and uncles, and grandma" across the Atlantic, the singer told an *Austin City Limits* crowd in 2005. Eventually they bought a cottage in a picturesque village on the west coast of Ireland near Galway. Prine became a regular at a local pub. "Most of my friends are musicians," he told Roddy Campbell. "We'll take our guitars and go down to Green's and give them a few tunes. It's a great little pub. But if you show up without your guitar, and into serious drinking, nobody bothers you."

In 2005 a surreal Cowboy Jack Clement documentary called *Shakespeare Was a Big George Jones Fan* surfaced. It contained footage of Prine dating back to the singer's beloved sessions with Clement in 1977—and the following conversation:

Clement: I remember that song "How Lucky Can One Man Get." What was that—the summer of '77?
Prine: That was the summer of '77. We were working on two records at once.
Clement: Yeah, mine and yours.
Prine: Yeah.
Clement: We sorta fiddled away the whole summer.
Prine: Yeah, we did.

Clement: Never finished a record.
Prine: Day after day.
Clement: Mmm-hmm.

Nearly ten years after the release of *Lost Dogs and Mixed Blessings*, Prine was badly overdue for an album of new, original songs. Inspiration didn't strike nearly as frequently as it once had. Decades had passed since he had been able to throw together a classic song while driving to a gig. "I'd write songs in batches of two or, at the most, three, and then it would be six to eight months before the next one would come along," he told Derk Richardson in a 2006 interview for *Acoustic Guitar*. "It was a very slow process. I'm not a disciplined writer and I'm prone to being lazy, so I never write all that fast. I tried to get this record going when I had about four songs. Then I had to wait until the next batch of songs came." Family responsibilities also changed his work habits. "I had to set time limits on myself," Prine said. "Like I had to say, 'Next Tuesday I'm going to write a song; I need it for this collection.' I would never do that before—I would just wait, and if a song came along at three or four in the morning, I would stay up and write it and sleep all day. But it's totally different with kids. Against my better wishes, I had to discipline myself to get up with the kids at six in the morning, and by ten at night you're tired like the rest of the world." He worked on his next album for most of the first decade of the twenty-first century. Gary Paczosa, who had previously engineered records by Alison Krauss and Union Station, Dolly Parton, Nickel Creek, and Gillian Welch, produced the album with Prine. They recorded at several studios around Nashville, including one in Germantown that Prine had set up with engineer Dave Ferguson, who began his career as an engineer for Cowboy Jack Clement—and portrayed Clement in the 1989 Jerry Lee Lewis biopic *Great Balls of Fire!* "I got my own studio in an old meat-packing plant on the Cumberland River outside of Nashville," Prine told Meg Griffin. "We call it the Butcher Shoppe."

Prine's road band, Jacques and Wilber, formed the core of his studio band. They were joined by veterans of previous Prine sessions such as multi-instrumentalists Phil Parlapiano and Pat McLaughlin, pedal steel player Dan Dugmore, drummer Paul Griffith, and fiddler Shawn Camp. Dobro player extraordinaire Jerry Douglas showed up with his Weissenborn guitar for one song, while Prine continued his tradition of attracting stellar female vocalists to sing harmonies. This time around it was country star Krauss and Mindy Smith, a singer-songwriter who hadn't even been born when Prine's first album came out. Smith sang on three songs, at times sounding eerily reminiscent of Rachel Peer-Prine. Prine also collaborated with other songwriters to a degree not seen since *The Missing Years*, cowriting one song apiece with Donnie Fritts and Keith Sykes, two with Roger Cook, and three with McLaughlin. "Pat is very much like me as far as subject matter," Prine told Richardson. "Anything that comes through the room, he'll grab it and write it. And he loves the sounds of words like I do, so sometimes he'll write a line that doesn't particularly make a lot of sense, but if it sounds good, we'll follow that star and see where it goes." As for Cook, Prine said they wrote more straightforward songs together when they weren't fishing or shooting snooker: "We argue about everything under the sun. Sometimes that's what a good song is—a good argument. When you're writing with Roger, anybody's gotta be able to sing the song; it's not just for you."

A month before the album appeared, in March 2005, Mr. Prine went to Washington. U.S. poet laureate Ted Kooser—a fellow Midwesterner, born in Iowa in 1939—honored the singer by asking him to appear with him at the Library of Congress. Kooser had been a fan since Prine's first album came out: "I played it as soon as I got home, and knew at once that here was a truly original writer, unequaled, and a genuine poet of the American people." He likened Prine's songs to Raymond Carver's short stories: "John Prine has taken ordinary people and made monuments of them, as I see it, treating them with great respect and love." Prine, dressed in black and wearing cowboy boots, his hair poofing up from a Don King widow's peak, ambled onto the Coolidge Auditorium stage with a big grin on his face and started the evening by singing "Fish and Whistle." Over the next hour and a half he played several of his best-loved songs and talked with Kooser about his early years, songwriting, his bout with cancer, and his family, asking Fiona, Jody, Jack, and Tommy to stand up and be recognized. He also talked to Kooser about his favorite songwriters, naming Dylan, Van Morrison, Kristofferson, and Gordon Lightfoot: "I been listening to a lot of Gordon Lightfoot lately. I always knew Gordon Lightfoot was a really great songwriter, but his stuff sounds better and better and better all the time. It's just really so good; some of it to me sounds like that's what should be in a dictionary next to a really good contemporary folk song, is a Gordon Lightfoot song."

Kooser told Prine he was diagnosed with "the exact same kind of cancer" about six months after the singer. Prine detailed his cancer treatment to Richard Harrington in a 2005 *Washington Post* feature. "Thirty years of smoking a pack a day obviously hadn't helped," Harrington wrote. "Giving up that habit affected Prine's voice as much as surgery and radiation. His voice coarsened a bit and dropped an octave, closer to his conversational level. The surgery involved removing a small portion of Prine's neck and refashioning his bite, and he's put on some weight. With his brushy mustache, the 58-year-old Prine looks like a friendly Joseph Stalin—except for standup shocks of hair that may be the most electric thing about him." A few weeks after the Library of Congress event, Kooser won the Pulitzer Prize for poetry.

Prine's new album, *Fair and Square*, appeared in April. The record's front cover photo showed the singer from the rear, dressed in black, carrying his guitar case down a rural lane in Ireland. He faced the camera on the back cover, framed by the road blurring off into the distance, his once-black hair now completely gray and white. Prine felt pressure to live up to the sound he and Epstein achieved together in the nineties. "He got such a big sound on me on *The Missing Years* and *Lost Dogs*," Prine told Jeremy Tepper. "So I was real careful trying to get a good sound on this, and I think we did it." In the liner notes he offered a dedication to Verna, whose death inspired "The Moon Is Down":

The stars in the skies
Fell out of her eyes
They shattered when they hit the ground
And now the moon is down

Prine thanked Bunetta "for thirty-five years of advice, direction, and friendship" and "for bringing Gary Paczosa and me together." He also thanked Paczosa "for bringing all this music alive" and "Fiona for putting up with me all these years." Now pushing sixty, Prine sounded energetic, gruff, lighthearted—and settled. The singer told Tepper it's "a really good-sounding, comfortable record." It was an unfailingly pleasant and well-crafted album that sounded every bit as domesticated as Prine's family lifestyle, with song titles such as "Glory of True Love," "My Darlin' Hometown," and "She Is My Everything." On that last one, an organ-soaked mid-tempo rocker, Prine offered a puppy-dog tribute to Fiona with a few clever lines: "I'd like to drive a Cadillac / The color of her long black hair." The sprightly Cook collaboration and album opener "Glory of True Love" worked better, though Prine's post-cancer vocals sometimes get a little slurred:

You can climb the highest mountain
Touch the moon and stars above
But Old Faithful's just a fountain
Compared to the glory of true love

"My Darlin' Hometown," another song written with Cook, was a slow waltz that paid tribute not to Maywood, but to an Irish town "far away over the sea." (Somewhere along the way the title got changed from "My Darlin's Hometown.") The McLaughlin collaboration "Crazy as a Loon" contained a series of vignettes that wouldn't have sounded out of place on *Bruised Orange*. The song also delved into the kind of character-defining detail largely absent elsewhere on the record: "Back before I was a movie star / Straight off of the farm / I had a picture of another man's wife / Tattooed on my arm." The vague description of sex in "Long Monday" ("We made love / In every way love can be made") paled in comparison to the vivid "Everybody Wants to Feel Like You" from *The Missing Years*: "I used to love you so hard in the morning / I'd make you stutter and roll your eyes."

Fair and Square also contained a couple of covers. The rocking closer (not counting bonus tracks), "Bear Creek Blues," was the latest in a long line of Carter Family songs Prine had recorded over the years, dating back to the title track of his second album. He took a circuitous route to find "Clay Pigeons," a lovely, wistful ballad sung from the point of view of a drifter in search of solid ground. Prine was struck by a Merle Haggard song called "If I Could Only Fly" and started looking for its author. Turned out Prine's friend Elizabeth Kemp used to sing backup for the songwriter, Blaze Foley, and she got Prine a bootleg recording of some of his material. "I wanted to hear his version of 'If I Could Only Fly' after I heard Merle sing it," Prine told Tepper. "So I listened to it, and right after, Blaze introduces this song 'Clay Pigeons.' And I thought, 'Man, this sounds like I wrote it! Where was I when that song came around?' It was the fingerpicking on it—I thought, 'Nobody fingerpicks that bad— it sounds like me!' It wasn't me—it was Blaze. And I thought, 'I gotta learn that song,' because I couldn't get it out of my head." Born Michael David Fuller in Arkansas in 1949, he grew up in Texas and performed under the stage name Blaze Foley—though his Austin friends in the seventies knew him as Dep'ty Dawg, Prine's old drinking buddy. "I never knew that I knew Blaze," Prine said. A couple of great songwriters paid tribute in song to Foley, who was shot and killed in 1989: Lucinda Williams with "Drunken Angel" and Townes Van Zandt with "Blaze's Blues." Foley's friends told Prine "that Blaze was just a big old bear of a guy with a big soft heart, and you can hear that on this song," he told Tepper. "He was fairly itinerant—he was homeless. They said on those dumpsters where it says BFI—in Austin it meant 'Blaze Foley inside.'"

The most striking song on *Fair and Square* was also its most controversial. On "Some Humans Ain't Human," Prine strayed far from the album's overarching theme of domestic bliss to write his first antiwar song in decades. He gave the song a doom-and-gloom feel by inverting the I–IV–V song structure, starting on the V chord as he slowly Travis-picked in G with a capo on the fifth fret that transposed the song to C. The gloomy feel was matched by the lyrics, a meditation on bad intentions. President George W. Bush launched an invasion of Iraq in 2003, accusing Iraqi president Saddam Hussein of maintaining weapons of mass destruction and supporting al-Qaeda, the terrorist organization behind the September attacks—neither charge turning out to be true. Prine took direct aim at Bush, not mincing words:

> When you're feeling really good
> There's always a pigeon
> That'll come shit on your hood
> Or you're feeling your freedom
> And the world's off your back
> Some cowboy from Texas
> Starts his own war in Iraq

In concert, Prine would sometimes substitute "hotshot" or "asshole" for "cowboy." He didn't anticipate the backlash he got from some fans. "Surprisingly, some people have written letters or walked out on shows and asked for their money back or given their T-shirt back," he told Richardson. "They usually preface it by saying they've been fans for years, and I would be thinking, 'If they've been listening all these years to "Sam Stone" and "Your Flag Decal Won't Get You into Heaven Anymore," I can't see how they would be aghast because I tore George Bush apart.'"

Critics greeted *Fair and Square* warmly if not effusively. David Wild gave the album the usual three and a half stars in *Rolling Stone*, labeling it "an excellent set of songs full of rootsy warmth and unpretentious wit." Robert Christgau gave it only an honorable mention in his *Village Voice* column, but awarded it three out of four stars in a *Blender* review, asserting that "She Is My Everything" and "Some Humans Ain't Human" rank with "Hello in There" and "Lake Marie" in the Prine pantheon: "While Prine's fans will admire how smoothly he downshifts from contentment to melancholy and back up again, the unconverted will wish he'd stop relaxing into indirection and Sunday drives down well-traveled roads."

By 2005 *Austin City Limits* had begun to stray from its country/ Americana roots after more than thirty years on the air, showcasing alternative rock acts such as the Flaming Lips, the Pixies, and Spoon. But the show still made room for Prine in a rare eighth appearance. Jacques and Wilber, his usual road band, were supplemented by Pat McLaughlin on guitar and mandolin. Prine, who seemed to have adopted the Kentucky colonel look as his uniform for the AARP years, stuck to songs from his new album, splitting the hour with Amos Lee, a singer-songwriter from Philadelphia nearly half his age. *Fair and Square* earned Prine yet another Grammy nomination, once again for Best Contemporary Folk Album. Sales-wise, the album was Prine's biggest hit since *The Missing Years*, cracking the Billboard Hot 100 for the first time since *Common Sense* thirty years before, peaking at No. 55 during a nine-week stay in the Top 200. The album topped the Americana radio charts for thirteen weeks, earning Prine the Artist of the Year award from the Americana Music Association. In early 2006 he won his second Grammy, besting Ry Cooder, Rodney Crowell, Nickel Creek, and Bruce Springsteen.

Acoustic Guitar ran an extended interview with Prine in early 2006, going into detail about his instruments (among many other topics). For fingerpicking Prine used a 1968 Martin D-28, while for rhythm work he played two Gibson J-200s, "one tuned down a whole step." At home he wrote songs on a 1993 Guild JF-100, "with Indian rosewood back and sides and Sitka spruce top." He strung his guitars with Martin phosphor-bronze mediums and amplified his Martin guitar with a Dean Markley ProMag soundhole pickup of indeterminate age.

On tour for *Fair and Square*, Prine explained a new limp by telling audiences he had recently undergone hip-replacement surgery. Over the previous decade he had also licked cancer and stopped smoking, leaving alcohol consumption the last major hurdle to improving his health as Prine approached sixty. (Well, that combined with his lifelong love of Orange Crush soda and aversion to vegetables, perhaps. A lengthy 2005 profile in *No Depression* magazine explained how Prine tracked meat loaf specials around Nashville, moving from diner to diner on different days of the week in *Endless Summer* fashion.) A 2005 *Paste* magazine profile asserted that Prine spent his twenties "in an alcoholic stupor." Prine eventually got serious about sobering up, banning alcohol sales in the area around the stage at his concerts—and angering some fans in the process. "Just because someone is a recovering alcoholic doesn't mean you can demand no one else drink," said one disgruntled concertgoer at a 2007 show in Charlottesville, Virginia.

Hot on the heels of *Fair and Square*, Prine returned to the studio to record a second album of duets on classic country songs. This time around he would have only one singing partner: Mac Wiseman, a country music veteran born in Virginia's Shenandoah Valley in 1925. Wiseman had started his career playing upright bass for Molly O'Day, later switching to guitar for stints with Lester Flatt and Earl Scruggs' Foggy Mountain Boys and Bill Monroe's Blue Grass Boys. Cowboy Jack Clement had planted the seed for a Prine-Wiseman project years before. "Cowboy said, 'I mentioned your name and Mac likes your music. You guys ought to get together and record some songs,'" Prine told Andy Ellis in a 2007 interview for CMA Closeup News Service. "I was amazed Mac even knew I existed, but when Cowboy says something, he's not just talking off the top of his hat."

They recorded at the Butcher Shoppe with Prine's partner and engineer at the studio, David Ferguson, coproducing. Jacques played bass, though Wilber sat out the sessions. Clement contributed rhythm guitar and Dobro to several songs. Other musicians were Pat McLaughlin on guitar, mandolin, ukulele, harmonica, and backing vocals; Jamie

Hartford, accomplished son of folk veteran John Hartford, on electric guitar; and bluegrass veterans Stuart Duncan (fiddle), Ronnie McCoury (guitar, mandolin), and Tim O'Brien (guitar, banjo). Songs included Kristofferson's "Just the Other Side of Nowhere," long used as the *Austin City Limits* theme; a couple of Western swing classics, Al Dexter's "Pistol Packin' Mama" and Bob Wills's "Don't Be Ashamed of Your Age"; and Tom T. Hall's "Old Dogs, Children and Watermelon Wine." No one would catch anyone sniffing anyone else's undies on this album of Prine duets. "We each agreed to draw up a list of fifteen songs and then get together to make the final selection," Wiseman told Ellis. "Well, John came over to my house, and seven out of the fifteen on our lists were duplicates. That seemed like an omen, you know? It meant we were on the same wavelength." They also cut some vintage crooner songs (Patti Page's "Old Cape Cod," Bing Crosby's "Where the Blue of the Night [Meets the Gold of the Day]"); a couple of religious standards ("Old Rugged Cross," "In the Garden"); and a 1925 ballad about a tragedy from the part of Kentucky that spawned Prine's family, "Death of Floyd Collins," telling the story of an explorer who got trapped near Mammoth Cave (and inspired one of the biggest media circuses of the early twentieth century). The studio musicians "were sitting all around us, and everybody could see each other's eyes," Prine told Ellis. "The stuff the guys played pretty much determined the arrangements, plus Fergy had a few ideas to go this way or that."

The modestly titled *Standard Songs for Average People* was released in April 2007. It's a delightful throwback to the prerock era, hardly groundbreaking but eminently listenable and enjoyable. Bill Monroe once called Wiseman "the strongest singer I ever had," and a *Nashville Tennessean* article by Peter Cooper called him an "acoustic music giant with a sonorous voice that lands him as some kind of bluegrass Sinatra." Prine, by contrast, had "a singing voice that sounds like sandpaper rubbed against a cowboy boot but manages to land pillow-soft on listeners' ears," Cooper wrote. While the album failed to make much of a splash with critics or CD buyers, reviewers generally gave it a thumbs-up. "Wiseman, 82, still has a honeyed tenor that gives itself so readily to the songs that it often verges on sentimentality," Geoffrey Himes wrote in a *Washington Post* review. "Prine, 60, has a small, scratchy voice that approaches the songs warily, as if suspicious of sentiment. Whether they're chuckling their way through Bob Wills's 'Don't Be Ashamed of Your Age' or soberly singing the hymn 'Old Rugged Cross,' the sensual pleasure of Wiseman's vocals and the skeptical intelligence of Prine's push and pull at each other to create a fascinating drama." John Milward, reviewing the album for *No Depression,* called it "an amiable picking party that evokes placid Sunday picnics more than rowdy Saturday nights. And while the results are pleasant enough, one can't help but wish somebody had spiked the punchbowl."

CHAPTER 15

Next to the Last
True Romantic

▼

As the second decade of the twenty-first century dawned, Prine appeared on the UK/Canadian TV show *Spectacle: Elvis Costello with . . .*, which aired stateside on the Sundance Channel. He joined such esteemed *Spectacle* company as Springsteen, Elton John, Smokey Robinson, U2 (well, half of them, anyway), Levon Helm, Allen Toussaint, Bill Clinton, Tony Bennett, and old buddies Mellencamp and Kristofferson. Portly and half bald at sixty-three, Prine sang with a spark, performing "Lake Marie" before sitting down with the host to talk about the song. "My diehard fans who have seen like a hundred shows, they treat it like *The Rocky Horror Show*," Prine told Costello. "'Sssssssizzlin'!'"

Forty years into his career as a performer, Prine had more diehard fans than he could count and enough awards to fill a mantle, most notably two Grammys. *Rolling Stone* named *John Prine* one of "The 500 Greatest Albums of All Time." (It came in at No. 458—just ahead of 1988's *Strictly Business* by the hip-hop group EPMD and just behind Jackson Browne's 1973 sophomore effort, *For Everyman*.) He had been inducted into the Nashville Songwriters Hall of Fame in 2003 and received a lifetime achievement award for songwriting from the Americana Music Association. A tribute website with roots that dated back to the days of the dial-up modem, John Prine Shrine (www.jpshrine.org), supplemented the official Prine and Oh Boy sites, offering fans forums, photos, lyrics, trivia, and an opportunity to trade concert recordings. In

March 2010 the first Prine tribute album appeared: *The Postman Delivers: A Chicago Musicians' Tribute to John Prine Vol. 1*, featuring regional artists covering seventeen classics, from "Spanish Pipedream" to "You Got Gold." Musicians and fans regularly staged live tribute shows to Prine, with annual affairs taking place in Toronto, Canada, and Parkersburg, West Virginia. In 2010, a theater company in Indianapolis produced *Pure Prine*, a theatrical tribute to his music in the vein of *Five Guys Named Moe* and *Beautiful—the Carole King Musical*.

He even had a plaque on the Proviso East Alumni Wall of Fame back home in Maywood, alongside ones for actor and singer Carol Lawrence, who played Maria in the original Broadway production of *West Side Story* (Class of '50); NASA astronaut Gene Cernan, the last man to walk on the moon (Class of '52); Green Bay Packer Ray Nitschke, a member of the Pro Football Hall of Fame (Class of '54); Sheila Crump Johnson, cofounder of Black Entertainment Television and owner of several pro sports teams (Class of '66); and NBA All Star Michael Finley, a starter for the 2007 NBA champion San Antonio Spurs (Class of '91):

MR. JOHN PRINE CLASS OF 1964
—RENOWNED SINGER, SONGWRITER AND GUITARIST
—GRAMMY AWARD WINNER
—HAS BEEN COMPARED TO THE GREAT AMERICAN
STORYTELLER MARK TWAIN
—"PARADISE" IS ONE OF HIS MOST FAMOUS SONGS

Actor Dennis Franz (*NYPD Blue*) also attended Proviso East, graduating two years ahead of Prine. In May 2010 the singer once again returned to the school, this time playing two benefit concerts for the Maywood Fine Arts Association. A film crew recorded the concerts and shot footage of Prine around town (à la his 1980 *Soundstage* appearance) for a planned documentary project. He closed the final show with "Paradise," joined onstage by his sons and three brothers. Dave played a fiddle solo and each brother sang a verse of the song.

Oh Boy released two collections of classic Prine songs in 2010. *In Person & On Stage*, Prine's third live album, appeared in May, showcasing his work with Jacques and Wilber, his touring band for most of the previous decade. The song selection ranged from his first album through

Fair and Square, and several guest vocalists joined Prine: Emmylou Harris ("Angel from Montgomery"); Sara Watkins from Nickel Creek ("The Late John Garfield Blues"); the brilliant Idaho-born rocker and wordsmith Josh Ritter, who had clearly learned a lot from his elder ("Mexican Home"); and Iris DeMent, adding the cracked, strangled beauty of her voice to "In Spite of Ourselves" and "Unwed Fathers." The band Kane Welch Kaplin backed Prine on the closing song, "Paradise." But the real stars of the record were Jacques and Wilber, who created a spacious, atmospheric sound perfectly sympathetic to Prine. Wilber, who had interviewed dozens of country, folk, and rock artists on his nationally syndicated weekly radio show *In Search of a Song*, seemed to have the entire history of country guitar picking at his fingertips, playing Don Rich to Prine's Buck Owens. Prine was one of many artists who contributed to *Coal Country Music*, a benefit album Wilber produced in 2009 to raise money for the Alliance for Appalachia, a coalition fighting the modern equivalent of strip mining, mountaintop removal. Later Prine sat down with Wilber for one of the most comprehensive interviews of his career, which aired in three parts on *In Search of a Song*.

The black-and-white cover of *In Person & On Stage* was like a photographic version of the rearview painting on the cover of his first live album twenty-two years before. Only this time Prine was flanked by Wilber and Jacques, and had his arms open wide to the crowd in an ecstatic pose. "Some people think putting out a live album is not that big a deal, but I worked on this for two years," Prine told Peter Cooper. "Sequencing took six months. I went purely for performance, not to try and make sure that we had specific favorite songs." The singer dedicated the album to "his number one fan, Tom 'Crusher' Reynolds (1953–2010)." "We'd be in the Midwest or San Diego or really anywhere, and there'd be Crusher, outside the building when it was time for soundcheck," Prine said. ". . . I'd always invite him in, even though I never invited any other people in for soundcheck."

The second collection of vintage Prine songs from Oh Boy came out a month after the live album. *Broken Hearts & Dirty Windows: Songs of John Prine* arrived in June, matching twelve tunes with some of the best young Americana artists around, with Watkins and Ritter revisiting their songs from the live album. Old Crow Medicine Show, whose rewrite of Dylan's "Wagon Wheel" was already well on its way to becoming the "Free Bird" of the early twenty-first century, covered "Angel from Montgomery." Rising North Carolina stars the Avett Brothers sang "Spanish Pipedream." Singer-songwriter Justin Townes Earle, well out from under the shadow of his father, Steve Earle, covered "Far from Me." Alt-country veterans Drive-By Truckers—whose Patterson Hood is the son of Muscle Shoals Rhythm Section bass player David Hood—tackled "Daddy's Little Pumpkin." Conor Oberst (formerly of Bright Eyes) and the Mystic Valley Band played one of the more obscure songs on the record, "Wedding Day in Funeralville" from *Common Sense*. Echo king Justin Vernon of Bon Iver sang "Bruised Orange (Chain of Sorrow)." My Morning Jacket, the Louisville, Kentucky, band whose Jim James (aka Yim Yames) had recently sung with Prine on *The Late Show with David Letterman*, covered "All the Best." The album closed with Those Darlins playing "Let's Talk Dirty in Hawaiian," featuring the slackest slack-key guitar around. (Despite the reference to the song in the album's title, no one covered "Souvenirs.") In the liner notes, Vernon recounted listening to Prine's *Great Days* anthology as a child on a family trip. "'Hello in There' somehow reached into my twelve-year-old frame and allowed me to feel the quiet devastation of the old man and Loretta," Vernon said ("as told to Michael Perry"). ". . . Your songs are still here, John, beautifully breathing and beating us up." That may have been the most striking thing about *Broken Hearts & Dirty Windows*: Hearing an array of voices breathe fresh life into songs of remarkable imagination and intricate wordplay, a reminder of what a revelation Prine's songs could be when heard with fresh ears.

Veteran critic Ken Tucker—who had interviewed Prine for *Rolling Stone* thirty-three years earlier—reviewed the live album and the tribute record as a package for the NPR radio show *Fresh Air*. He liked the concert record much better than the tribute. Prine "sounds pretty great on almost every cut on this live album, and he could teach the whippersnappers with juicier vocal cords on his tribute album a few things about how to sell a song," Tucker said. Most of the songs on the tribute record, he said, substituted "flat-footed awe" for Prine's emotional subtlety: "Because he started out strumming an acoustic guitar, and because one of his first well-known songs was the Vietnam War–era song 'Sam Stone,' Prine gets pegged as a folk singer-songwriter. In fact, he has always had at least as much country music in his rhythm and his rhymes. That's another thing that his kind admirers on the tribute album don't seem to get: You can convey sincerity through something besides emoting. It's called detachment—a detachment that roots a soaring, ringing song such as 'The Glory of True Love' in an earthiness that really enables it to lift off."

Just before *Broken Hearts & Dirty Windows* hit the streets, Prine performed at the annual Bonnaroo Music and Arts Festival, held about an hour south of Nashville in Manchester, Tennessee. Bonnaroo had evolved into one of the biggest festivals in the history of American music, attracting an estimated seventy-five thousand music fans in 2010. Other performers that year: Stevie Wonder, Steve Martin and the Steep Canyon Rangers, Jay-Z, Weezer, John Fogerty, Conan O'Brien, Aziz Ansari, Mumford and Sons, the Avett Brothers, the Black Keys, Norah Jones, the Nitty Gritty Dirt Band, Carolina Chocolate Drops, and Daryl Hall with Chromeo. Prine was joined during his set by Ketch Secor and Willie Watson of Old Crow Medicine Show, with Kristofferson (now well into his seventies) also turning up for "Paradise" during the encore. "The applause from the audience as we walked on stage for the encore was deafening!" Wilber wrote in his blog.

Prine continued to tour, though for the previous fifteen years or so he had worked to balance personal appearances with family life at home. "The road will wear you out, and if your body gets worn down, your mind gets worn down," he told Alex Rawls. "It doesn't become fun anymore." He started limiting his concerts to weekends so he could be home during the week to drive his boys to and from school when they were young. He and Fiona spared no expense for their boys, sending them to the exclusive University School of Nashville. They contributed more than five thousand dollars per year to the school's annual fund, and Fiona served on the school's board of trustees. She also worked with an Irish foundation to combat addiction, did poetry readings with the likes of Roy "Future Man" Wooten of Bela Fleck and the Flecktones, and in recent years pursued a BA in liberal studies from Belmont University in Nashville.

Tragedy struck the Oh Boy family the night of 8 January 2011. Juri Bunetta, Al's nineteen-year-old son, a high school senior, rolled his car off of I-65. He was reportedly driving at a high rate of speed, and died from his injuries the next morning at Vanderbilt University Medical Center. Al and his wife, Dawn, adopted Juri at age five and brought him to the United States from his native Latvia. His parents wrote a public letter of appreciation for the support they received after his death: "To all of you who have comforted us and helped our family navigate through this unknown, we thank you. We are truly humbled by your sustained love and prayers. Let us all move forward with love and forgiveness for one another. We will turn this sorrow and anger into joy and understanding." Later they created a nonprofit organization, the Juri Bunetta Friendship Foundation, "to help the homeless, teens in crisis and people facing life-changing emergencies."

In October 2011 Oh Boy reached into its archives to release some of Prine's earliest recordings—if Prine's random boxes of old stuff counted as an archive. "I found these tapes because my wife Fiona made me clean out our garage the last time we moved!" he wrote in the liner notes to *The Singing Mailman Delivers*, a double CD that showcased Prine's early studio demos recorded at WFMT in Chicago in August 1970, as well as a live performance from the Fifth Peg, recorded three months later. (Prine wrote that he recorded the demos at WFMT the same day Studs Terkel interviewed him. Either he did more than one interview with Terkel or he got his chronology mixed up. A photo of the tape box in the CD package indicated that Prine recorded the songs at WFMT on 1 August 1970, while the only readily available bootleg recording of Prine and Terkel clearly dated from 1971, after Prine had signed with Atlantic Records but before he had begun recording his first album.) The CD package also contained a wealth of color photos of Prine with his family around 1969–1970—including a shot of a wide-eyed Prine building with an Erector set on a kitchen table, and one of him seated on a sofa with his brothers. The singer thanked his ex-wife, Ann Carole, for providing most of the photos (misspelling her name, adding an "E" to the end of "Ann"). Prine dedicated the album "to the memory of a beautiful boy—Juri Bunetta."

The CD cover was a cartoon silhouette of a mailman, looking like a rounder version of Zippy, the skinny old U.S. Post Office mascot, hauling a sackful of letters below a mock 1970 postmark. Critics hailed *The Singing Mailman Delivers* as a memorable origin story. "His songs, to anyone [who's] ever heard them, are like creation myths, part of our shared vocabulary, holding more weight than they can sometimes bear, from their very moment of inception," Jonathan Bernstein wrote in a review for *American Songwriter*. Jon Dolan, reviewing the release for

Rolling Stone, gave it three and a half stars (naturally): "It's a fine introduction to a richly imagistic Midwestern everyguy whose languid good nature defied singer-songwriter smugness."

Death becomes all too common after a certain age, and Prine had to say goodbye to more and more people who made a significant impact on his life. His brother Doug, who retired from the Chicago Police Department in the late nineties after rising to lieutenant and watch commander, died 1 May 2012 at the home outside Sacramento, California, he shared with his second wife, Suzanne. He was seventy, and had four children and seven grandchildren. Early Prine booster Roger Ebert died 4 April 2013, also at the age of seventy. For years he had undergone treatment for cancer of the thyroid and salivary glands, and multiple surgeries had dramatically altered his appearance and robbed him of his ability to speak or eat by conventional means. Yet he continued to write, occasionally publishing stories about his early years in Chicago listening to Prine. In January 2013 Prine joined an all-star crew of musicians who gathered at Nashville's War Memorial Auditorium to pay tribute to Cowboy Jack Clement. The bill featured several longtime Prine collaborators, among them Kristofferson, Emmylou Harris, and Sam Bush. "Perhaps the pindrop standout of the night, if not the most emotional, was John Prine— himself a weathered troubadour—clad head-to-toe in black, lending his vulnerable rasp and delicate fingerpicking to a mournful, solo-acoustic take on Clement's 'Ballad of a Teenage Queen,'" Adam Gold wrote in *Rolling Stone.* Clement died at age eighty-two on 8 August 2013 after years of health problems.

In early 2013, fellow Old Town School veteran Roger McGuinn gave Prine credit for inspiring him to become a better performer. "I was opening for John Prine in Texas back in the early-to-mid-'80s," McGuinn told Ed Condran in an interview for the *Asbury Park Press.* "John is a wonderful storyteller who engages the audience. The day after the show my wife and I read the review and it said, 'Unless you're a really big fan of Roger McGuinn, it (his performance) was kind of boring.' The reason for that was the contrast to John Prine, who was so great telling his stories. At that point, I decided to tell stories and I've been doing it ever since. My shows have been so much better."

Well into his fifth decade as a performer, Prine kept rolling, putting on energetic ninety-minute shows despite his own health battles. In late 2013 and early 2014 he had to cancel a few shows to get treatments for lung cancer. "I've been diagnosed with non–small cell carcinoma of the lung," he wrote in a letter to fans. "Doctors here in Nashville have caught it early, and it is operable. They see no reason why I won't fully recover. This is a different form of cancer, unrelated to what I had in 1997." After his successful surgery, Fiona posted a series of updates to the John Prine Shrine website and on social media. "We are both amazed at the amount of love coming at us," she wrote. "We can actually honest to god feel it . . . life is goodness and we are beyond grateful for the Grace in our lives." His old cohort Johnny Burns weighed in with a slightly less reverent "get well soon" message on Facebook: "Dear Johnny Trouble, know that I'm pulling for you as you go into surgery today and hoping for a quick recovery . . . know that I'm there with you today and if you should require me to resume wingman status, I can still summon demons at a moments notice. We'll be friends for a long time, like it or not. Well, I better go, get well and hey, while they're in there have them check you for worms. Hang in there. Much love, Carl Fire." A few weeks later Prine was back on the road.

The traveling gets old, Prine told Peter Cooper at the Country Music Hall of Fame, "but once you get out there, and the lights go down, and the spotlight comes on, and you start dancing around, it feels like the first time that spotlight ever hit me in that little folk club." His songwriting muse appeared to have abandoned him in recent years—as of this writing, he hasn't unveiled any new original material since the release of *Fair and Square* in 2005. Speaking to Peter Cooper at the Country Music Hall of Fame in 2014 about his prolific early days as a songwriter, Prine said, "The guy that wrote those songs is way back in Maywood, Illinois, somewhere." But Oh Boy continued to come up with creative ways to package Prine's old material. In July 2013 the label released a deluxe vinyl reissue of *The Missing Years*, complete with a bonus track from the Epstein sessions, a moody ballad called "The Third of July." The current Nashville generation clearly looks to Prine as an elder statesman. Miranda Lambert covered "That's the Way That the World Goes 'Round" on her 2009 album *Revolution*, and sang the song for a TV audience of millions at the 2010 CMA Awards. Rising star Kacey Musgraves cited

Prine as one of her primary influences, and she obviously wishes she had had a chance to hang out with him during his wild years:

> I'm not good at being careful
> I just say what's on my mind
> Like my idea of heaven
> Is to burn one with John Prine

The same month Prine announced his lung cancer diagnosis, the Country Music Hall of Fame unveiled *John Prine: It Took Me Years to Get These Souvenirs*, a special exhibit scheduled to run for six months. It displayed handwritten song lyrics, concert posters, Grammy Awards, doodles, a street sign from John Prine Avenue in Drakesboro, Kentucky, and Prine's first guitar, the 1960 Silvertone Kentucky Blue archtop his parents gave him for Christmas decades before. The exhibit also included a broken *Missing Years* CD along with a typewritten letter from the ex-fan who snapped it in two: "Words to songs such as Jesus The Missing Years may sound clever but they are insidious in that they chip away at the limited remaining respect that many of our young people have for God, faith and religion." According to the exhibit sign, "Prine had the letter and broken CD framed."

When he's not touring, Prine spends his time these days hanging out with his family in Tennessee and Ireland, shooting snooker at his favorite Nashville pool hall, eating meat loaf at his favorite diners, and fishing. (He owns property in Florida and keeps a fishing license paid up in Arkansas.) He's clearly not ready for assisted living, and he makes it clear that, if he ever does end up in a retirement home, he doesn't want to hear any reminders of a certain song from a generation ago that helped earn him a name as one of America's finest songwriters. "Well God, man, I just hope I'm not sitting there, eighty-five years old, having kids standing outside my window singing 'Hello in There' to me," Prine once told David Wild. "I'll probably throw rocks at 'em."

Acknowledgments

▼

Writing a book like this involves countless hours of isolation, but it also takes a village. A lot of people helped me bring my first book home, none more than Gwen Gosney Erickson, whose support, enthusiasm, research skills, companionship on the road, and feedback helped make this book dramatically better than it would have been without her involvement. (I'll never discount the importance of vertical files again!) I love you, Gwen, and I can't thank you enough for all your contributions. My old friend and journalism colleague David Menconi first approached me about writing a book for this series, for which I am eternally grateful, and he introduced many improvements through several close reads of the manuscript. (He and I are probably both glad he won't have to ask me "How are the rewrites coming?" next time we cross paths at Cat's Cradle or the PNC Arena.) Thanks to David and the coeditor of this series, Peter Blackstock, for making me a part of the team. Casey Kittrell of UT Press was an unfailingly enthusiastic, patient, and sharp-eyed editor. Close scrutiny by Paul Spragens improved the manuscript in small but crucial ways.

Musician relatives, friends, and acquaintances have helped me shape my understanding of the creative process and the music business. My son Rhett, a fine keyboard player currently establishing himself in the Atlanta music scene, helped with technical details. My son Sam, a fine musician in his own right, provided encouragement, enthusiasm, and welcome breaks for a game of disc golf as I brought the book home. Over the years I have learned a lot and had a great time arguing and trading stories with Andy Ware, Britt "Snüzz" Uzzell, Jeffrey Dean Foster, Phil Lee, Jamie McLendon, Jon Shain, Ken Mickey, Tom Meltzer, Jeff Hart, and Mike Nicholson. Bass god Steve Eisenstadt gave me valuable insight into Prine's musical techniques (and a free television, to boot!). My primary technical adviser was an outstanding guitarist, teacher, singer, and songwriter who has more than a little Prine in his musical DNA. (In one of his songs he sings, "I'll do anything for you except the thing that I won't do.") Sam Frazier spent hours listening to Prine's songs and documenting their keys, structures, and quirks for me. He gets full credit for any technical insights, and he helped me flesh the book out in crucial ways. Many thanks, Sam.

Several people helped as I researched the book. David Jordan showed me around Maywood, Illinois, and its environs and shared his abundant enthusiasm for Prine's music, as well as stories about Prine and Goodman concerts dating back to the seventies. Mary Linda McKinney and Mark Wutka were gracious enough to put me up on two research trips to Nashville. The thumbpickers and thumbpicking enthusiasts in Muhlenberg County couldn't have been kinder or more helpful, particularly Joe Hudson and Marilyn Kirtley. The John Prine Shrine website was a constant companion as I double-checked lyrics and track listings. I got invaluable assistance from several libraries and institutions. Grover Baker at Middle Tennessee State University's Center for Popular Music went way beyond the call of duty, as did Kathy Casey, the librarian at Proviso East High School in Maywood. I'm also grateful for the help I received from the staffs at the Genealogy and Local History Annex of Harbin Memorial Library in Greenville, Kentucky; the Harold Schiffman Music Library at the University of North Carolina at Greensboro; and, at my alma mater, the Music Library and Southern Historical Collection at the University of North Carolina at Chapel Hill.

More than anyone else, my brother Steve first fired my enthusiasm for music as a child. The writing of Dave Marsh and Robert Christgau sparked my interest in Prine's music long before I had ever actually heard much of it. Reading the work of other music journalists and talking with them through the years helped me focus my interests and passions. The encouragement I received from Peter Guralnick over the past two decades helped keep me going through the most difficult period of my life. I'm also grateful for encouragement from and friendship and good conversations with John Dougan, Dan Heilman, Parke Puterbaugh, Rick Clark, Ed Bumgardner, Mark Segal Kemp, Erin Murphy, and Tom Graves. My colleagues at the *Greensboro News & Record*, Mel Umbarger, Nancy Sidelinger, and Tim Myers, were patient and supportive despite my odd schedule and frazzled nerves as I juggled work on this book with newspaper and freelance work.

Many friends have also helped tremendously along the way, whether reading the manuscript and providing valuable suggestions, sharing their enthusiasm, or simply helping me carry on through hard times. They include Mick Scott, Erik Dobell, John Elderkin, Cheryl Morgan Maxey, Mike Smith, John Pharo, Lynn Inman, Lee Wallace, Bill Curry, Madison Taylor, Elena Barnes, Angie Smits, Russ Clegg, Charlie Berry, and Robbie Schultz, along with the rest of the Boys' Night Out crowd. This book wouldn't have happened without crucial support from Martin Clark, the late Don Payne, and my parents, Sybil Huffman and the late Dick Huffman. Last but not least there's my oldest and best friend, Phil Collins (the American one), who has shaped my views on music and life in more ways than I can count, and who has been my biggest cheerleader down through the years, right up through writing this book. Thanks, Boob!

Select Discography

▼

Having his own record label has allowed John Prine to avoid a fate common to modest-selling artists: out-of-print records. You may have to check used record stores or eBay to find a couple of his albums (*Pink Cadillac* is conspicuously absent from Oh Boy's online catalog as of this writing), but in general Prine's output remains readily available more than four decades after his debut album.

Unfortunately, one cutout casualty is the finest introduction to Prine's work ever released: the 1993 collection *Great Days: The John Prine Anthology*. It's a wonderful overview of Prine's music, complete with detailed song notes from the singer and a wealth of photographs. Copies are out there, but they're likely to set you back fifty bucks or more.

The next best thing? The crystal-clear 1988 live album *John Prine Live*. While it leans heavily toward the solo-acoustic, storytelling singer-songwriter side of Prine, it's a sweeping introduction to his music and persona, and a great listen. His subsequent live albums—1997's *Live on Tour* and 2010's *In Person & On Stage*—are solid records, but lack the scope and intimacy of that first one. (And couldn't a wordsmith as creative as Prine have come up with at least one memorable title for a live album at some point in his career?)

Which brings us to his studio albums, ranging from 1971 to 2005. (As of this writing, *Fair and Square* remains Prine's last hurrah as a collection of new songs.) During his Atlantic years, in the early seventies, he was a precocious kid gradually figuring out how to put his brilliant songs across in the studio. Recording for Asylum on the cusp of the eighties, he made two records that courted commercial success (*Bruised Orange* and *Storm Windows*) and one that didn't (the aforementioned *Pink Cadillac*). Since releasing *Aimless Love* in 1984, his first record for Oh Boy, Prine has done consistently good work, framing the nineties with two of his best albums.

Prine has never put out a really awful or embarrassing album—the murky *Pink Cadillac* may be light on memorable songs, but even it rocks hard. While some other albums go off the rails for a song or two (1975's *Common Sense*, 1995's *Lost Dogs and Mixed Blessings*, 2005's *Fair and Square*), Prine fans will find plenty to like on all of his studio albums. Here are the ones I consider the cream of the crop.

John Prine (Atlantic, 1971)

Precious few artists ever shot out of the gate with as strong a set of songs as Prine put together for his debut. Alternately funny ("Spanish Pipe-dream"), wistful ("Angel from Montgomery"), and harrowing ("Sam Stone"), *John Prine* showcases a stunningly powerful, fully mature songwriter . . . who wasn't quite ready to make a record. Prine hadn't found his singing voice, and he never meshed with the hit-making pros at American Sound Studio. With songs this strong and characters this memorable, however, it's easy to overlook the album's shortcomings.

Sweet Revenge (Atlantic, 1973)

Third time's the charm. By the time he made *Sweet Revenge*, Prine had learned how to front a band, and he wrote a set of songs nearly equal to the ones on his debut. On this album he mixes humor, drama, and quiet reflection, writing a song Elvis would end up loving ("Please Don't Bury Me"), throwing away his best-ever shot at a hit single ("Dear Abby," which probably would have typecast him, as Prine feared at the time), and bringing it all back home with a song by Muhlenberg County's own Merle Travis.

Bruised Orange (Asylum, 1978)

Wee Steve Goodman kicked Prine's ass all up and down Michigan Avenue and got a great record out of him. A bit too whimsical at times, but once again Prine delivers a set of brilliant songs, with lyrics that look back with mixed emotions at his Midwestern childhood and his crumbling marriage.

Storm Windows (Asylum, 1980)

Ignore the album cover, where Asylum tried to fool fans into thinking they were getting a new Bob Welch record. This may be the most overlooked gem in the Prine catalog, the singer making one great album with the Famous Potatoes before he moved to Nashville and left the band behind. Strong songs, sympathetic production by a Muscle Shoals Swamper, and a title track it's a shame Dylan never covered. (Maybe he was afraid critics would label him the new Prine.)

Aimless Love (Oh Boy, 1984)

Prine launched his new label with an album rooted in inspired Nashville professionalism. This is the singer at his most relaxed and comfortable, singing songs mostly about love—and, less frequently, its absence. He finally got around to putting "The Bottomless Lake" on an album, and with "Unwed Fathers" he fully caught up to his country music heroes.

The Missing Years (Oh Boy, 1991)

Our hero hits his stride. For my money, this is the one Prine album to own, recklessly ambitious songs meeting perfectly sympathetic production from Howie Epstein. Prine is relaxed enough to write some of his most outrageous lyrics . . . which he mixes with everyday colloquialisms such that it seems perfectly reasonable and inevitable when he gets around to describing Esmeralda having sex with the Hunchback of Notre Dame. Then he turns around and sings devastatingly plainspoken songs about love and loss. Would that every divorce spawned something as worthwhile as *The Missing Years*.

In Spite of Ourselves (Oh Boy, 1999)

Worth owning for the sweetly perverted title duet with Iris DeMent alone, but it contains so much more. Prine gets intimate with the members of a heavenly chorus, resurrecting Nashville's duet tradition and taking it into uncharted territory. Old pro Jim Rooney builds a perfect honky-tonk bed for the singer and his paramours, who team up to create as delightful an album as Prine has ever made.

Select Bibliography

▼

Baird, Robert. "Missing No More: John Prine Makes Up for Two Decades of Lost Time." *Phoenix New Times*, 2 October 1991, http://www.phoenix newtimes.com/content/printVersion/159553/.

Bangs, Lester. "John Prine: The Troubadour, Los Angeles, CA." *Phonograph Record*, January 1972.

Boyer, Peter J. "John Prine Knits the Ragged Edges." *St. Joseph (MO) News-Press*, 1 July 1978.

Bridges, Les. "John Prine, a Folkie Comer." *Rolling Stone*, 9 December 1971, pp. 16–18.

Campbell, Roddy. "A Return to Prine Time." *Penguin Eggs*, Summer 2005.

Cannon, Bob. Review of *Great Days*. *Entertainment Weekly*, 10 December 1993, http://www.ew.com/ew/article/0,,308894,00.html.

———. Review of *Lost Dogs and Mixed Blessings*. *Entertainment Weekly*, 5 May 1995, http://www.ew.com/ew/article/0,,297078,00.html.

Christgau, Robert. "Really Glad to Be Here: John Prine Gets Well on an Apple Pie Diet." *Village Voice*, 28 September 1999, http://www.village voice.com/content/printVersion/217551/.

Cocks, Jay. "John Prine's Best Album." *Rolling Stone*, 7 September 1978.

Compton, Joe F. "Modern-Day Mark Twain." *Dirty Linen*, August/September 1992.

———. "Prine Time." *Acoustic Guitar*, September 1995.

Cooper, Peter. "John Prine and Mac Wiseman Make Beautiful Music Together." *Nashville Tennessean*, 6 May 2007.

————. "John Prine Still Delivers." *Nashville Tennessean*, 7 June 2010.

————. "Master at Work: After a 10-year Hiatus, John Prine Is Back to Making Music with Renewed Vigor." *Nashville Tennessean*, 19 June 2005.

Cronin, Peter. "Oh Boy! It's a New Prine Album." *Billboard*, 18 February 1995.

DeLuca, Dan. "Old Master Back on Top of His Game." *Nashville Banner*, 20 April 1992.

————. "Prine in His Prime: Singer-Songwriter John Prine Is Anything but Slick." *Philadelphia Inquirer*, 4 April 1992, http://articles.philly.com/1992 -04-04/news/26006056_1_memphisto-german-afternoons-big-old-goofy-world.

Ebert, Roger. "Singing Mailman Who Delivers a Powerful Message in a Few Words." *Chicago Sun-Times*, 9 October 1970.

Ellis, Andy. "John Prine and Mac Wiseman Visit the Great American Standard Songs." CMA Closeup News Service, 2007, http://www.gactv.com/gac/cda /article_print/0,3008,gac_26068_5766621_ds-article-with-groups,00 .html.

Everett, Todd. "John Prine: New Moustache, New Band, New Music." *Los Angeles Free Press*, 9–15 May 1975.

Flanagan, Bill. "John Prine." *Written in My Soul: Rock's Great Songwriters Talk about Creating Their Music*, pp. 130–138. Chicago: Contemporary Books, 1986.

Flippo, Chet. "John Prine: Avery Fisher Hall." *Rolling Stone*, 5 June 1975.

Freedland, Nat. "John Prine: Troubadour, Los Angeles." *Billboard*, 1 January 1972, p. 8.

Friskics-Warren, Bill. "Happy Marriages: John Prine Teams Up with a Host of Female Singers for New Duet Project." nashvillescene.com, 11 November 1999, http://www.nashvillescene.com/nashville/happy-marriages/Content ?oid=1183691.

Ghianni, Tim. "John Prine Finds a Fan at the Snooker Table." *Nashville Ledger*, 2 August 2013, http://www.nashvilleledger.com/editorial/Article.aspx?id =67943.

Goldsmith, Thomas. "The Pride of John Prine." *Nashville Tennessean*, 28 September 1991.

Gregory, Ted. "Prine Returns Home to Boost Center for Arts." *Chicago Tribune*, 27 February 2000.

Grise, Cynthia. "Pure Paradise: John Prine's Way with a Music Lyric Is a Bit of Listening Heaven for His Many Fans." *Central City (KY) Leader-News*, 22 September 1993.

Guarino, Mark. "John Prine on His Song 'Lake Marie.'" *Chicago Daily Herald*, 19 November 1999, http://www.mark-guarino.com/chicago-daily-herald /1387-john-prine-on-his-song-qlake-marieq.

Harrington, Richard. "John Prine, Vox Populi: After Beating Cancer, a Poet's Poet Savors the Fanfare He's Given the Common Man." *Washington Post,* 18 June 2005, http://forums.stevehoffman.tv/threads/great-article-on -john-prine.55253/.

Himes, Geoffrey. "John Prine." *The Encyclopedia of Country Music,* 2nd ed. Oxford: Oxford University Press, 2010.

———. "John Prine & Mac Wiseman: 'Standard Songs for Average People,' Oh Boy." *Washington Post,* 15 June 2007, http://www.washingtonpost.com /wp-dyn/content/article/2007/06/14/AR2007061400414.html.

Hoekstra, Dave. "John Prine: Makin' Hometown Hopes Come True." *Chicago Sun-Times,* 9 May 2010.

———. "John Prine, Songs from the Heart." *Chicago Sun-Times* (online blog), 4 May 2010, http://blogs.suntimes.com/hoekstra/2010/05/it_has_been_ 30_years.html (accessed 30 June 2013).

Holden, Stephen. Review of *Common Sense. Rolling Stone,* 22 May 1975.

Hull, Tom. "Back from Fishing: John Prine Returns to a World Stripped of His Favorite Subject Matter—Humanity." *Village Voice,* 9 August 2005, http:// www.villagevoice.com/2005-08-09/music/back-from-fishing/full/.

Hurst, Jack. "Prine Time: Songwriter Tries Acting as Well as Keeping His Show on the Road." *Chicago Tribune,* 22 August 1990, http://articles.chi cagotribune.com/1990-08-22/features/9003100318_1_prine-time-boy -records-label-unscripted-introductions.

Hutchinson, Lydia. "Behind the Songs of John Prine." *Performing Songwriter* 12 and 46 (orig. May/June 1995 and June 2000; 10 October 2013), http:// performingsongwriter.com/john-prine-songs/ (accessed 1 June 2014).

Knowles, Clark. "A John Prine Story." Blog post, 3 April 2011, http://clark knowles.wordpress.com/2011/04/03/a-john-prine-story/.

Kot, Greg. "A Happier Song: Recovered from Cancer, John Prine Returns to His Musical Roots." *Chicago Tribune,* 14 November 1999, http://articles .chicagotribune.com/1999-11-14/news/9911140416_1_john-prine-steve -goodman-grand-ole-opry.

———. "John Prine: The Bard of Old Town Returns." *Chicago Tribune,* 26 February 2010, http://fridaynightboys300.blogspot.com/2010/03/john -prine-in-chicago-tribune.html.

———. "John Prine Live on Tour." *Chicago Tribune,* 25 April 1997, http:// articles.chicagotribune.com/1997-04-25/entertainment/9704250370_1 _missing-years-illegal-smile-john-prine.

———. "John Prine Recalls His Chicago Folk Roots." *Chicago Tribune,* 28 February 2010, http://articles.chicagotribune.com/2010-02-28/news/ct -ae-0228-john-prine-20100228_1_john-prine-folk-music-existentialism.

Kruth, John. "John Prine: One of the Good Guys." *Sing Out!*, Winter 2006, p. 54.

Mabe, Chauncey. "Prine's Success: A Mixed Blessing. Folk Singer Makes Adjustments for Bigger Audiences." *Fort Lauderdale Sun-Sentinel*, 9 June 1995, http://articles.sun-sentinel.com/1995-06-09/entertainment/9506070 311_1_prine-s-success-john-prine-songs.

Marcus, Greil. "John Prine's *Common Sense.*" *Village Voice*, 21 April 1975.

Marsh, Dave. "Prine Cut." *Rolling Stone*, 29 November 1979.

Martin, Frank. "John Prine Goes Back to What's Left of Paradise." *People*, 28 October 1974.

Milward, John. Review of *The Missing Years*. *Rolling Stone*, 23 January 1992.

Mitchell, Justin. "Oh Boy, Prine Now Has His Own Label and a New LP." Scripps-Howard News Service, 6 April 1985, http://articles.chicagotribune.com/1985-04-06/news/8501190771_1_aimless-love-bottomless-lake-boy-records.

Nelson, Paul. "Nice Guy Prine Almost Finishes First." *Rolling Stone*, 7 September 1978.

Nolan, Tom. Review of *Sweet Revenge*. *Rolling Stone*, 31 January 1974.

Ochs, Ed. "Tom [*sic*] Prine, Steve Goodman: Bitter End, New York." *Billboard*, 20 November 1971, http://books.google.ca/books?id=5Q8EAAA AMBAJ&q=prine#v=snippet&q=prine&f=false.

Patterson, Jim. "Surviving Cancer Gives John Prine a Fresh Voice." Associated Press, 9 October 1999, http://www.southcoasttoday.com/apps/pbcs .dll/article?AID=/19991009/NEWS/310099936&cid=sitesearch&templ ate=printart.

Pollock, Bruce. "John Prine." *In Their Own Words*. New York: Macmillan, 1975.

Prine, John. Interview. *Music Business Radio*, 8 May 2008, http://blog.music businessradio.com/2008/05/bonus-content-.html.

———. Interview. In *Steve Goodman: Live from Austin City Limits . . . and More!* Red Pajamas Records, 2003.

———. Interview with Bob Edwards. *Morning Edition*, National Public Radio, 26 October 1999.

———. Interview with Kara Manning. *Rolling Stone*, 21 September 1995.

———. "A Personal Message from John Prine." Oh Boy Records, April 1999.

Prine, John, and Meg Griffin. "Sirius Disorder." Sirius Satellite Radio (Channel 24), June 2005, http://www.johnprine.net/audio/prine.sirius2.mp3 (accessed 28 June 2013).

Prine, John, and Ted Kooser. "A Literary Evening with John Prine and Ted Kooser." Library of Congress, 9 March 2005, http://www.loc.gov/today/cy berlc/feature_wdesc.php?rec=3677 (accessed 28 June 2013).

Prine, John, and Ken Paulson. "John Prine, Part 1." *Speaking Freely*, First Amendment Center, Nashville, TN, 30 March 2004, http://www.first amendmentcenter.org/john-prine-part-1-2 (accessed 29 June 2013).

Prine, John, and John Platt. "John Prine." WGLD (Oak Park, IL), 19 December 1971, http://beemp3s.org/download.php?file=13663547&song=John +Prine+Interview+-+WGLD+12-19-71 (accessed 1 June 2014).

Prine, John, and Nick Spitzer. "John Prine." *American Routes Radio*, WWNO (New Orleans), 13 August 2008, http://americanroutes.wwno.org/player /show/543/hour/1 (accessed 29 July 2013).

Prine, John, and Jason Wilber. "In Search of a Song: John Prine, Part 1." *In Search of a Song with Jason Wilber*, ISOAS Media Group, 30 July 2011, http://www.prx.org/pieces/118837-in-search-of-a-song-john-prine-part -1 (17 May 2014 rebroadcast) (accessed 1 June 2014).

Prine Sorkin, Anne. "Biography of My Grandmother, Verna 'Cotton' Hamm Prine." http://www.hammbook.com/verna-valentine-cotton-hamm-prine -biography/ (accessed 29 June 2013).

"Question & Answer with John Prine." *The Prine Shrine*, http://www.jpshrine .org/biography/prine_QnAf.htm (accessed 30 June 2013).

Rawls, Alex. "Back Talk with John Prine." *Offbeat*, December 2002.

Richardson, Derk. "Acoustic Classic: Angel from Montgomery." *Acoustic Guitar*, January 2006.

———. "Big Ol' Goofy World." *Acoustic Guitar*, January 2006.

Rooney, Jim. *In It for the Long Run: A Musical Odyssey*. Urbana: University of Illinois Press, 2014.

Ruhlmann, William. "John Prine: Prine Time." *Goldmine*, 11 December 1992.

Salamon, Jeff. Review of *Lost Dogs and Mixed Blessings*. *Spin*, August 1995.

Shewey, Don. Review of *Aimless Love*, by John Prine. *Rolling Stone*, 20 June 1985.

"A Sort of Homecoming for a Really Cool Guy." *John Prine Shrine*, 26 February 2000, http://www.jpshrine.org/red/proviso/index.html (accessed 4 July 2013).

Tucker, Ken. "John Prine: Midwestern Mind Trips to the Nth Degree." *Fresh Air*, WHYY, 7 June 2010, http://www.npr.org/templates/story/story .php?storyId=127368704.

———. "John Prine Cracks an Illegal Smile." *Rolling Stone*, 3 November 1977.

———. Review of *Storm Windows*. *Rolling Stone*, 30 October 1980.

Whitman, Andy. "John Prine: On the Outskirts of Paradise." *Paste*, June/July 2005.

Wild, David. "Tuning into Prine Time: John Prine Scores High in the Ratings with *The Missing Years*." *Rolling Stone*, 20 February 1992.

Wilson, Alan. "Musical Sounds of John Prine May Not Be Familiar, but Can Be." *The Robesonian* (Lumberton, NC), 31 January 1974, http://news.google .com/newspapers?id=T21WAAAAIBAJ&sjid=H0ENAAAAIBAJ&pg =7395,2707015&dq=john-prine&hl=en (accessed 30 June 2013).

Zollo, Paul. "John Prine: The Bluerailroad Interview." *The Bluerailroad: A Magazine of the Arts*, http://bluerailroad.wordpress.com/john-prine-the-bluerailroad-interview/ (accessed 29 June 2013).